Stone Boy

ALSO BY RONALD LEVITSKY

The Love That Kills
The Wisdom of Serpents

Stone Boy

RONALD LEVITSKY

Charles Scribner's Sons
New York

Maxwell Macmillan Canada
Toronto

Maxwell Macmillan International
New York Oxford Singapore Sydney

Charles Scribner's Sons   Maxwell Macmillan Canada, Inc.
Macmillan Publishing Company   1200 Eglinton Avenue East
866 Third Avenue   Suite 200
New York, NY 10022   Don Mills, Ontario M3C 3N1

Macmillan Publishing Company is part of the Maxwell Communication Group of Companies.

Library of Congress Cataloging-in-Publication Data
Levitsky, Ronald.
    Stone boy / Ronald Levitsky.
        p.   cm.
    "A Nate Rosen mystery."
    ISBN 0-684-19554-2
    I. Title.
    PS3562.E92218S76   1993   92-42073
    813'.54--dc20   CIP

Macmillan books are available at special discounts for bulk purchases for sales promotions, premiums, fund-raising, or educational use. For details, contact:

Special Sales Director
Macmillan Publishing Company
866 Third Avenue
New York, NY 10022

10 9 8 7 6 5 4 3 2 1

Printed in the United States of America

For Sonia

Acknowledgments

The author wishes to thank the following people: Dr. James Gillihan, expert on Lakota burial rites; Fran Lambert, champion reiner; Brother Simon of the Holy Rosary Mission, Pine Ridge Reservation; the Native American Education Center of Chicago; and, especially, Kathy, Jim, and Stuart Hood of Spearfish, South Dakota.

June

Chapter 1

MONDAY EVENING

The starlings perched on the corral could have warned her, but Grace didn't know their language. The way they watched, silent and dark as judges, made her believe something was wrong. Maybe the weather. It was too hot for so late in the day—too hot for rain, yet far in the horizon, lightning glinted off a flint-colored sky. Yes, the starlings could have warned her about whatever was coming, but she was only a woman and a half-breed and didn't know their language.

She shifted in the saddle, as her horse's ears pricked.

"What is it, Curly? Smell rain?"

He pawed the ground, impatient to continue.

"All right, boy, one more time."

Brushing back her long braids, Grace brought in her heels to put Curly into a full run. Half-closing her eyes, she smiled, loving the way his long mane billowed in the wind. She turned him sharply, did two standing circles, changed leads as they loped around the corral, then, turning again, put him into another run. Leaning forward, Grace wrapped her reins around the saddle horn, spread her hands like wings, and flew with Curly across the corral. She watched the red wraps of his forelegs flash and sensed they were nearing the railing. Suddenly she shouted, "Whoa!" and leaned back. Curly's hind legs locked, while his front hooves churned to a halt a foot before the fence, directly in front of the starlings, who didn't so much as flutter a wing. A perfect slide.

"Tell me that wasn't worth eighty points," Grace challenged the birds. "That was nice, Curly. Do as well this Saturday, and we'll win it. There's an extra bag of carrots in it for you." She patted his neck, filling the air with dust. "Ooh, we'd better get you a nice cool shower before supper's ready."

3

RONALD LEVITSKY

Dismounting, Grace opened the corral gate and walked her horse to the hitching post in front of the barn. She put away the saddle and bridle, removed the wraps on his forelegs, and, picking up the hose, adjusted the nozzle to a cold hard stream. She sprayed Curly from braided tail to neck. He shook his head and, sticking out his tongue, lapped the water, then suddenly nuzzled against her, soaking her T-shirt.

"Curly, you slob!" But she hugged him back and murmured, "You're a good boy, aren't you."

Sighing, she scraped the water from his coat, combed the tangles from his mane, and led him back to his stall.

"You stay inside tonight—might rain. I'll come see you before going to work." Petting his nose, she added, "Love you."

Grace walked across the yard to the porch steps. Turning, she gazed past the corral, up the long sloping prairie to the top of the ridge. Most of the grass had already been cut and rolled into bundles; she'd finish gathering them tomorrow. Only the very top of the ridge had been left alone, as always. "For our brothers, the buffalo," her father said, even though the buffalo had been gone a hundred years. The grass stood long and dark against the gray sky, almost as dark as the Black Hills in the distance. Her father's sacred land, surrounded by their people's sacred land, or so he said. To her it was a waste of good hay.

He was up there now, but it wouldn't do calling him for supper. He'd shake his head, as if talking to a naughty child, and say, "Lakotas eat when they're hungry. Only white men eat when the clock tells them to."

Kicking a clod of dirt from the porch, she muttered, "Let him wait for his damn buffalo," and walked into the house.

"Stevie, you'd better wash up for . . . !"

Something was burning. She hurried into the kitchen, through smoke billowing from the pot of chili on the stove.

"Damn it!" She shut off the stove and flicked on the overhead fan. "Stevie, didn't I tell you to turn down the heat at 6:30? You're twelve years old, not a baby! I hope to hell you like peanut butter and jelly for supper! Stevie?"

Her son didn't answer, and, after waiting for the smoke to clear, Grace went into the dining room, where she'd left him an hour ago doing homework. Books, pencils, and crumpled papers were spread like a battlefield across the table; directly in front of his chair lay the same math

4

problem he'd copied in an angry scrawl just before she'd left for the barn. There was no answer. With him, there never was.

No need to wonder where he'd gone—he'd snuck out to play Indian with his grandfather. She thought about going up the ridge to drag him home, but that would've meant another fight, and she was just too tired. No more fights, not with her shift coming up in a few hours.

In her room, Grace sat on the bed and struggled with her boots. It was the time of day she always thought about her husband, Steve—the way he'd pull her boots off, laughing at "how such tiny feet could get so damn stuck." She stripped off the rest of her clothes, stiff from dirt and dried sweat, like the shed skin of a snake, and dropped them into the hamper. Her hair unbraided, she took a long cold shower.

She lay back in bed, still nude, and looked at herself in the full-length mirror while caressing her shoulders and arms. After years of baling hay, her hands were rough, and her skin, still young and soft, tingled as if being touched by a man. Her thick black hair hung loose around her breasts. "Injun hair," Steve would whisper, as he brushed until it shone like ebony. That and her dark eyes and broad cheekbones were her father's. Only the straight nose and light skin belonged to her mother. "Pretty for a half-breed," the women in town always said. She must've been; enough of their men had bothered her ever since she was a girl. They still did; somehow being a widow made her even more desirable. Like she was hungry for a man, any man.

Grace reached for the brush, beside Steve's picture on the night table, and stroked her hair as he used to do. The breeze through the window felt warm against her cheek, like his breath just before they kissed. She stroked her skin the way he used to with his rough hands. Her legs stirred, as if under him, and her breath quickened.

"No," she almost sobbed, rubbing her eyes with the base of her palms, the way her Lakota grandmother did.

Tossing the brush onto the night table—she heard it knock his picture over—Grace quickly got dressed, choosing a clean pair of jeans, a T-shirt, and sandals. She pinned her hair back with a large wooden barrette and hurried from the room.

She opened a can of tuna, made a salad, and sat at the dining room table, across from where Stevie was supposed to be doing his homework. Through the window, the sky hadn't grown any darker; it might not rain after all. He'd be all right on the ridge. Her father had enough common sense . . . No, she'd better ride up there after dinner.

Ten minutes later, as Grace walked into her room for her boots, the screen door slammed.

"Mom! Mom!"

"Where've you been?"

He ran through the house into her room.

"Mom, you . . . you gotta . . . come!"

He leaned over suddenly, his lanky frame working like a bellows to catch his breath. His hands were dirty, as were his clothes, jeans torn at the knee.

"What have you gotten yourself into?"

"Mom, you gotta . . . "

"I'm not going anywhere, and neither are you. Do you know you almost burned the house down? And since when can you leave your homework . . . ?

He grabbed her arms, his eyes widening.

"Stevie, what is it?"

"There's a skeleton up on the ridge, near Grandfather's sweat lodge. You gotta come!"

"A skeleton? Is your grandfather all right?"

"Yeah. He's up there. Mr. Gates is there too."

"Oh, God. All right, let me . . . "

Before Grace finished her sentence, Stevie had already run from the house. She thought about calling the station, but to tell them what? Besides, Albert Gates being with her father . . . She couldn't call the police just yet.

By the time she left the house, Stevie was halfway up the ridge. It was hard running in sandals, but the grass was short, the ground unbroken, and the breeze a little cooler than before. Before she reached the tall grass near the top, Stevie had disappeared on the other side, where her father's sweat lodge stood, but she could hear a soft murmuring.

For a moment, feeling the tall buffalo grass brush against her legs, Grace remembered as a little girl walking with her father while they listened for the spirits who lived upon this holy place, especially her father's brothers, the elk, that he'd seen on his first vision quest. He'd sworn he heard them, and she, in the foolishness of childhood, thought she had too. But it had just been the wind.

What she heard now wasn't the wind, nor was it spirits. They were human voices, and topping the ridge Grace saw, about fifty feet past the sweat lodge, her father sitting very straight across from Albert Gates, who knelt while brandishing something in his right hand. Stevie, his hands clenched tightly behind his back, stood beside his grandfather and stared at the ground.

Gates shifted his bulk from knee to knee while wiping his pug face with a large handkerchief. A few white hairs, long and curly, covered the crown of his head like dried foam. His dress shirt was splotched with sweat.

" . . . deal's a deal, whether with you or another member of your family. Just like at my business—salesman sells you a car for a certain price and maybe makes a mistake in your favor. Don't matter, 'cause I stand behind it. Maybe I kick his ass later, but the deal stands. You understand what I'm saying, Chief?"

Her father replied so softly that Grace couldn't hear. She moved past the vision pit—the deep trench where he would sit for days in meditation—and stood beside the sweat lodge, laying a hand upon one of the bent willow trees and smelling the old deerskin hides mixed with the aroma of Bull Durham tobacco offerings. As a child she had gone into the hills with him to cut and peel the twelve white willow trees, then bend them into a dome covered with hide and canvas. Despite herself, she smiled at the memory and could almost understand why Stevie kept running up here—running to him.

Gates shook his head. "I'm not backing away from this baby! Maybe I can sweeten the pot a little. Whaddya say to another c-note, Chief?"

Her father said, "I'm not a chief. For over forty years we've known one another, and you still make the same mistake."

"C'mon, you know I don't mean nothing . . . "

"I'm just Saul True Sky, a Lakota or *ikce wicasa*—simple Indian. Just as you are *wasichu*."

"What the hell you mean by that?"

"He just means you're white," Stevie muttered. "That's all. Just that you're a white man and don't understand."

"Oh." Gates crinkled his brow, then caught sight of Grace. "Kid, glad you're here. Maybe you can talk sense to your old man. You're the only one in the family got any real brains."

Her father turned. He had on his work clothes, a blue cotton shirt and faded jeans. His white hair, threaded with a few raven strands, was brushed back nearly to his shoulders, except for the small braided hoop above his right ear. No wonder Gates was frustrated—her father's face was smooth and hard like a stone, as it always looked when he was dealing with the whites. The deep wrinkles about his eyes and lips showed only when he was smiling. Looking from one man to the other, she took a deep breath and demanded, "What's this all about?"

Gates said, "C'mere and take a look at this baby. Believe you me, it's some beauty."

He was motioning with the object in his right hand—a small trowel. That tool told her exactly what Gates was talking about.

It lay between the two men, half buried and surrounded by a small pile of earth. Its skull, mottled green and copper, grinned obscenely. The collarbone had been broken, but around what had once been its throat was a necklace of small colored stones. There were gaps in the loop where shells might have been strung. Small pieces of rotted buckskin clung to the ribs, several of which also were broken.

"Well?" Gates said, leaning forward.

She shrugged. "Body of a dead Indian, I guess. We never seen nothing like this on our property. It's like the ones found on your wife's ranch, back when I was a kid."

"That's right. Two of them down by that dried-up riverbed we use for pasture—one a woman and the other a young boy. Figured they might've wandered away from Big Foot's band, when he went down to Wounded Knee back in 1890. This one here looks just like them other two, sort of the third pea in the pod. If I didn't know better . . . " Gates shook his head. "Probably like them two, he died from fighting, maybe from hunger or the cold. The stories he could tell, heh? We'll know more, once one of them college professors has a look-see."

Her father shook his head.

As Gates grew even redder, Grace asked, "Why're you so interested? There're hundreds of remains like this in museums. Even in your collection, you must have . . . "

"Hell, yes, I got four of these here skeletons, plus another half-dozen skulls. But it ain't really the body I'm interested in. Look closer. Here."

Dropping the trowel, he took a small paintbrush and carefully removed some dirt on the left side, where the skeleton's third rib emerged from the earth. Grace knelt beside him and saw what appeared to be part of a long, narrow package that had been double-wrapped in rawhide. The outer layer had nearly rotted away, but the inner one, decorated with beadwork and a design she couldn't make out, looked intact.

"Know what that is?" Gates asked, his grin wide as the skull's.

When she shook her head, her father replied, *"Wotawe."*

"That's right," the other man said, "a genuine *wotawe*—medicine bundle. Ain't many of those around, and it'd just about make my collection complete."

"It's *wakan*—holy. You must leave it alone."

"Chief, your boy Will and me made a deal."

Grace asked, "What's my brother got to do with this?"

"Why, he's the one who found it. A few hours ago I saw him, out by my tool shed, pulling out my digging box. This one here." He pointed to a large tool chest behind him, filled with trowels, brushes of assorted sizes, metal and bamboo picks. "He told me what he'd stumbled across up here. Said he'd begun digging it out with a shovel—can you believe how stupid, using a shovel on something old and delicate as that? No wonder some of them bones is broken. When he saw what it was, he run over to my place for the proper tools."

Her father said, "The boy had no right to disturb this resting place."

"Why not? He's Indian too. Leastways, he's half-Indian."

"The boy is an apple." They all knew what that meant—red outside but white inside. "He'll do anything for money except work—even step on the graves of his people."

"The dead's dead, Chief. Might as well get some use outta them. Why, when I go, they can make a flowerpot outta my head, for all I care. Know what I mean?"

"Yes. That would be an improvement. Then maybe you would finally stop talking and listen to what people say."

Gates clamped his jaw shut. The edges of his lips turned up slightly as he drew a folded sheet of paper from his shirt pocket. He spread the paper on the ground.

"This here's a receipt. Recognize the signature, Chief? It's your son Will's chicken scratches. Up at the ranch, after he described to me what he'd found, he agreed to sell me the medicine bundle for $500. I already gave him a $50 advance. Wasn't gonna give him a dime more until I saw the *wotawe* for myself. But I'm satisfied—you'll get the rest of the money. I'll even make out the check to you, Chief. Won't Will be surprised.

Knowing that boy, he probably wasn't gonna tell you and keep the $500 for himself. That Will," Gates chuckled while reaching into a back pocket for his checkbook, "maybe I should make him one of my used-car salesmen."

"This is my land," Grace's father said, "not Will's. I want you to leave now. My son will return the money you gave him."

"But I don't want the money, Chief. I want the *wotawe*. If I don't get it—if it ain't your son's to sell, then I guess he's guilty of fraud, and I'll have to go see the police."

"So that's it," Grace said. "If my father doesn't give you what you want, you're gonna cause trouble for Will."

Gates nodded. "It won't be his first visit with the cops. There were those drunk-and-disorderlies—well, boys will be boys. But that check-cashing problem—he did a little time for that, didn't he? So how about it, Chief? Let me just dig this little bundle out, and I'll be on my way. Like I said before, I'll even add $100 for old time's sake."

Her father shook his head.

"And Will?"

"My son must learn that, for a Lakota, there are worse things than jail. Now get off my land."

The two men stared at one another for a long time. Finally, Gates moved back a few inches, but only to reach into his toolbox for a long bamboo pick. Bending over the skeleton, he carefully scraped dirt away from the bundle while muttering, "A deal's a deal."

When her father reached to push the other man's hand away, Gates jabbed him with the pick, breaking the slender stick in two.

"Get the hell away . . . Jesus!"

Something flashed against Gates's right hand; a small blade left a thin crimson trail between his wrist and knuckles. Looking up, Grace saw Stevie standing over them, a small pocketknife in his hand. The boy chewed on his lower lip until speckles of blood appeared on his teeth. His hand jerked forward, as if to strike again.

"No, Stevie!" she cried, but it was her father who stood and took the knife away.

Putting his hand on the boy's trembling shoulder, he said what she knew he would say—what he used to tell her. Her lips formed the words silently. "It is not done."

For a moment there was silence, and Stevie began to relax, as if her father's hand was drawing all the fear and anger from him.

"Damn!" Gates exploded.

Stevie jumped back and seemed on the verge of running away. Grace grabbed him tightly.

"It's all right, honey. Just take it easy. Remember what Dr. Arens says—long, deep breaths. That's it. That's right."

Gates cupped his wounded hand. "All right? Jesus H. Christ, your boy cut me! Look at this! I'm bleeding, for Chrissakes!" Shaking, he carefully twisted his handkerchief around the wound.

"It's nothing," Grace's father said.

"Nothing?"

"A good scar. It will make you look manly. The women will like it."

"You're as crazy as the kid here. Folks say he oughta be put away."

Grace held Stevie closer. "You shut up about that!"

Staring at his hand, he seemed not to hear her. "Yeah, put away where he can't hurt anybody else. And the rest of you, off this land. It's coming, it's coming real soon." He took a step forward, almost stumbling into the skeleton. Blinking hard, he looked from the remains to Grace's father.

"I tried to be nice, even put in a good word with my wife about that hearing next week. But now, I don't give a damn if they kick your ass outta here. Blast that highway right through your house. Right through this here pile of bones." Squinting, he looked down one side of the ridge, then the other. "Yeah, that road'll come right on through here."

"They'll build no road here. This land is *wakan*."

"My ass. It's more than *wakan*—it's commercial."

Grace said, "I think you better leave right now."

Gates flexed his hand gingerly. "I oughta get the cops out here on your kid."

"You hit my father first. Stevie was just protecting him."

He nodded slowly. "All right, but we still got a deal about that medicine bundle. You hear me? I'll be back with the cops if I have to."

Gates took several steps backward, his gaze darting from Grace to her father and son. Finally he trudged down the ridge to where his Cadillac was parked. Grace watched his car grow smaller as it followed the ribbon of dirt road winding its way to the interstate.

With Gates gone, Stevie stopped trembling and, head lowered, stood very quiet beside her. It was almost worse this way, when the boy with-drew into himself; his body felt fragile, like one of those dolls made of paper and wire.

Grace lifted his face and brushed back his hair.

"You okay?"

He nodded stiffly.

"You didn't take your evening medication, did you?" When he shrugged, she said a bit louder, "Of course not. You take it with your supper, but you weren't at home. You were out somewhere with your grandfather, instead of doing your homework like we'd agreed."

"You agreed," Stevie said. "I never did."

She felt her face grow warm but knew arguing would only make it worse. Instead she turned to her father. "What were you doing out here with the boy? I thought you were on a job today."

"I was. I went to help Ike build a fence in Rapid City. In the afternoon he got sick . . . "

"You mean drunk."

"I put Ike in his truck and drove him home. I told him he needed to do an *inipi*—the sweat would purify him—and that I would go collect the stones. I walked to the hills for them. On my way back, I met the boy. He helped me take the stones the rest of the way up here. That's when we found Gates."

"You should've sent Stevie right home. It was time for supper."

"The boy wasn't hungry. Why eat when you're not hungry?"

"And his medication?"

Her father smiled, showing the deep creases in his face. "He's sick in spirit. What better place for such an Indian to be than here, in this holy place?"

Releasing her son, Grace stepped closer to her father. "How many times do I have to tell you—Stevie's no Indian. His grandmother was white, his father was white. The only Indian blood in him is yours."

"And some of yours, daughter. Besides, I look at him and see the face of my people. His spirit is restless, that's all. You let the doctors put fences around it like the cattle on Gates's ranch, when it needs to roam free, like my brothers the elk."

"It's exactly that kind of talk that's making him the way he is. As if the way his father died weren't enough, you have to fill him full of that mumbo jumbo. I had to grow up with it, but Stevie doesn't. He's white. He doesn't have to live like this."

He gently cupped her face in his hand, and she half-closed her eyes, wanting to nuzzle against him. But there was Stevie. She pulled away.

"What's going to happen when they build the road through here? When all this is asphalt?"

"It will never happen."

"Like you always say—the law is white."

Her father nodded toward the skeleton. "He will save us. I feel his spirit. It's come for a purpose."

She shook her head slowly. "Gates is right—you are crazy. I want you to leave Stevie alone."

Grace turned, but her son was no longer there. She ran a few steps and then stopped, seeing him squatting beside the stones piled between the vision pit and the sweat lodge. Each stone was round and about the size of a man's hand. As she knelt beside him in the tall grass, he held one up to her.

"Look at this one, Mom. Look at the design on it, like someone paint-ed a man's face with green moss. The face looks familiar."

She stroked his hair. "Yes, it's pretty."

"Grandfather calls it a bird stone. He says his friends the starlings paint these designs on the stones and that some people, looking into them, can tell the future. Do you think so?"

"I think your grandfather is full of stories. We'd better go home—I'll make you supper. Let's put that back."

As Grace reached for the stone, he stopped her, bringing it closer. His finger traced the mossy image. "I know who that face reminds me of." She watched his eyes grow wide. "It looks just like Mr. Gates."

13

Chapter 2

MONDAY NIGHT

Each night walking into the police station, through the rear entrance of Bear Coat City Hall, Grace knew how Curly felt inside his stall. The squad room wasn't much larger than her living room, and the khaki-colored walls made it appear even smaller. In the center of the room, surrounded by a three-foot-high plywood wall, stood the dispatch unit, computer, copier, fax machine, file cabinets, and telephone. To her right, under a window, was the assistant chief's desk, as well as a few chairs resting against the wall, where the off-duty cops drank coffee and gabbed with one another. The chief had his own office through a door to the left.

Wendy, the second-shift dispatcher, sat alone in the squad room. Giggling over the phone, one hand idly playing with a blond curl, she reached into her purse and, without skipping a beat of conversation, reapplied her lipstick. The clock on the desk read 10:58.

Wendy's voice went husky. "I'll be outside in five minutes, honey. Don't make me wait. Bye."

Before Wendy could hang up, Grace grabbed her hand and whispered, "Is that my brother? I want to talk to him."

The other woman put down the receiver. "No such luck. I ain't seen much of Will lately. I think there's somebody else—there always is. Bet it's either Caroline from the travel agency or else Andi. He tell you?"

"Believe me, I got other things to talk to him about. So who's the guy?"

"Kenny—you know, that cowboy from Fort Pierre. He's taking me out for a few drinks."

"Is that all?"

She smiled, fluffing her hair in the desk mirror they shared. "Say, why

15

don't you get yourself a date for Saturday night, and the four of us will go into Deadwood."

"Thanks, but I don't think . . . "

"Oh, come on, it'll be fun. When's the last time you were out?"

Grace shrugged.

"Look, I could ask Kenny if he's got a friend."

"No."

"You really should get out. It's been over a year since Steve . . . "

"Maybe another time." She scanned the log book. "Anything going on tonight?"

"You gotta be kidding. What can happen in a town with two traffic lights? Elroy called in a few speeders and some kids out after curfew. Tom's working tonight."

Switching places with Wendy, Grace asked, "How come?"

"Said he had paperwork to catch up on, but he's been out most of the evening. Went over to check on the lumber mill. You know Tom—after that attempted break-in last month, he likes to make sure everything's okay. I tried to raise him a few times, but no answer. Probably nothing, but you better keep trying. How do I look?"

"Good enough to be hog-tied and branded. Now get outta here. Have a good time."

After Wendy left, Grace called Tom, but no response. That wasn't like him. Having alerted the two squad cars on duty, she spent the next few minutes staring at the phone, then dialed Jack's number.

"This is Jack Keeshin. Sorry I'm not in to take your call. Please leave a message, and I'll get back to you. Thanks."

She'd been hearing his answering machine for the past two hours, and, once again, she hung up without leaving a message. It was reassuring just to hear his voice, even if only a recording. Almost 11:15; where could he be? Maybe a late business meeting, or maybe, like Wendy, he was on a date. What kind of woman did he go for?—probably blond, long-legged, and wearing a cocktail dress like they did back in L.A. She found herself sketching his face on a notepad, crumpled the paper, and threw it away. What business was it of hers what he did at night?

She spent the next few minutes straightening the desk beside the computer, where Tom had installed a cubbyhole for each of the three dispatchers. Wendy's was jammed with cosmetics. Edna, who had been on the day shift for forty years, kept hers neatly arranged with medication

16

and an extra pair of bifocals. Grace's held a piece of charcoal she sometimes used for sketching and two photographs—one of her, Steve, and Stevie taken two years ago; the second showing her riding Curly in last year's reining championship.

There was one other item. Putting her hand deep inside the cubbyhole, she touched the turtle doll woven into a checkered pattern of green and yellow yarn. It had been made by her Lakota grandmother when Stevie was born. Not only was it his first doll; more important, it contained a piece of his umbilical cord. He had worn the turtle until he thought it too babyish, but for years afterward she carried it in her purse to guarantee him a long, healthy life.

She had brought the turtle doll here months ago, because in the long, quiet nights she needed something to give her hope about Stevie. A silly superstition, still it made her feel better. Just as when her mother died, her father had delayed the dead woman's passing by cutting a lock of her hair, tying it to a post, and making food offerings in her name. For a month Grace herself had kept the cooking pot in front of their house filled for passersby, who spoke of how good her mother had been, even for a white woman. Another superstition, yet during those weeks Grace had felt her mother's spirit slipping away so slowly, death didn't hurt quite so much. Not like when her husband died.

Swallowing hard, she slid in front of the dispatch unit to try Tom again. Then the door opened wide.

"Cir-cle the wagons! In-juns! Woo, woo, oww!"

Something crashed against the door, then her father's friend Ike stumbled in. Even from across the room she could smell the cheap whiskey on his breath. His hair, the color of gunmetal and nearly as long as hers, was tied in a ponytail. He wore jeans, work boots, and a Denver Broncos T-shirt so frayed that the emblem seemed tattooed to his chest. Unlike most Indians' faces, his was narrow and hollow-cheeked, the chin coming to a point like a goat's. The way he hopped around at the old-way dances was like a goat too.

"Hi, Gracie. Bet you didn't expect to see me tonight."

She couldn't help but smile. "My father said you were sick."

"Ah, sick. That's right. Bad spirits in me, your father said. Guess I went looking for a bottle of the right spirits. Found 'em too. Good-quality stuff. Ain't that right, Chief Cross Dog?"

Tom walked in yawning. "Yeah, it must've been $1.49 a gallon. You take it easy, Ike. Don't want you to hurt yourself in your condition. Hello, Grace. After 11:00 already?"

Maybe how he stood made Tom seem taller than most people, or how his shoulders almost filled the doorway. He wasn't one to mess with, but Grace liked him best this way, when he was a little tired and gentle with a poor old drunk. He rubbed his hair, cut short, and gave a weak smile. His face was dark as her father's and as broad, with large, sad eyes that reminded Grace of a draft horse.

As he brought Ike past the counter, she said, "We was plenty worried. Wendy called you, then I tried. Where've you been?"

Before he could answer, Ike spun around, did his little goat dance, and pointed to each of them. "Well, I'll be. Lookee what we got here." He began singing, "One little, two little, three little Indians—one little, two little, three little Indians—one little . . ."

"All right, Ike, that's enough," Tom said.

" . . . two little, three little Indians. What's the matter? Tom-Tom don't like bein' called an Injun? Maybe you ain't an Indian chief, but police chief's even better. Makes you almost white, like Gracie here."

Tom suddenly grabbed Ike, lifting him off the ground. The old man looked down at his feet paddling air, then smiled. "Lookee, I'm flying."

Grace leaned over the wall and touched Tom's shoulder. "He's drunk. He didn't mean nothing by it."

After a moment Tom nodded and gently set Ike down. "Sorry, old-timer. Come on. Let's give you a chance to sleep it off."

"Can I have the cell on the left? It's got a nice view of the junkyard, and I like talking to Samson, the guard dog."

"All right. Just don't keep that dog up past his bedtime."

"Thanks, Chief." Ike smiled at her. "How'd that comedian always used to end his shows? 'Say good night, Gracie.' 'Good night, Gracie.'"

"Good night, Ike."

While Tom took the old man through the station into the lockup, Grace dialed Jack again. She heard his recorded message but this time said, "This is Grace. It's almost 11:30. I'm at work. Please call me as soon as you get in. It's important." Her face grew warm. Maybe he'd think it was personal—that she was checking up on him. She quickly added, "It's about my father and the hearing."

Hanging up, she saw that Tom had returned. Instead of going into his office, he poured a cup of coffee and sat behind the desk across from her.

18

"Ike busted a window at the Quik Mart. I'll talk to the owner. Maybe he'll drop the charges, once Ike is sober and willing to work the damage off."

"You found him by the Quik Mart?"

"Yeah, on the way to your place. He was wandering along the highway. Pretty dark out there. Good thing I found him, before he became somebody's road kill."

"What were you doing over by my place? Wendy said you went to check on the lumber mill. That's on the other side of town."

He began fingering his coffee cup. "We're not talking about New York here; ain't much distance between one place and the next. I checked the mill out, then drove around a little. Just like to see everything's all right."

She smiled. "You're lying. Look at the way you're fiddling with that cup. Just like in school, when Mrs. Duran asked for your homework and you played with your pencil while telling her some lie about the wind blowing it out of your book."

Through the half-open door to the lockup, they heard Ike crooning, "Beautiful dreamer, wake unto me . . . ," while the junkyard dog across the alley howled a reply.

"So what were you doing?" Grace persisted.

"I told you, just out checking the town to make sure . . . "

"You were out with a girl!" When the cup almost fell from his hand, Grace slapped her desk. "Why, Tom Cross Dog, you tell me this minute who she is!"

"It ain't . . . Just forget it, Gracie."

"Oh no. If you think for one minute . . . "

"I said forget it!"

He stared at her, until she looked away. "Sorry, Tom, I didn't mean to pry."

"Beautiful drea . . . mer!" Ike's voice cracked trying to reach a high note, while the dog howled in mournful harmony. "Beautiful . . . "

Tom walked to the doorway. "Shut up before I rip your throat out!"

Grace shook her head slowly; it was like watching a stranger. "Ike doesn't mean any harm."

"They never do—none of these drunken Indians. Lazy and shiftless and good for nothing, like Ike here sitting in the slammer. Probably hasn't washed in weeks, and his brain's pickled in alcohol, but what the

19

hell do you expect of an Injun? Don't it ever bother you, Gracie, or do you forget that you're part Injun too?"

"No, Tom, I don't forget."

"I wonder. I . . . " He stopped suddenly and walked back to the desk, sitting heavily in the chair.

"Go on," she said.

"Forget it." He looked down at the desk. "I heard you calling Jack Keeshin. Something about the hearing?"

"Uh . . . yeah, I was calling him about that . . . and about my father." Immediately she regretted mentioning her father to Tom.

"Anything wrong?"

"Not really. Well, we found the skeleton of an Indian up near the sweat lodge. Body must be a hundred years old."

"That all?"

She thought about mentioning Gates, but that would only bring in Will and maybe what Stevie did with his pocketknife. "Yeah, just that. I wondered if having the remains on the ridge would make any difference at the hearing. What do you think?"

"I think whatever the white man wants he'll get. They've been stealing our land since Custer found gold back in the 1870's. A few more acres won't make any difference. Make the best deal you can, take the money and run."

"My father won't."

Tom straightened in his chair. "No, he got religion. Too bad he wasn't always that way."

"Sorry. I shouldn't have brought it up."

Tom's body rocked slowly in the chair. Grace remembered that too from school, whenever he got nervous.

"You seeing Keeshin?" he asked.

"He's acting as Father's attorney."

"You know what I mean."

"You mean, like going out?"

He nodded.

"I don't see how that's any of your business."

At that moment, Al sauntered into the station and flipped his patrolman's cap onto the old hat rack in the corner. His shift started at midnight, but he always came in a half hour early with a milk shake from the Big Freeze. Despite his sweet tooth, he was thin as the nightstick he carried. He sat in the chair nearest the desk and worked the straw like a suckling kitten.

Grace said, a little too loudly, "I better check on our two units. Shift changes pretty soon. Besides, they'll want to know you came in."

As Tom walked into his office, she began making her calls. Neither squad car had anything to report. She logged their responses while Al slurped the bottom of his shake; then the phone rang.

"Police. How can we help you?"

"It's me, Will."

Turning away from Al, she half-whispered, "I need to talk to you, but later when I get home."

"Gracie . . ."

"Of all the jackass ideas, trying to sell Albert Gates something that ain't yours . . ."

"Gracie, it's about Gates."

"What did you do, find another skeleton up there?"

The line went dead. "Will? Will, you there?"

Finally he replied, "I found him up on the ridge."

"What're you talking about?"

"He's dead, Gracie. Albert Gates is dead."

She felt cold inside; her lips couldn't move to speak.

"Gracie, you hear me?"

She swallowed hard. "What happened?"

"I came home from the gas station a little while ago and saw a light on the ridge. Figured it was Dad. I wanted to bring him back to the house—thought it might rain tonight. When I got up there . . . It's terrible. You better send the cops."

"Is Father up there?"

"Yeah."

"Is he all right?"

"I guess so. He's . . . Just send somebody out here right away."

"Tom!" she called. When he appeared in the doorway, she told him what Will had said.

"Tell him not to touch anything, and you contact the paramedics, Doc Gustafson at the medical center, and forensics in Rapid City. Ask Andi if she can take some pictures."

"I'm going with you," she said.

"I don't think . . ."

21

"My father's up there."

He hesitated only a moment. "All right. Al, make those calls and cover for her."

Still chewing on the straw, Al asked, "Should I have Elroy get over there? That's part of his patrol area."

Tom looked at Grace, then shook his head. "He's probably on his way in. I'll take the call myself."

He didn't bother with the siren. At ten minutes to midnight Bear Coat had long ago tucked itself into bed, except for the five bars whose lights winked like fireflies, a last call before closing. A block ahead a tavern door opened, and in the warm night air, Grace heard a man and woman giggling. Passing the door as it closed, she smelled stale beer and cigarette smoke and shivered, because once Steve would've walked from such a place, his face suddenly illuminated in the darkened doorway as he lit a cigarette and smiled at somebody's joke.

As they reached the north end of town, the road went from concrete to gravel. Slate-colored clouds obscured the moon and stars; in the great blackness of night, even the car's headlights drifted away like smoke. Somewhere ahead lay the ridge and the Black Hills, but at that moment Grace felt bound neither by space nor by time. Around her she sensed the prairie grass blowing gently in waves, and the car seemed to drift in a great ocean. Then no longer the ocean; she might have taken flight, tiny dashboard lights the constellations she was leaving far behind.

Any moment the vast darkness would open and she would see the spirit world with its tall grass, herds of buffalo, tipis of her ancestors, and the faces of those who had gone before her. Maybe even her husband; some of the old ones believed that there would be a place for those whites good of heart. She needed somebody to confide in, and her father . . .

Will had said their father was all right, or had he? It couldn't be happening again, not after so many years. She heard her fingers drumming on the car door. Tom must've heard it too. Could he be thinking the same thing? Would it start all over again?

Light shone through the first-floor windows of her house. Will appeared suddenly in the headlights. He blinked hard and pushed back a black wave of hair as they stepped from the car. Grace's brother leaned heavily against the hood; his undershirt, soaked with sweat, stuck to his chest. Tall and well built, still he looked like a little boy standing next to Tom.

Tom asked, "Where's Gates?"

"Up on the ridge."

"Your father up there too?"

"Yeah."

While Tom went into the trunk for a flashlight, Grace pulled her brother aside. "What's Father got to do with this?"

"I don't know."

"Oh, God, I can't go through this again. What'll it do to Stevie? You haven't told him, have you?"

Will looked down at his shoes. "Stevie's not here. I went upstairs to his bedroom, and he's gone."

"He isn't up on the ridge with . . . ?"

"No, I checked. At least he ain't there now. Maybe we oughta tell Tom."

"You don't say one word about Stevie. You understand?"

"But . . ."

She shook her head to silence him, as Tom returned. They drove slowly up the ridge.

Will pointed from the back seat. "That light up there's Gates's flashlight. Ain't too strong anymore—I left it when I ran to call you."

A few minutes later they parked at the top of the ridge, beside the sweat lodge. Will hurried out. He picked up the flashlight and walked a few yards to their left.

"Over . . . over here."

Grace followed Will's gaze to the ground. She thought of Halloween, the way Gates's head lay like a pumpkin in the darkness, illuminated only by the dim light. She could barely see the body stretched behind.

Tom examined the corpse. "Back of his head's smashed in. He's dead, all right. Been awhile—body's getting stiff." He searched Gates and removed a piece of paper from an inside coat pocket. "Some kind of bill of sale"—he looked up—"between Gates and Will."

He ran his flashlight back and forth across the ground between Gates's corpse and the Indian remains to their right. He followed his beam of light toward the skeleton. "It looks like there was a struggle over here—a toolbox is knocked over. Then Gates dragged himself as far as he got and gave out. Don't see what killed him, though. Will, you sure you didn't touch anything?"

Will's gaze was transfixed by the corpse.

23

"Will, you all right?"

His brow furrowed. "Yeah."

Tom went back to the corpse. "You touch anything?"

"No."

"Hmm—his right hand's bandaged. What's this?" He pried something from Gates's hand and held the object to the light. "It's some dirt—no, too hard. Maybe an old piece of rusty metal." After putting it in his shirt pocket, he walked over to Will. "You said your father was here. The sweat lodge?"

"No, over there."

Tom took a few steps, then stopped suddenly, bending his knees. "There's a stone here, and it looks like some blood's on it. We'd better see your father."

Grace walked with Tom to the vision pit. He shone his flashlight into the blackness. "Saul True Sky."

Her father looked up.

"What're you doing?"

"I'm talking to White Bear."

Tom's light crisscrossed the pit. "Who's White Bear?"

"The one who's been dug up over there. His *wanagi* called me."

"*Wanagi*—his ghost?"

"I've been flying with him, through the clouds, back to our ancestors. I've seen the buffalo chewing on this grass."

"Come on out of there."

Her father crawled from the pit and stood beside Tom, who asked, "Do you know why I'm here?"

"It must be about something bad, or you wouldn't have come."

"Albert Gates is dead. His body's over there—back of his head's crushed. You know anything about that?"

"No. I've been with White Bear."

"You know why Gates came here in the middle of the night?"

Grace stepped beside her father. "You don't have to say anything."

"He came here for White Bear's *wotawe*. He came this afternoon, but I wouldn't let him take it."

Sirens wailed in the distance.

Tom asked, "The two of you fight this afternoon? Gates's right hand is bandaged—you do that?"

"No."

"Did White Bear?"

Her father's face slowly broke into a smile. "You think I'm crazy."

"Did you kill Gates?"

"That's what's wrong with you. You don't believe in the spirits. You are a full-blood, more than my own children, yet you are too much of this earth. You need to fly with the spirits. When you finally fly, then you will truly be Lakota."

He tried to put a hand on Tom's shoulder, but Tom grabbed it and stared at the sleeve.

"That looks like dried blood. There's blood on a stone back there. Could be what smashed Gates's head in. You know anything about it?"

"It's one of the stones for Ike's *inipi*."

Taking the flashlight from Will, Grace looked at the stone and recognized its pattern—the face in green moss resembling Albert Gates. She held her breath, not daring to look at either man. Where was Stevie?

Far below them, points of light punctuated the darkness. For a moment Grace imagined they were stars and pictured herself above them, flying with the spirits to find her son. Blinking, she realized they were the headlights of the paramedics. The ambulance jerked to a halt, as did several cars behind it. Men ran toward Gates's body.

Tom took the small piece of metal from his pocket, holding it in an open palm. "Do you know what this is?"

Her father shook his head.

Suddenly light flooded their eyes.

"Jesus!" Tom said. "What the hell are you doing?"

Andi stood beside them with her camera. "Isn't it evidence?"

"Just take the usual pictures of the body and send them over. I keep telling you, the town's not going to pay for a hundred shots of the crime scene."

Returning the piece of metal to his pocket, he glanced at the corpse, then said, "True Sky, you'd better come with me."

Grace shook her head. "Tom, this is crazy! Father couldn't kill anybody!" She put a hand to her mouth, knowing it was the worst thing she could've said.

He grabbed her so close, she could feel his heart pounding. "No? It's not like he never done this before."

Chapter 3

WEDNESDAY MORNING

All morning the airplane wing had played tag with the sun slipping through clouds as it moved west. Now, as the jet began its descent, Rosen saw from his window the southern end of Lake Michigan. Its azure water shone smooth and fragile as glass; drop a stone from this height and the lake might shatter. The three of them used to skate on the frozen lake, laughing while their blades made designs in the ice. He shook his head. Of all the airports in the world, he hated O'Hare the most.

"Are you finished with this, sir?"

The flight attendant was pointing, across an empty seat, to his cup of tea.

"Yes." He checked his watch. "We'll be arriving a few minutes early."

"Uh-huh. You flying in for business?"

"Just making a connection," he said, again looking out the window.

He hadn't quite told the truth, but then he hadn't quite lied either. Anywhere else there was never any thought of lying. He would've been, as always, a stranger among strangers, like them slipping through the airport to grab a taxi to some hotel. Inside the gray or green room, with its paintings bolted to the wall, he would unpack quickly before going downstairs to eat, and no one would see that he hadn't called home, because there was no one at home to call.

Chicago was different; in the city where he'd spent most of his life, he could play the stranger only by lying to himself. There were times when he did—running through O'Hare to make a connection without even a phone call, without daring to look around for fear he might meet someone who had known him long ago, when he wore his *peyot,* curled sideburns. How many times, as a boy, had he been told by the rabbi that

27

emet, truth, was God's seal. Still Rosen committed the abomination and lied to himself, because there were some things worse than a lie.

He watched the small houses and baseball diamonds near the airport grow larger as the plane dropped lower, until, skimming a highway overpass, its wheels suddenly touched concrete and it roared along the runway to a long, slow halt. Rosen took his time, straightening the blue plaid tie she'd given him last Hanukkah. He wouldn't have to lie today. After the aisle had cleared, he took his briefcase from the overhead rack and walked from the plane into the airport.

She was in his arms before he even saw her. Turning up her chin, he kissed her gently, then they hugged again.

Sarah looked up at him, and her eyes glimmered, bleeding the mascara. "Daddy . . . Daddy."

She wore her long black hair in a ponytail, the way she had as a little girl—the way he liked it. But the ponytail seemed out of place with the mascara and blush, and the earrings. When had she gotten her ears pierced?

They walked into the waiting area, and he sat beside her, still holding her hand. She wore a Cubs T-shirt that hung over her cut-offs. She looked at him for a long time, then giggled and wiped her eyes with a tissue.

"You look terrific," he said. "I can't believe . . . "

"You can't believe how much I've grown. Daddy, you always say that. I suppose you wouldn't recognize me walking down the street."

"That's right, especially with all that makeup."

"It's not that much. Besides, in a few more weeks I'll be in high school."

"I know, all grown up. Pretty soon you'll be needing a face-lift and cellulite removal." He looked past her. "Where's your mother?"

"Parking the car. We were running a little late, so she dropped me off. Do you have much time?"

"About forty minutes. I have to make a connection for South Dakota."

"What kind of case is it this time?"

"An American Indian's been accused of murder."

"How many people did he kill?"

"Isn't one enough? Your mother isn't letting you watch all those slasher movies, is she?"

"No. I didn't mean anything."

He sighed softly, stroking her hair. "I shouldn't have snapped at you. It's just . . . I worry about you. How's everything?"

"Great. I'm taking tennis in summer school—it's a way of getting acquainted with the high school. I really like it. Mom and I've been playing. I can almost beat her."

"She's probably afraid of breaking a nail. You're keeping up with piano?"

"Uh-huh. In fact, I took a three-week course at the music center on advanced theory. It was pretty interesting."

"Your mother didn't mention anything about the class."

"It was a kind of spur-of-the-moment thing. You're coming to my fall recital?"

"Have I ever missed one? How's everything else?"

"Oh, Daddy, did I tell you I've learned to play stride piano? One of the albums you left me—Joe Turner, you remember."

"Sure."

"I've been fooling around with the keyboard, playing like he did. Sounds like a waterfall and drives Mrs. Chang crazy. She says, 'Stop that racket! That not your lesson. You waste your time. You waste my time. Very bad girl!'" Sarah giggled nervously.

"I'd love to hear it. How's everything else?"

Her toes dug into the carpet. "Okay."

"Are you getting used to Shelly?"

"I guess. He doesn't expect me to call him Dad or anything. He tries to be nice. We all went to a ball game last week. I like his house. He's got a Jacuzzi in the backyard he lets me and my friends use."

"That's good."

"He's still kind of geeky. I mean, like a podiatrist's supposed to be a real doctor, or what? And he's got all this elevator music on tape—sometimes I think I'm living in a shopping mall. You know, he used to play the accordion as a kid. Talk about being a dork."

"It's all right, Sarah."

"Huh?"

For the second time, Rosen lifted her chin. "It's all right to like him."

He looked into her eyes and smiled his best liar's smile. Sarah seemed about to say something but, instead, wiped her eyes again. He moved his hand toward her, hesitated, then clicked open his briefcase.

"Here's a little something you said you wanted. It's extra large; I know you like them big."

He handed her a Georgetown University jersey, with the Hoya bulldog emblem covering the front.

Grinning, she pulled it over her Cubs shirt. "This is great, just great. Thanks."

"The bulldog kind of reminds me of my boss, Mr. Nahagian."

Her index finger traced the emblem. "It looks like the dog on 'Tom and Jerry,' the one that's always chasing Tom. I used to watch the show Saturday mornings while Mom graded papers and you worked on some legal stuff. Then you'd take me to the park. Remember?"

Rosen nodded but said nothing. Those memories were like scar tissue; words, any words, scratched them raw. So he clicked his briefcase shut and sat quietly.

"Oh," Sarah said, reaching into her pocket, "this is for you." She handed him a plastic key chain in the shape of a quarter note. "I remember how you were always misplacing your car keys. It glows in the dark. The quarter note's just a little something to remind you of me."

"Thanks, I can really use it."

As he put the key chain into his pocket, Bess approached them.

"Hello, Nate." She sat beside their daughter. "You look good."

"You too."

In a way, she did. Short hair cut into a flip, an even tan, a powder-blue blouse with matching shorts, and jewelry including her piece of the rock—the diamond engagement ring and wedding band from Shelly.

"Nate, I know you don't have much time, but there're a few things we need to talk about."

"Sure."

She handed a five-dollar bill to her daughter. "Honey, get me a cup of coffee with two sugars, tea with lemon for your dad, and whatever you want. No candy—we're going to meet Cousin Donna for lunch in an hour."

"But I want to stay with Daddy. He'll be leaving in a few minutes."

"I promise this won't take long. Then you can have him all to yourself."

After Sarah left, they both shifted from the empty chair between them.

He said, "I'm surprised you remembered—about the tea with lemon."

"I remember a lot. Like all those years picking you up here at O'Hare, at God knows what time of day or night."

"That was good exercise. You've gained a few pounds since then. Better start taking your coffee without sugar, or pretty soon you'll be lumbering into Weight Watchers, measuring your food like gold dust and eating zucchini whip. Does Shelly like his women plump, or just their feet?"

She allowed herself a small smile. "That's good, Nate, those smart-aleck remarks of yours. Keeps me from getting too sentimental. You wouldn't like that—neither of us would."

Rosen watched Bess absently reach for her hair to play with the tresses no longer there, the ones she had let down slowly on their wedding night. Suddenly he wanted to touch her hair and kiss her, to see if she'd respond. She would. They had loved each other all those years—not just devotion, but the heartbeat quickening and blood pumping. Grappling in the tangled sheets . . .

"I just wanted to let you know about the school psychologist's final report concerning Sarah. They're mailing you a copy, but basically things have been much better. It's been . . . what? . . . almost eight months since I married Shelly. The psychologist believes that Sarah's showing the usual symptoms of anger and guilt as a result of our divorce, but he thinks there's something more, something Sarah's not telling. In any event, both he and I agree she's been adjusting. It'll just take time."

Still watching Bess's hand, Rosen said nothing.

Finally she brought it down to her lap. "Well, I thought you'd be glad."

"Sure."

"The psychologist has alerted the high school, and someone there will be monitoring her progress for the first semester. But her final grades were good, she's practicing with her usual concentration, and she's having a great summer. I'm very pleased, and you should be too."

He nodded.

"Things would be even better if you were more accepting of the situation."

"Situation?"

"My marriage. I know, more than anything, you want what's best for Sarah. If you could just . . ."

"Just what?"

"I don't know, maybe have dinner with us, Shelly too, the next time you're in town."

He shook his head.

"At least stop with the podiatrist jokes. Every time we go to McDonald's, Sarah says it must be Shelly's favorite restaurant because of its golden arches. That's one of your adolescent cracks."

"All right."

"Look, I know I hurt you, but for Sarah's sake we should try to make the best of it."

"Of what? You sleeping with another man?"

Her eyes widened. "What in God's name are you talking about? Shelly and I are married."

" 'In God's name'? That's a strange way for you to put it. You know we never received a *get*."

She rubbed her forehead, flashing the rings in front of his eyes. "*Get*— a Jewish divorce? You never mentioned it when we went through court. Knowing how you feel about your family, I never thought a *get* would even cross your mind. What's done is done. Why in the world would you bring it up now?"

Why would he? He must be crazy to say things like that. Still, for a moment he saw her smiling shyly, dressed in white and standing with him under the *huppah*.

He asked, "You know why a Jewish groom steps on a glass at the marriage ceremony?"

"My mother said it was the last time the husband ever puts his foot down."

"It symbolizes what discord between husband and wife can do to their family."

Bess shook her head slowly. "So, after all these years, your head's still in that ghetto of your father. People go through divorces all the time. They adjust, and their children adjust."

"Do they?"

"I never said you were the only one at fault. We just didn't get along. Irreconcilable differences . . . God, I don't know why we're rehashing all this."

"Irreconcilable differences? What does that mean—you wanted a boat on Lake Michigan and I settled for one in the bathtub? The only real justification for a *get* is something serious like adultery, and there was never any of that."

Crossing her arms, Bess stared at him for a long time. Finally, she said, "Well, I'm sleeping with Shelly now, so go ask for your *get*."

He turned away, pretending to look for Sarah. It was a mistake to have come, to have seen Bess with those rings, fresh from another man's bed—even if the man was her husband.

Her hand was on his arm, slowly pulling him around.

"Nate, I had no idea my marriage bothered you."

"Forget it. Like you said, 'what's done is done'."

"Maybe you should get some help. If therapy helped Sarah, it could probably help . . . "

"I said forget it."

"But if . . . "

"Here's Sarah." He took the tea from her. "Thanks."

She sat between her parents, and they sipped their drinks for a few minutes.

"Everything okay?" she asked.

"Sure," he said, checking his watch. "I'd better get going."

"Oh, Daddy, you just got here!"

"Walk me to the gate." To Bess, "Sarah mentioned a music theory class. You know I pay for all her lessons." He took out his checkbook. "How much was it?"

"It was just something extra we fit into her schedule. Shelly and I . . . I've taken care of it."

Pen poised over the checkbook, he asked again, "How much was it?"

She hesitated, then said, "A hundred dollars."

Bess was lying. It must've cost at least twice that much, but they both knew he didn't have that kind of money. He handed her the check.

She asked, "Have you spoken to any of your family lately?"

"No."

"It's just that Shelly heard your brother Aaron might be the new head of cardiology. They're both on staff at Highland Park. Quite an honor for someone not much over forty."

"He was always the smart one in the family."

"Funny, he always says that about you. You should call him. And . . . your father's been ill. Just the flu, but anything at his age . . . I thought you should know."

33

Lifting his briefcase, Rosen stood and, taking Sarah's hand, led her away. Bess remained seated, finishing her coffee and looking at a newspaper strewn on the carpet near her feet. Halfway down the corridor, he glanced back to see her watching them.

"Sarah, do you remember when you were a little girl, your mother and I used to take you ice-skating? We'd make little designs on the ice with our skates."

"Like what?"

"Oh, clowns and stars. Sometimes you'd sit on the ice and make big circles with your tush. Everybody thought you were so cute."

"Daddy, I didn't seriously do that in public."

They looked at each other, then both burst out laughing.

He held her hand tightly all the way to the gate, where a few businessmen had lined up for boarding.

"I'd better go."

She nodded, and tears welled in the corners of her eyes.

Cupping her face in his hand, he kissed her forehead. "It's all right. I'll be in for your recital in a few months."

"That's so far away."

"Maybe I can come through O'Hare on my way back from South Dakota."

"Promise."

"Sure. Now you promise me not to let this new situation—your mother's marriage—bother you. All right?"

She nodded, swallowing hard. "It doesn't bother me—really. It's you I'm worried about."

"Me?"

"Uh-huh. I just can't stand for you to be alone."

He suddenly grew very warm and, feeling his heart beat heavily, loosened his tie. "I'm not alone." He stared deep into her eyes and thought of how the Torah described wearing the phylacteries. He touched his heart, then his forehead. "I keep you here and here, before my eyes always."

They hugged tightly, he kissed her once more on the cheek, then pulled away from her arms. Before leaving he said what he'd always told her, ever since she was a baby. "Be a good girl."

Handing his boarding pass to the attendant before entering the gate, he looked back and waved.

The attendant said, "She's a pretty girl."

"My daughter. She's come to see me off."

Walking into the plane, he thought, "At least today I didn't lie. I wasn't a stranger."

Chapter 4

WEDNESDAY AFTERNOON

Flying over Wisconsin, Minnesota, and South Dakota, Rosen saw farm-
land that went on forever, an enormous checkerboard of yellow and green
fields bigger than most countries, big enough to feed the world. It was a
monument more wondrous than those of marble he saw every day in
Washington. His father would have said, "Of course it is more wondrous,
because all that you see is a gift from God."

Then he would have quoted the Psalms: "'How manifold are Thy
works, O Lord! In wisdom hast Thou made them all.'"

It always came back to his father. Even the words Rosen had spoken to
Bess, about adultery and the need for a *get,* might have been his father's.
She had said the old man was sick, but Aaron lived nearby—the eldest
son and a doctor. He'd take care of everything, like the dutiful son he
always was. If the illness became serious, Rosen would get a call. Would
even that bring him home?

"How manifold are Thy works . . . "

He thought of Sarah—how wondrous she was, and how she was growing up without him. And Bess. What talmudic passage had the rabbi
quoted at their wedding—"He who has no wife abides without goodness
and joy."

"Leave it alone," he muttered, remembering what Bess had said.
"What's done is done." Besides, there was the case. He needed to concen-
trate on that, or he'd be of no use to anyone, especially to the man
charged with murder . . . this Indian, Saul True Sky. Putting on a pair of
headphones, he listened to the all-jazz channel while reading the murder
account that had been faxed to his office the day before.

During the next half hour, Rosen occasionally glanced out the window
and noticed the landscape changing. The greens and yellows weren't

quite so vibrant; in the distance, the land rose into a series of hills darkened by forests.

"We're beginning our descent into Rapid City," the pilot said over the intercom, as the seat-belt sign flashed.

Walking through the gate into the waiting area, Rosen scanned the terminal, looking for the woman who was supposed to meet him.

"Mr. Rosen?"

He turned, then blinked as a flash went off in his face.

"You are Nate Rosen, from the Committee to Defend the Constitution?"

"Yes."

Another flash. After his eyes cleared, he saw a woman with a camera standing before him.

"I'm Andi Wojecki. Thanks for coming."

She was tall and slender, in her mid-twenties, wearing a white blouse with puffy sleeves, blue jeans, and sandals. A purse on a long leather strap hung from her shoulder. Her face was pretty, almost delicate with its cat's eyes and turned-up nose, but a strong jaw gave it character. Her straw-colored hair was cut short, which emphasized the jaw even more, as did her broad smile.

"I hope you had a good flight. That airplane food can be seriously dangerous. Let's get your luggage, then I'll take you into Bear Coat. It's about an hour's drive."

Rapid City Airport could have fit into O'Hare's car-rental lot, but it was clean and modern, with low slat ceilings exposing the walkways above. Andi walked a little ahead of him. She moved like a cat, bending one knee and stretching gracefully to photograph anyone catching her fancy—a businessman wearing a cowboy hat, an old man whose cane had a pistol-shaped handle, and an Indian woman whose small children trailed behind her like ducklings.

Rosen said, "My boss, Mr. Nahagian, mentioned you own the town's newspaper. I take it you're also its photographer."

"Dad owned the paper, but I sold it after he died. I stayed on and, in a hick town like Bear Coat, do a little of everything—photography, reporting, even paste-up." She reached into her purse. "Here's yesterday's edition. It's got the best coverage of the murder."

The *Bear Coat Chronicle*'s headline screamed: ALBERT GATES MURDERED, and most of the paper's eight pages were taken up with the

38

crime. A photograph of Gates had been placed directly under the word MURDERED, and, below it, another photo showed paramedics rolling the body away from "the scene of the crime." Both photos were credited to A. Wojecki.

The lead story gave details, most of which Rosen knew from the fax. The police chief, Tom Cross Dog, was quoted as saying that Saul True Sky had been arrested for the murder and that police had "strong physical evidence" linking him to the crime. Other stories carried background information on the victim, who owned a car dealership in Rapid City and a ranch outside of Bear Coat, and his wife, Belle Gates, the town's current mayor. All that was mentioned of the accused murderer was his name, age—"probably 67"—and the fact that he had been a resident of Bear Coat his entire life.

"Not much here," Rosen said, returning the newspaper to Andi. "What else can you tell me?"

"Well, like it says, they found Gates's toolbox by the Indian remains, and his Cadillac parked down the other side of the ridge."

"What about this 'strong physical evidence'?"

"Gates was hit on the back of the head, and his blood type was on Saul's sleeve. A stone with blood on it was found near the body. That's about all I know. Tom's playing this pretty close to the vest. He's no Barney Fife."

"Excuse me?"

"You know, Barney Fife. The bogus deputy sheriff on 'Andy Griffith.' The TV show, 'Andy Griffith.' "

"Sorry, I don't know it."

Andi shook her head sadly. "You grow up on the moon?"

"Sort of. The *Chronicle* didn't say much about True Sky. Normally, a paper would play up the killer angle for all it's worth. I expected to see his sullen face staring back at me on the front page with some deep-background about his sordid past."

"Yeah, well, things are like a little complicated. Do you know why you're here—I mean, why I called the Committee to Defend the Constitution?"

Rosen nodded. "My boss Nahagian said he knew your father. They worked together on one of the CDC's first cases, back in the fifties."

"Uh-huh. It had something to do with the county jail making Indian prisoners cut their hair, and the Indians saying it was against their religion. Dad was very young, he'd just taken over the paper, and he wanted to do something good. Nobody gave a damn about Indians back then. Finally he found this new organization, the CDC, and your Mr. Nahagian. They lost the case, but I guess they became good enough friends to exchange Christmas cards. When I went to D.C. on my junior class trip, Mr. Nahagian showed me around. He sent me a real nice letter two years ago, when Dad died."

"You think this True Sky is being framed for the murder, because he's an Indian?"

She looked down at her camera before answering. "Maybe. Saul True Sky was one of the Indian prisoners my father tried to help with Mr. Nahagian. And . . . there could be another reason."

They had reached the baggage-claim conveyor belts. While Rosen waited for his suitcase, Andi went to a nearby candy counter. She came back smoking a cigarette and offered him one.

"No, thanks," Rosen said, as he pulled his luggage from the conveyor.

"I hope you're not one of those antismoking fanatics. They really freak me out. They're usually chewing gum and bulging out of their spandex."

"No, I think it makes you look like Humphrey Bogart."

"Huh?" She grinned. "You know, you're kinda cute."

It was a beautiful day, the breeze making it just cool enough for his sport coat. Following Andi into the parking lot, he tried to guess what kind of car she drove. They passed a number of Jeeps and pickup trucks, and he figured her for one of them, maybe with fuzzy pink dice and a Grateful Dead bumper sticker.

"Here we are," she said.

It was an old yellow Mercury—beat up, rusted, and the size of a gunboat. She unlocked the trunk, which yawned open to reveal its contents: a spare tire, lawn chair, snow shovel, several camera cases, a tripod, boots, books, stacks of old newspapers, and a man's boxer shorts.

She pushed the newspapers to one side. "You can put your suitcase in here."

"You can put the entire airport in here. Some car."

"Dad's. He said if he couldn't afford a Cadillac, at least he could buy something as big. Well, get in."

The car's interior was a faded green vinyl, the cracks in the seats covered by long strips of black duct tape. Even with the windows open, everything smelled of stale cigarette smoke; the ashtray was overstuffed with butts. The clock didn't work, he wondered about the gas gauge reading empty, but he had more leg room than in a swimming pool.

Andi quickly pulled from the parking space, turning the steering wheel with both hands, and the car rumbled forward.

"Original muffler," she said, leaning back and taking a long drag of her cigarette.

Suddenly she hit the brakes, grabbed her camera and snapped a photo of a wizened cowboy passed out against a pickup, an empty whiskey bottle resting like a candle between his hands. Then she continued, through the parking lot, onto the highway.

Rosen said, "You're really serious about this photography."

"It's gonna be my ticket out of here. I'm putting together a portfolio to send to newspapers in Denver, San Francisco, Chicago—anywhere that's got streetlights and men who don't act or smell like bulls."

"I thought the great photographers came out West to take pictures. Like Ansel Adams."

"He didn't have to live here. I'm gonna be like Annie Leibovitz— spend all my time taking kinky photos of Mick Jagger and Clint Eastwood. No more cowboys and Indians."

They drove for a few more minutes, then Rosen said, "You mentioned there was another reason why someone might want Saul True Sky framed for the murder."

Andi nodded. "You ever hear of George Manderson?"

"No. Should I have?"

"He discovered a tin mine around 1890, after the Indians were driven onto their reservations, and built Tin Town. Was the big man around here for awhile. After he died, his son Owen got into a feud with the owner of the Homestake Gold Mine down by Lead. Guy by the name of William Randolph Hearst."

"I can guess what happened."

"Hearst squashed him like a bug. Cut off his transportation routes, hired away his miners, while Owen kept pouring his money into the mine, even after the tin began to run out. Talk about being a jerk. He went broke, and, if that wasn't bad enough, his daughter hurt him the way Hearst never could."

Andi stubbed her cigarette butt into the ashtray, then lit another one. "Eleanor was an only child, and Owen spoiled her rotten. Folks say she was a helluva tomboy—great rider, used to hang around the rodeo. Her old man didn't like that and spent the last of his money to send her East for an education. Guess he wanted her to become Queen of South Dakota or something. Instead, she came back full of her own ideas about the Golden West and how the white man had screwed the red man. She helped my dad defend those Indians I told you about.

"Then she did the damnedest thing. She married one of the prisoners, Saul True Sky. A white woman just didn't do that back in the fifties. Well, Owen kicked her out and never spoke to her again. When he died, though, his will left everything to her. Of course, by then he'd lost most of Tin Town to taxes. Eleanor and Saul lived in the house her grandfather had built, though Saul stayed on the ridge most of the time. Said it was holy. They seemed happy enough, had two kids, then Eleanor died from a bad fever. That was about twenty-five years ago. Her kids, Grace and Will, still live up there."

"Sounds like you know the family pretty well."

"We've been close ever since my dad helped Saul that first time. I'm an only child—my own mom died when I was young, and now they're about the only family I got. Grace has always been kind of an older sister."

"What was True Sky in jail for?"

She hesitated. "I guess a lot of things, but no matter what folks tell you, he's a good guy. Some of the Lakota around here even consider Saul a holy man. You got to help him. Look, you must be tired. Relax and enjoy the ride."

Flicking her cigarette ash out the window, Andi turned on a rock-and-roll station and tapped in time to the music. She wasn't going to talk about True Sky anymore, so Rosen loosened his tie and took in the scenery through the Mercury's panoramic window.

It was as beautiful as people always said. A canvas of sky, powder-blue with wisps of drifting clouds, spread far as he could see, dwarfing the dark hills, which the highway split far into the distance. A limitless, immutable sky; from such a place could the voice of God whisper. In comparison, everything else seemed inconsequential, like the rows of tract houses and trailer parks just outside of Rapid City, even the occasional two-story home with its wooden deck and swimming pool.

As they rode farther from town, he saw fewer buildings and more open land. Most of the hay had already been gathered into rolls. A few had dried to an ashen color, probably overlooked from the previous year's harvest. Occasionally the car passed a stretch of tall grasses, where small groups of cattle grazed peacefully behind rail fences.

The beauty of sky and land made the billboards along the highway even uglier. They came rushing up to the car, one after the other, an endless stream of beggars in loud clothing. "Sturgis Motorcycle Classic," "Mt. Rushmore," "Homestead Gold Mine," "Spearfish Passion Play," "Gambling in Deadwood," and advertisements for dozens of hotels and restaurants.

From a distance, the hills peeked over the signs, as if afraid to get too close. They rose one upon the other, dark from the clusters of evergreens covering them.

Rosen said, "Now I know why they're called the Black Hills. They're very beautiful."

Andi nodded. "They were nicer before all the tourism. You know, they're sacred to the Lakota. I forget just why."

"Because of the *el*."

"Huh?"

"The spirits inside the hills."

"You know about the Lakota?"

"I understand their worship. It's not so different from my ancestors."

"So you're an Indian too! Which tribe?"

"One of the Ten Lost Tribes." He nodded toward the sign they had just passed. "Wasn't that the turnoff for Bear Coat?"

"Uh-huh, but I want to take you by the scene of the crime. Besides, bet you've never seen a real ghost town before."

Passing a gas station on their right, Andi slowed the car and reached over to wave at a mechanic getting out of his pickup. Smiling, the young man waved back.

"That's Saul True Sky's son, Will," Andi said. "He's the one who found Albert Gates's body on the ridge."

After traveling another two miles, they exited onto a narrow gravel road that swung back below the highway through a timber underpass. A hand-painted sign, reading "TIN TOWN," had been tacked to one of the crossbeams. A quarter mile later, the gravel petered to a dirt road bisecting a field of grass and scrub trees.

Andi stopped the car and took her camera. "Well, what do you think?" When he shrugged, she added, "Over there, don't you see it?"

He followed her into the grass and saw something broken into shadows around one of the trees. It had once been a frame house but now tilt-ed precariously, with a loose side board fluttering in the breeze. Bending on one knee, Andi snapped a picture.

"The tin mine's about a mile straight ahead, up in the hills. It's been closed since before World War I—that's about how long this place has been abandoned. You know, I've been out here dozens of times and taken a thousand photos, but it always gets to me." She pointed, about twenty feet from the house, to a large stone fireplace standing amidst a pile of rubble. "My grandmother's best friend grew up in what used to be that house. I'm going across the way to shoot the old school. There's plenty to see around here, unless you're bored."

"On the contrary."

As Andi crossed the road, Rosen strolled past the lone fireplace to the next house, which looked solid except for a large hole broken through the middle of the roof. Inside, the walls were water-stained and cracked, bookshelves broken, and the furniture rotted.

A tattered easy chair, its springs poking through the stuffing, had been drawn near the fireplace. He pictured a miner coming home, lighting his pipe, and sitting wearily in the chair while his wife cooked in the kitchen. Rosen stepped to the front door, where the woman must have called her children for supper just as, up and down the street, a hundred other women were calling their children. He listened—were their voices still caught in the wind? He walked through the grass, parallel to the road, passing ruin after ruin, and remembered the stories his grandfather had told of the pogroms in Russia. How the Cossacks would sweep like fire through a town—looting and killing and driving the people away. Was this how those towns looked? He saw a small spade half-buried in the ground, where perhaps once a woman had worked her garden. An old cotton shirt, torn and faded, hung from a nail under the eave of the next house. It waited patiently for its owner, as it had been waiting since before Rosen was born, perhaps even before his father was born.

Behind one of the houses stood a shed with one large window, shel-tered by a bower of tall evergreens. The building appeared intact, and, stepping inside, Rosen sensed something different about its interior. The floor, dappled with light shining through the branches, had been swept clean recently; he saw an old straw broom against a wall near the door-way.

Something lay in the shadows of a far corner—an Army duffel bag.

Rosen unzipped it and found a khaki bedroll inside, which looked relatively new. There was something else about the bedroll, a smell he couldn't quite distinguish in the shed's mustiness. He inhaled deeply—something sweet, but what was it?

Hearing Andi call his name, he returned the duffel bag to the corner, then walked back to the road.

"What do you think?" she asked.

"Like you said, it can really get to you. Take some interesting pictures?"

"Nothing I didn't have before."

"Do many people come up here?"

"A teacher might bring her class for a history lesson. Maybe a few teenagers mess around, but folks haven't paid too much attention to this place. Of course, all that's changing."

"You mean, because of the murder."

"No, because of the gambling. C'mon, the ridge is this way."

As they walked up the dirt road, Andi said, "You must've seen all the signs for gambling in Deadwood. It's an old cowboy town, where Wild Bill Hickok was shot in the back. Like lots of places around here, the town was slowly dying, but it had one thing going. It's on the National Register of Historic Places. The state legislature passed a law allowing gambling in any such town, if that's what its residents want. Now Deadwood's making money hand over fist."

Rosen asked, "And this ghost town?"

"Tin Town's on the historical register too. They say Hearst had it done, as a kind of finishing touch to Manderson's ruin. Nobody thought much about it, until Deadwood got rich."

"Sounds like a real windfall."

"Yeah, but there were a couple big problems. You've never seen Deadwood. A lot of its residents don't like what happened. Along with the money came crime and congestion—school kids sneaking over to play the slot machines with their lunch money. See, Bear Coat's about two miles over the ridge. It grew up later, first as a home for some of Hearst's gold miners, then the timber company came in. This ghost town's technically within Bear Coat's city limits, which is what gave the town council its bright idea—a way to get rich and keep Bear Coat itself from becoming a cheap little Las Vegas."

She pointed back to the gravel road from where they'd come. "What if all the gambling and most of the traffic could be kept in this area? It's the real historical part of town anyway, and with the money generated from gambling, it could be restored into the mining town it once was. That would bring in even more tourists. See what I mean?"

"Sure, a perfect compromise."

"There's only one problem. The man who owns the land between Bear Coat and Tin Town hasn't been willing to go along with the town's plans."

"Wouldn't it make him rich?"

"Probably, but for some people, money ain't everything. Care to guess who that person is?"

"My client, Saul True Sky."

"Uh-huh. So the town council's trying to take over Saul's land and build a proper road to connect to the highway. Of course, once these houses are restored, they'll be the perfect places for poker, blackjack, and slot machines."

"Who'll get the gambling licenses?"

She shrugged. "I don't know all the details, only that it's not just the casino owners who are supposed to get rich, but everybody in town—restaurants, motels, gift shops. Property values will shoot sky high."

"That's if the town council wins its condemnation case."

"Oh, it will. Who ever heard of an Indian winning a court case? Besides, now Saul has more to worry about than just losing his land."

"What's True Sky's argument in the suit?"

"What do Indians always use as an argument? The land is holy, and the spirits shouldn't be disturbed. What judge in South Dakota's going to buy that?"

Rosen stopped and turned Andi toward him. "I'm surprised you didn't call Nahagian about that case instead of the murder. It's more clearly an issue for my organization—freedom of religion."

"I probably would have, except Grace already got my editor, Jack Keeshin."

"A newspaper editor?"

"He's a lawyer too. Came here from Los Angeles about six months ago. Bought the paper and settled into the quiet life. He calls it semi-retirement."

"He doesn't care about getting rich from bringing gambling in?"

"Jack's already pretty well off. He came here to get away from the fast lane."

"And Mr. Keeshin didn't want to defend True Sky on the murder charge?"

"No, I don't think Jack does criminal law. Besides, Mr. Nahagian said you were the best he had. This case is a hell of a lot more important to Saul than a piece of land." She took a step forward. "Who's that?"

Shielding her eyes, Andi looked toward the top of the ridge. Suddenly she broke into a smile and waved.

Something squatted where the ridge crested. At first thick and solid, the shape gradually unfolded into a gangly boy.

Rosen said, "He looked like a rock."

"Yeah, like Stone Boy," Andi replied, waving again. "From an old Lakota legend. That's really Grace's son, Stevie. He's . . . "

Before she could finish, the boy disappeared over the ridge.

She shook her head. "He's kind of strange. Not a bad boy, just . . . well, it's hard for him to settle down. He lost his dad last year—road was icy and Big Steve's truck jackknifed. Now this trouble with his grandfather Saul. It'd be tough on any kid."

Rosen asked, "Was Stevie around the night of the murder?"

"Guess so. I mean, he must've been in bed. It was late and a school night. He couldn't have seen anything. You want to go on up? That's where Albert Gates's murder took place."

Rosen looked up the ridge. Stevie might still be there. That would mean talking to him without knowing what questions to ask and, worse, without having the chance to gain his confidence.

"No," he said, "I'd better see True Sky first. Hey . . . " She snapped his photo again. "What's that for?"

"Force of habit." She grinned. "Besides, like I said before, you're kinda cute."

Chapter 5

WEDNESDAY EVENING

Over the years Rosen had come to believe that one nameless individual had built the same generic restaurant in every American town. Such a restaurant was invariably located on the corner of Main Street; included the word "village" or "country" or "cafe"; had green or red vinyl booths, plastic menus with the prices changed in black marker, and cracked tile on the floor. The same picture frames hung along the walls, the only difference being the paintings, which gave each establishment its particular dime-store ambiance. Some depicted the Greek isles, some Florence, some the Alps, some the Great Wall of China.

He sat in a booth of Bear Coat's Village Diner, under a painting of Mount Rushmore. A Western motif dominated the restaurant, with pictures of the Rockies and Yellowstone, as well as the head of a buffalo mounted on the wall above the cash register. It was after seven. The dinner crowd had thinned to a few families, who ate at various tables arranged in checkerboard fashion from one end of the restaurant to the other. Nearly everyone was blond, and every male over twenty-one wore a cap—except him.

He pushed his plate away, then sipped his lukewarm tea, as Andi slid onto the seat across from him. Head tilted and forearms crossed on the table, she looked like a marionette.

"Figured you'd be here," she said. "Why didn't you leave a message at the motel?"

"I didn't know what restaurants were within walking distance. With your keen reportorial instincts, I knew you'd find me."

"Do you like V.D.?"

"Excuse me?"

"That's how we townies affectionately refer to the Village Diner. Enjoy your meal?"

"The best in continental cuisine. As you can see, I had the french dip and french fries."

Pulling his plate to her, Andi spanked the end of the ketchup bottle until it engulfed the remains of his dinner. Her fingers fished out one fry at a time, and she chewed thoughtfully.

As a family of four left their nearby table, they nodded hello, the husband adjusting his Denver Broncos cap. Andi waved back.

Rosen asked, "Why do all the men wear caps? Is it a custom, like the Chinese binding their women's feet? Are their heads really pear-shaped?"

"No."

"Do they ever take them off? How about when they go to bed?"

Her mouth spread into a wicked grin. "Sometimes, but not always. It kinda tickles. Once I almost broke a rib when this guy's brim . . . "

"I get the idea. Are you finished, or should I order another bottle of ketchup with fries on the side?" He handed her three napkins from the dispenser.

"All done." She wiped her mouth, then leaned back and lit a cigarette. "I thought we'd go over to the station, so you could meet Saul. His bail hearing's tomorrow morning in Deadwood. That's the county seat. Hope that gives you enough time."

"It'll have to. After you."

They passed a table where three men in cowboy hats were finishing their coffee. The oldest, maybe fifty, took Andi's arm.

She said, "Hello, Gil."

His eyes narrowed, and a web of wrinkles spread over his leathery face. "Got a cigarette?" he asked.

"Here."

"Thanks. So what do you think about that Indian murdering my boss?"

"Shouldn't a jury be deciding that?"

He flashed a smile, then took a long drag on his cigarette. "They's all bad—that Indian and his half-breed kids. Never did like Will hanging around the ranch."

Andi started to walk away, but he pulled her back. "Just don't want your editor trying any of his lawyer tricks."

"Jack's not defending . . . " She stopped suddenly.

Gil looked slowly from her to Rosen. "Me, I like the old ways. Give 'em their choice—a bullet or a rope. Never did understand this legal bullshit. Know what I mean?"

"Uh-huh." She twisted her arm free. "For that, you'd have to know how to read. Come on, Nate."

As they reached the door, Rosen said, "You didn't introduce us."

"Consider yourself lucky. That's Gil McCracken, foreman of the Double G—Gates's ranch. After talking to him, I could use some fresh air."

The sun was beginning to set. Copper-colored awnings hung like drowsy eyelids over the stores, and second-floor windows yawned half-open to catch the evening breeze. The buildings were brick with wood trim painted white; a few storefronts simulated front porches with white-washed pillars and short picket fences. There were several gift shops, a gunsmith, and Whistler Realty displaying advertisements in its windows for several area homes and commercial properties.

Rosen studied the ads. "Pretty inexpensive compared to Chicago and D.C."

"Expensive enough for a hole-in-the-wall like this. Actually, prices have risen. Guess some folks are betting that Bear Coat will bring in gambling. 'Course, it takes money to make money. Biggest property owner in town's probably the Judge and Pearl. Pearl's the realtor, but her husband's got the money."

"He's a judge?"

Andi nodded. "In fact, he's trying Saul's case. His family's been here as long as those trees covering the Black Hills. Yeah, the Judge is straight as a tree, and as boring."

"And his wife?"

She grinned. "Besides the age difference, Pearl's . . . Well, you'll have to see for yourself."

They continued past a small movie theater specializing in old Westerns. The feature that evening was John Wayne in *Stagecoach*.

"Nice town," Rosen said.

"If boredom's your thing. City Hall's just down the block."

"How did this place get the name 'Bear Coat'?"

"Depends who you talk to. Indians like Saul will tell you a legend about a Lakota maiden who got lost in a snowstorm and was about to die, when the Great Spirit took pity on her and sent a bear to keep her warm until the storm ended and her people could find her. Saul says it happened up on his ridge, the one we saw earlier today. That's why it's so holy."

"It's a beautiful story."

"Make-believe's always prettier than the truth. The town's really named for General Nelson A. Miles. After the Custer massacre, he chased the Cheyenne and Sioux, including Crazy Horse, all over these parts, until they finally gave up. The Cheyenne called Miles 'Bear's Coat,' and that's really how we got our name."

"I can see why True Sky prefers the legend."

"Uh-huh. Otherwise, it's kinda rubbing the Indians' noses in it. That's Town Hall. Police station's in back."

The street lights blinked on, as Rosen followed Andi around the corner and inside.

Sitting behind the dispatch unit, a young woman with curly blond hair was reading a romance novel. She pointedly ignored a policeman who, leaning over the plywood wall separating them, was trying to make time.

"Hi, Wendy . . . Elroy," Andi said.

They both looked up, the policeman blushing violently. A little over-weight, he had brown hair, a slight mustache, and eyes pale as his com-plexion. The kind of man whose name you'd keep forgetting.

Andi continued, "This is Mr. Nate Rosen. He's the lawyer I told Tom about—the one who's going to defend Saul True Sky on the murder charge."

The policeman quickly walked forward. His handshake felt doughy. "I'm Assistant Chief Elroy Baker. Pleased to meet you." He spoke with a slight Southern accent.

"Thank you. Since the bond hearing's tomorrow, I'd like to see my client now."

Baker rubbed his jaw. "Tom—that's Chief Cross Dog—didn't mention anything about letting the prisoner see a visitor after hours."

"I am Mr. True Sky's attorney."

"Hmm. Wendy, call Chief Cross Dog and get clearance for Mr. Rosen, while I fill out the necessary papers."

While Baker walked to his desk, Andi whispered, "That's the way Elroy is. Always making a big deal out of nothing."

"I can't raise Tom," Wendy said. "I'll try again in a few minutes."

Rosen shook his head. "I shouldn't be denied access to my client."

"Go ahead, Elroy. We always let Margie Travers come by at night whenever her no-good husband's sleeping one off."

"But this here's a murder charge." Baker drummed his fingers on the desk, then walked back to Rosen. "Oh, all right. Guess it can't do any harm. I have to search you first."

As Baker patted down Rosen, Andi said, "Watch his hands. Ain't that right, Wendy?"

Again blushing, the policeman quickly finished. "Okay. Follow me. Not you, Andi."

"But I'm the press."

"Sorry, but you ain't got no business . . . "

"What about the First Amendment? Tell him, Nate."

"Officer Baker's right. Besides, it's in the best interest of my client to see me privately. I'm sure you understand."

"No, I don't!" Her face colored, and she stared at him the same way she'd stared at Gil McCracken. "I brought you here. This is my story. Nobody's getting in the way of . . . " She stopped suddenly, biting her lower lip.

"Get in the way of what?" She shook her head, and Rosen continued, "Saul True Sky's my client, not yours. He has the right to see me in private. Officer Baker."

Andi looked away, as Rosen followed the policeman through a back door.

The jail was small—a narrow corridor with two cells on the right. The only illumination was the gray twilight drifting through the barred windows.

In the far cell, a man leaned out the window and sang, "When the moon hits your eye like a big pizza pie, that's *amore*."

Somewhere in the distance, a dog howled a reply.

Baker said, "No more of your caterwauling, Ike. After two days in here, I thought you'd finally be sober."

"Bells will ring, ting-a-ling-a-ling . . . !"

"I said shut up!"

The prisoner walked to the bars. He was an old Indian, his long hair tied in a ponytail. "I was only singing to Samson, the junkyard dog. He's chained up like me. We talk to one another about what it's like to be free. One day soon, I'm going to cut him loose."

"You're nuttier than a fruitcake. You do that, and you'll be right back in here for messing with another man's property."

"You don't understand. That dog is my brother. We have to look out for each other. Ain't that right, Saul?"

"Yes," someone replied from the first cell.

Rosen hadn't seen the other prisoner because, sitting on the floor, the man was obscured by shadows.

Opening the cell door, Baker said, "This is your lawyer." To Rosen, "Want me to turn on the lights?"

Rosen looked at his client, sitting in the dark like an animal, watching him with animal eyes. "No."

He stepped inside the cell and leaned against the bars while the policeman left the corridor, closing the door behind him. For a few minutes neither man spoke. Rosen would wait as long as it took. He was the stranger, the outsider.

Finally, True Sky said, "You're the one my daughter's friend Andi spoke about. The lawyer from Washington."

"That's right."

"Where's your briefcase? A lawyer without a briefcase is like a vulture without talons."

"I'm saving it for court. For now I just want to get acquainted."

"Sit down."

Rosen sat cross-legged on the floor opposite True Sky. The old man was eating a bowl of soup with the thick smell of beef and onion. He held the spoon with his fist like a child.

From the other cell, Ike sang softly, "Everybody loves somebody sometime, everybody falls in love somehow."

True Sky said, "He's always liked Dean Martin."

"That's right," Ike agreed. "Elvis wanted to sing like Dean Martin. Your lawyer friend here looks a little like Jerry Lewis."

"This man's taller, I think."

Ike hummed the rest of the song, while True Sky again lapsed into silence. Rosen stifled a yawn. The airplane trip, the long car ride with Andi, and now this—sitting stiffly on a cold concrete floor. He felt impatient to get on with the case, to do something beside watching the shadows slowly weave themselves into a veil of darkness between him and the old man.

The old man slowly ate his soup.

"Is that all they gave you for dinner?" Rosen asked.

"It's all I need. The water once came as rain from the sky. The fire to cook it came from the sun. The meat is from our four-legged brothers who sustain us. And the steam is the breath of our grandfathers that will join the sky."

Watching the old man eat, Rosen remembered the Passover seder. At that meal the horseradish, the mixture of apples and nuts, and the roasted egg were all symbols of a people's faith. As the youngest, he'd always asked the Four Questions which, with the food, reminded man of God's goodness and mercy. The same way that the old Indian's simple bowl of soup did. Could such a man, believing as True Sky did, be a murderer?

Rosen asked, "Did you kill Albert Gates?"

The Indian put down his bowl of soup and looked him in the eyes. "No."

That word, more than any other, Rosen listened for in court. Sometimes it was shouted over and over like a hammer; sometimes it scurried from the accused's lips like a frightened mouse. Even the best liars said it a bit too quickly, as if it were a coal too hot to stay in the mouth. True Sky's "no" walked out quietly and stood very still.

"Why did the police arrest you for the murder?"

"I don't know. Somebody killed Gates. I sat nearby in my vision pit, so they arrested me."

"According to the newspaper, you admitted having an argument earlier in the day with Gates."

"He wanted to take the *wotawe* from the bones of White Bear. I wouldn't let him."

"Those are the Indian remains on the ridge, that the paper mentioned. So Gates came back that night to get this medicine bag. The police say they have physical evidence tying you to the murder. Do you know what that is?"

The old man put his right hand, palm upward, upon his lap. "They found a stone, about this size, near the pit. It was one of the stones I had gathered into a pile near the sweat lodge for Ike's *inipi*. This stone, they say, killed Gates. And there was some of his blood on my shirt-sleeve."

"How did the blood get there?"

"I didn't kill him. I was with my brothers, the elk. We stood in the tall grass and spoke with the spirit of White Bear."

"And you didn't see who killed Gates?"

"I wasn't there."

Shifting his weight, Rosen stretched his back. He wasn't getting anywhere, but he couldn't help but smile. It was like studying the Talmud. A good mind and a good heart weren't enough; he would need patience.

"We'll talk more another time. Tomorrow, I go before the judge to discuss your bail. I understand you've lived around Bear Coat all your life, but that you've been in trouble before with the law."

"That was a long time ago."

Rosen decided not to press the old man about his past. He would probably get a convoluted answer; it would be easier to check the police records.

"Mr. True Sky, is there anything you can tell me that will help secure your bail?"

It had grown so dark that Rosen barely saw the old man's face crinkle as he broke into a smile. "I'm innocent. Will that help?"

Rosen stood and flexed his knees. "That always helps. In the meantime, is there anything I can do for you?"

"See that nobody disturbs White Bear. His remains must be given a decent burial."

"All right. I'll see you tomorrow morning."

Rosen walked stiffly toward the cell door, keeping his hands outstretched in the darkness until they touched the bars. He was about to shout for the policeman when he saw a crack of light at the corridor entrance. Someone was listening.

"Officer Baker, I'm ready!"

He called Baker's name again, and the door slowly opened. The policeman flicked on a switch, and light, fine as talcum powder, filtered through a dusty overhead fixture.

Unlocking the door, Baker asked, "Everything go all right?"

"You should know. Why weren't any lights on, before I came in here?"

"Dunno. We just never thought about turning them on. Doesn't seem to bother these two. Ain't like they're reading the paper or nothing."

Ike said, "I want a newspaper or one of them *Playboy* magazines. I like to read the advice column. That Playboy Advisor's a very wise man. Once one of my testicles was hanging lower than the other, and I read . . . "

"Shut up," the policeman said. "Any of that filth comes in here, I'll just confiscate it."

"You'd like that."

Baker took a step toward Ike; then, eyeing Rosen, he hesitated.

"C'mon, I got work to do."

The two men walked down the corridor to the doorway.

Putting his hand on the light switch, Baker shouted, "Well, you two want the light on or not?"

"No," Ike said. "I'm tired. But you get me some magazines tomorrow. Maybe the *Enquirer.* A man loses track of world events in here."

The squad room seemed as quiet as before. The dispatcher was shaking her head at Andi, who sat on Baker's desk.

"I just don't believe you," Wendy said.

Andi stuck out her jaw. "I really care."

"If he ain't going out with you, then who?"

Andi was about to answer, when she saw that the two men had returned. She shook her head at Wendy, who began typing at the computer.

"Well," Andi asked Rosen, "what did you think of Saul?"

"He's not an easy man to get to know."

"You know he's innocent, don't you?"

"I think so."

From the other side of the control center, someone said, "The hell you do."

Another policeman stood in the doorway of an inner office. He was Indian, with massive shoulders and biceps almost tearing the short sleeves of his blue shirt. He walked across the room and stood a few inches from Rosen. Baker quickly returned to his desk and busied himself shuffling papers.

Andi said, "This is Mr. Rosen, Saul's lawyer from Washington. Nate, meet Police Chief Cross Dog."

Rosen decided not to offer his hand, uncertain how the policeman might respond. "I'd like to ask you some questions about the murder."

"What makes you think he's innocent?"

"My personal opinion isn't the issue. What I need to know . . . "

"You think he's just another victim of white man's justice—that it?"

"It could be that his race or religious beliefs . . . "

"That ain't it, you understand." Cross Dog moved so close, Rosen felt the other man's breath. "That ain't it at all."

"Do you want to whisper the real reason in my ear now, or should we wait until our second date?" The policeman blinked hard, but before he could respond, Rosen said, "I need to see your files on Mr. True Sky. If you're not willing to cooperate, I'll get a court order."

Cross Dog moved suddenly, and Rosen took a step back. The chief pulled a large folder from the file cabinet and slapped it into Rosen's hands.

"Take a look. Take a long look at the man you're claiming is innocent."

Rosen opened the file, which went back almost fifty years. The first few entries dealt mostly with drunk-and-disorderlies and several speeding tickets. There was one barroom fight involving another man being cut by a knife, but no formal charges had been filed. Turning the page, he blinked hard at what he saw and read the words again very carefully.

"That's right," Cross Dog said. "Your client killed a policeman."

Rosen read the next few pages very carefully. "It was judged second-degree murder—an accident."

"The hell it was. True Sky got drunk and was tearing up the bar. When the policeman, John Little Thunder, tried to arrest him, True Sky grabbed John's gun and shot him dead."

"That was back in 1964. He was given a twenty-year sentence."

"Yeah, and only served seven. Andi's bleeding-heart father got True Sky a new trial—got him off."

Andi shook her head. "People at the bar finally came forward and said Little Thunder was beating on Saul, that Saul only grabbed the gun in self-defense."

"John Little Thunder was an officer acting in the line of duty. He was a good man."

"He was your uncle," she said softly. "Saul's been sober for years. A lot of your people see him as a holy man. Why can't you just forget the past? What's done is done."

Andi used the same words that Rosen's ex-wife had a few hours before. "What's done is done." He wondered if he had grimaced the same way Cross Dog was doing just then. He understood the other man's pain of not being able to escape the past. For a moment, he wanted to put a hand on Cross Dog's shoulder, but he knew what the Indian's reaction would be. The same reaction Rosen would have given Bess.

"I'd like a copy of both True Sky's police record and the Albert Gates murder file."

Cross Dog nodded curtly. "I don't want you complaining later about some nickel-and-dime police irregularity." He handed the file to Wendy. "Make the copies he wants."

For the next few minutes, the only sound was the copier's soft humming. Finally, Wendy handed the papers to Rosen.

"Anything else?" the police chief asked.

"No. Thanks for your help."

Andi touched Rosen's elbow, and they walked to the door.

Cross Dog blurted, "I don't want you thinking that True Sky's some poor beaten-down Indian. I've been hearing that crap all my life—not just from whites, but from my own people. Nobody ever gave me anything, but I never got drunk and busted up a bar. And I never killed nobody. You just remember that."

Opening the door, Rosen nodded.

He walked quickly ahead of Andi, around the building to the sidewalk.

"Hey, wait for me," she said. "What's your . . . oww!"

Rosen pulled her toward him under a streetlight. "Why didn't you tell me that True Sky had been convicted of murder? Murdering the police chief's uncle, no less."

Looking at the ground, she shrugged.

"You made me look like a fool. The last thing in the world I need is the town's top cop angry with me. Your camera's got more brains than you. At least it's idiot-proof."

She pulled away and, jutting her chin, squared off as if ready to take his best punch. "What would you have thought of Saul if I'd told you all that? I wanted you to meet him first, so you could see he couldn't kill anybody."

"But he did kill somebody."

"Jesus, you're worse than Tom! I expect it from him, but Mr. Nahagian said you had brains."

Rosen shook his head.

"Well, what're you gonna do? Fly back to Washington with your tail between your legs?"

Rubbing his eyes, he said, "I'm going back to the motel and get some sleep. Are you going to drive me into Deadwood for the hearing tomorrow morning?"

She relaxed her stance and smiled. "Yeah. I'll even buy you breakfast."

Her eyes strayed from him, and he turned to follow her gaze across the street. Above the door of the building directly opposite them, a sign read BEAR COAT CHRONICLE. A light glimmered from a second floor window; it formed the outline of a man who was watching them.

Andi waved. "That's my boss, Jack Keeshin, the one who's trying to help Saul keep his land. If you're as smart as Mr. Nahagian says, the two of you ought to really get along. Well, my car's across the street. I'll be at the motel at seven a.m. sharp. Bye."

Rosen looked back at the window, but the light had been switched off. Hearing a sudden clap of thunder, he scanned the sky but, as the rumble continued, realized it was only Andi's muffler. A minute later, the noise ended, and the street was once again silent.

He walked under the cold gray streetlights, then turned the corner, where the only illumination was the distant neon glow of the motel sign. In one day he had traveled from Washington to Chicago and now stood in the very center of America. A stranger once again, he felt buried, as if the black sky of night were so much dirt shoveled over him.

Above, a full moon glowed serenely. It looked perfectly clear and round, reminding him of the book *Goodnight Moon,* which he had read to Sarah as a little girl. Sarah. He took out the key chain she'd given him, which glowed in the darkness like an amulet. Holding it tightly, Rosen smiled as he walked back to the motel, and even though he lay in a strange bed, he fell asleep the minute his head touched the pillow.

Chapter 6

THURSDAY MORNING

Having driven the first fifteen minutes from Deadwood in silence, Grace glanced at Rosen, who stared out the window, occasionally shifting his long legs against the Corolla's glove compartment. Her father was no better; sitting in the back seat, eyes closed and arms crossed, he might have been asleep. The only sound was the cold air streaming through the vents.

She stifled a yawn. Usually at 11:15 she was sound asleep, not waking up until Stevie came home from school. Would there be time for any sleep today—what with meeting Belle Gates and the others at twelve? Once again she glanced at Rosen. Whoever heard of a lawyer who didn't like to talk?

Clearing her throat, she said, "You were great at the hearing. We really can't thank you enough. Isn't that right, Father?"

"I'm innocent. Why should I pay to stay out of jail?"

"It's a murder charge, and they could have set a high bail. What if it had been $100,000—even more?"

"I'm innocent."

"But he got you out with no cost, on your . . . your . . . "

"On his own recognizance," Rosen said.

"It was a miracle, what with the way folks feel about Indians. Not to mention that Albert Gates had plenty of friends, or that Judge Whistler's married to a member of the town council."

"That would be Pearl, the one who has the realty office in town."

"The one who has everything. Have you met her?"

Rosen shook his head. "I'd like to. She and her husband sound like an intriguing couple."

"That's one way of putting it." Grace didn't want to think about Pearl;

she was too happy about her father coming home. "Yeah, what you did was a miracle."

"Not really," Rosen said. "Your father is an established resident of Bear Coat, he's considered by many to be a religious leader, and he's had a clean record for the last three decades."

"I thought his having spent time in jail for killing John Little Thunder would just about guarantee a high bail or none at all."

Again Rosen tried stretching his legs. He grunted softly, then said, "It had the opposite effect, because he was later found innocent. An innocent man who spent seven years in prison and didn't come out embittered, but rather turned to religion."

"The way you put it all together for the judge. We're lucky Andi got you."

"This is only the beginning. I read the police report last night. There's strong evidence against your father—his argument with Gates, the murder weapon found near him, and the blood on his sleeve."

"Maybe Father cut himself on something."

"It's Gates's blood type, not your father's."

Could her father really have committed the murder? The only other way he could've gotten the blood on his sleeve was earlier that same day, when Stevie cut Gates and her father took the knife away. But if she told Rosen, he might think . . . No, she couldn't.

"Grace?" Rosen was staring at her.

She swallowed hard. "Sorry. What were you saying?"

"Did you see the object clutched in Gates's fist?"

"Uh . . . just for a second, before Tom put it in his pocket. A small piece of metal, I guess. It looked all rusted. Probably something Gates grabbed on the ground while he was dying."

Rosen said nothing, and his silence made Grace nervous. She said, "Hope Andi didn't mind you driving back to town with us."

"No, she had to file her story on the hearing."

"What do you think of her?"

He tried to stifle a smile. "She's quite a character."

"She thinks you're cute."

"That's only because I'm wearing pants."

"Andi's not like that. A girl on her own—it's hard in a town like Bear Coat. All that big talk's just her way of acting tough. She wouldn't give the time of day to most men around here. She really likes you."

He shook his head.

"Really, she—"

"Let's talk about this meeting you want me to attend."

"It's with the committee in charge of the Tin Town development project. Jack thought it might give you some background on what's been going on between Father and the town council."

"This meeting—"

"Stop the car," her father said.

Grace knew better than to argue, even though there was nothing for miles except mown fields and a few trees. Maybe he had to relieve himself. She parked on the gravel shoulder of the road.

He stepped from the car. "Give me my knife."

She handed him a large knife in a leather sheath from the glove compartment. He walked deep into the field and, reaching one of the trees, cut at a thick branch until it broke loose, then trimmed it. He returned to the car with the branch.

As Grace drove back onto the highway, her father said to Rosen, "I know the truth doesn't always matter in a white man's court. You did a good job."

Rosen smiled. "I had my briefcase with me."

"Yes, that makes a difference—you looked like a lawyer. This branch is from a good ash tree. I'm carving you a present that will make you very happy."

"Thank you. Now, about this meeting?"

Grace said, "It's to see if Father will let the highway go through our property. If he doesn't, there'll be a hearing next week. Jack thinks the town council might want to make some kind of deal."

"Can something be worked out?"

Grace nodded toward the back seat. "Whatever Father says."

"What's your opinion?"

She shrugged. "Mother left the land to him, so it's his decision."

"And if she'd willed it to you?"

"She didn't. She came to believe in the Lakota way—the man makes the decision, and the rest of the family obeys."

Looking into the fields, Rosen said, "Mr. True Sky, after the meeting I'm going up to your ridge. I'd like you to be there, to tell me whatever you can about Gates's murder."

"I'll be there."

"I'd also like to talk to your grandson, Stevie. He . . . "

"No," Grace blurted.

"Shouldn't he be home from school by then?"

"I don't want you talking to him."

"Why not?"

"I don't want him bothered—that's all."

"But I just—"

"He doesn't know anything. He was asleep when the murder took place, and I just don't want him bothered anymore. He's been through enough trouble in his life for a whole busload of children. I don't want you bothering him. Understand?"

When he didn't respond right away, Grace glanced at Rosen, who was staring at her.

"Well?" she demanded.

"I understand."

No one spoke; her father's whittling joined the soft hissing of the air vents, as Grace drove the rest of the way into Bear Coat. She parked a half block from the town hall. Holding the branch in his right hand, her father walked beside the lawyer. Grace followed the customary step behind. The breeze, unusually warm and humid, seemed to lap against them.

Her father said, "I'm not going to this meeting."

Grace wasn't surprised; nothing he did surprised her anymore. She asked, "Who's going to speak for you? Will's not coming."

"You do it. It's your mother's land. You're half-white—you can speak to those folks at the meeting."

She tried keeping the edge from her voice. "I'm surprised you're letting me talk for you. After all, I'm only a woman."

"You can tell them no and not be hurt. You're not going to talk about anything important—only money." He touched Rosen's arm with the branch. "I'm a brother to the elk. Me talking to the whites about money is no good. You understand?"

Rosen nodded.

"Long time ago, before the Little Big Horn, the Cheyenne almost wiped out a group of soldiers defending a small island in a river. Twice the Cheyenne charged without their war chief, Roman Nose, because he had eaten bread that had been touched by a metal fork—a white man's tool. The metal broke his good medicine, which protected him. On the third charge Roman Nose couldn't hold back, even though it meant he would die. He rode with the other braves and was killed by a bullet. It had to end that way."

"Yes," Rosen said. "It was the same with the ancient priests of my people. There were certain objects they weren't allowed to touch, for fear of contamination."

"You explain it to that other lawyer, the one my daughter likes so much."

"Jack will understand," Grace said. "Hasn't he stood with us right from the start?"

Her father shook his head. "It's bad enough I have one lawyer. Now there's two. I feel like a rabbit walking down the road between two coyotes."

They had reached the town hall. Grace watched the American flag's shadow flutter like a wounded bird on the hot concrete. It was nearly twelve, time for the meeting.

Her father said, "Ike got out of jail this morning. I'm meeting him at Chris Chasing Horse's body shop. Later, he'll drive me home. I'll see you up on the ridge, where White Bear lies."

Grace said, "Be careful going to Chris's. Stay away from Tom Cross Dog. He's not gonna be happy seeing you out of jail."

She watched her father cross the street and disappear around the corner. He moved with the slow, sure step of an old tomcat who knew his neighborhood.

"He'll be all right," she half-whispered. Still, she wished he were up on his ridge, talking to his starlings and dug-up skeleton. Crazy but safe. "You have to understand the kind of man he is—what the old ways mean to him."

"You don't have to explain," Rosen said. "He reminds me of someone I know."

"He's a little strange, but . . . "

"Be grateful at least you're a family."

Grace tried to smile. Resisting the impulse to let him go first, she led Rosen into the town hall. They walked up a narrow wooden staircase to the town council's meeting room, directly across from the mayor's office.

The door opened into the center of the room, where a long conference table stretched in either direction. A map of "Historic Bear Coat" covered most of the wall near the doorway. Along the opposite wall hung the portraits of every town mayor since 1920. All were male, except the last one, who stared into the room with such determination that, in comparison, the others seemed like a kindergarten class called before the principal.

At that moment, the real face was far different from its portrait. Mayor Belle Gates leaned against a corner window, the bright sunlight deepening the shadows under her eyes. She wore a long black dress with a round collar and big buttons—probably something she'd found in the back of her closet. She'd had her hair done; in the air-conditioned room her auburn curls, streaked with gray, remained tight around her head.

Chick Cantrell, the engineer the town had hired to lay out the road and help with Tin Town's renovations, stood beside her. A fireplug of a man, he was stroking his thick salt-and-pepper beard. Grace had never seen him in a suit before. He usually wore an old flannel shirt, torn pants, and heavy boots. He stood very close to Belle, his big hand resting on her shoulder.

Belle limped over to Grace and hugged her. "Good to see you, honey."

"I'm so sorry about Mr. Gates. I would've come to the funeral yesterday, except . . . well, it just didn't seem right. You know, my father . . . " She looked away.

Belle reached up and brought Grace's face back. "I don't know if Saul did it. If he did, the law will punish him. But that's got nothing to do with you. You know how I got this limp."

Grace nodded. Thirty years before, Belle's horse had fallen on top of her. She would've died, except Grace's mother had kept the horse from moving, lifting its body just enough so Belle could breathe. Her mother had kept the horse up for almost an hour, until help came.

"Your mother saved my life. You never forget something like that." Belle looked at Rosen. "This must be that Eastern lawyer Andi Wojecki called in. This is Chick Cantrell, our project engineer."

The two men shook hands. "Well, let's get on with it."

Grace and Rosen sat down, while Belle walked around the table. Cantrell moved to the far corner, directly below Belle's portrait. Just then the door opened. Pearl Whistler and Roy Huggins joined the mayor, sitting on either side of her. Grace introduced Rosen to them.

Huggins nodded curtly. "I'm a member of the town council, as well as its attorney."

Interlacing his fingers, he hunkered over the table. It was always easier for Grace to imagine Huggins's large frame in a football jersey than in a steel-gray suit. He had been handsome once, but that was before the long nights of gambling and drinking had softened his features and blurred his eyes red. Even though it was only noon, from across the table she smelled the whiskey on his breath.

Unlike Huggins, Pearl looked better every year. Her red hair curled softly at her shoulders, just as it had when she and Grace were in high school. When Pearl had gotten all the boys, worn the best clothes, and ridden the best horses. She'd kept her cheerleader's body as well as her smile, which she worked on Rosen like oil on a rusty hinge.

Grace said, "You met her husband, Judge Whistler, at the hearing." Grace and Rosen exchanged glances. Yes, her eyes told his, that old man is Pearl's husband.

Huggins tapped his hands impatiently on the table. "I've got another meeting at two. We know your father's out of jail for the time being. Where the hell is he?"

"He's not coming. He wants me to speak for him."

"Jesus. All right, let's get started."

"Where's Jack?"

Belle said, "He called to say he'll be a few minutes late. He's at the newspaper office, making sure the story on your father's bail hearing is typeset properly."

"I don't want to start without Jack."

Huggins shook his head. "How many lawyers do you want?"

"I just don't feel right . . . "

Belle held up her hand. "Why don't we start? We'll do the talking. You don't have to say anything until Jack gets here. All right?"

Grace looked at Rosen. When he nodded, she said, "All right."

"Good. You know how much I don't want to go to court, but this is scheduled for Judge O'Hara next Monday, if we can't reach an understanding. We want to do whatever's possible to make your father happy, but we've got to have right of way. Without a new road going from the interstate through Tin Town and on into Bear Coat, there's no project. And, Grace, that pretty much means there's no Bear Coat."

"This town's been here a long time. Whether or not gambling comes to Tin Town, Bear Coat'll still go on."

"Will it? Tell me, what do folks do with a horse that breaks its leg?"

She hesitated, then said, "Shoot it."

"Bear Coat's broke all four of its legs. Only but a few ranchers can still make a decent living. Tourism's drying up with most people going to Deadwood for gambling or south to Mount Rushmore. Timber company's cutting back—you know about last month's layoffs. Now the federal government's taking out its nuclear missiles from their underground silos. The government helped pay for keeping up the roads and generating electricity to the ranches way out in the sticks. How're those people gonna be able to afford power now?"

Pearl said, "You can imagine what all this has done to property values. Every year a family's home is worth less. What businesses will want to locate here?" She turned to Rosen and smiled coyly. "I'm sure you must understand our concern."

Rosen asked, "Who's getting the gambling licenses?"

Pearl's smile melted away like morning dew, while Huggins grumbled something under his breath.

Belle said, "Nobody's out to make a killing. When Grace's grandfather went broke and couldn't pay his taxes, Bear Coat took over Tin Town. He only kept the land from the ridge down to where his house and barn are. Because Tin Town's on the National Register of Historic Places, Bear Coat held on to it, hoping one day it might be restored and bring in tourism. Now, with it being able to have gambling—well, we figured to develop it for the benefit of the entire town. Grace, wouldn't your father sympathize with something like that?"

Before she could answer, the door closed behind her.

"Let's all get out our violins and tissues, shall we?"

Jack sat beside her and squeezed her hand under the table. He was dressed casually, with an emerald-green polo shirt and brown slacks. The shirt looked good against his tan skin and brought out his green eyes. He brushed back his thick blond hair, slightly gray at the temples, and smiled. Grace smiled too.

Belle said, "We were just discussing why this development is so desperately needed. No one's out to make a killing. The whole point is to bring back Bear Coat. I don't want to be mayor of another ghost town." Her gaze drifted up to the map behind Grace. "My grandfather fought Indians, drought, and blizzards to keep his ranch going. He even outfoxed my husband's grandfather—salted a stream with gold nuggets and sold him the claim. How Albert and I laughed over that. Our roots go deep. We just don't want this town to blow away like so much dust."

Still gazing at the map, Belle lapsed into silence.

Pearl said, "That's why we've moved so carefully on this project. We want it to be done just right. Tasteful, respecting the environment and the feelings of all those concerned, especially Native Americans like Saul True Sky. Isn't that right, Mr. Cantrell?"

The engineer shifted in his chair. "That's right. The first thing Mayor Gates and Mrs. Whistler said, when they hired me, was to treat the land with respect."

"Oh, really?" Jack said. He placed his briefcase on the table and clicked it open. It had the same rich smell of leather as a new saddle. He unrolled a long blueprint, so that it faced Pearl.

"Recognize this?"

She blanched. "Where'd you get this?"

He drew his finger across the block letters at the top of the document. "Is this how you're going to tastefully maintain the environment of Bear Coat—by building Wild West World?"

"What?" Grace studied the upside-down blueprint.

Jack pointed to different parts of the plan. "This is Panner's Paradise, where you can pan for gold nuggets, here's Big Bronco Ranch, which offers trail rides—your place, isn't it, Belle? Over here is Buffalo Bill's Shooting Gallery. There's the Buffalo Petting Zoo, adjacent to Buffalo Chip Bingo. I believe that's where the pasture is divided into numbered squares and one bets where the buffalo will place its next dropping. Biodegradable—is that where your concern for the environment comes in?"

Pearl said, "We were just toying with some ideas."

"And let's not forget your empathy for the Native American. Right there, up on Saul True Sky's ridge, you're toying with Injun Land—including the Crazy Horse Gift Shop. I particularly like this drawing in the corner. I suppose if you're making a Western version of Disneyland, you should have an Injun Joe mascot instead of Mickey Mouse."

Pearl's lip trembled, but she only shook her head, tossing the curls from her shoulders.

Huggins said, "Look, Mayor Gates told you the economic problems Bear Coat faces. You're from out of town, Los Angeles no less. I don't expect you to understand . . . "

"Bear Coat's my home," Jack said, "as much as it is any of yours. Certainly more than Mr. Cantrell's, who is, I believe, also from L.A. and no doubt will be returning there as soon as his masterpiece, Wild West

World, is completed." He looked at each member of the town council. "I'm not sure how the profits from this enterprise are going to be divided, but finding out is just a matter of time. However, it's clear this project represents far more than the mere survival of a town. It's about what these things always are about—money and, ultimately, power."

Huggins banged his fist on the table. "What if it is? We've got the whole town behind us, and what have you got—one crazy old Indian."

Jack smiled at Huggins, as if waiting for a store clerk to make change. The other man started to say something, when Belle grabbed his arm. He sputtered; then, assuming his usual posture, he leaned over his clutching hands.

Jack said, "I don't believe Saul True Sky is crazy, and I don't believe the media will find him crazy either. He's a holy man, one who sees visions and can heal people."

Huggins grimaced. "The hell he can. He's not much more than a vagrant who's already served time for one murder and may be put away for good this time."

"I have faith in Mr. True Sky, his lawyer here, and the American judicial system. Besides, with the usual lengthy appeals process, the case may go on for another five to ten years. Wouldn't you agree, Mr. Rosen?"

The other lawyer nodded.

"There, you see? From my knowledge of Saul True Sky, I can assure you that nothing will dissuade him from defending both the land he loves and the religious principles it represents to him."

Huggins was about to reply, when Belle said, "Shut up, Roy." Leaning over the table, she looked directly at Grace. "We don't want to hurt your father, but we've got to have that road run through his land. These plans are just somebody's jackass ideas that'll have to be scaled down to size. We're all willing to do what we can to accommodate Saul—isn't that right?"

Pearl nodded emphatically.

"The bottom line is—we've got to have that road. What do you say, Grace? For the sake of the town. It's your future too—yours and Stevie's."

Grace felt her face grow warm, as everybody looked at her. Under the table, Jack's fingers curled around her hand and held it tightly. That was all she needed.

"My father says no. I'm sorry, Belle."

"But you could talk to him. If he'll listen to anybody, it'd be you."

She almost smiled. "Father only listens to his spirits. There's nobody on earth that can tell him what to do."

Sighing, Belle leaned back in her chair. "Then we'll see you in court."

Almost before she'd gotten the words out, Huggins was on his feet. Bending close to the mayor, he whispered hoarsely, "Told you it was a waste of time."

Pearl gazed at the blueprint like a coyote over fresh kill, as Jack rolled up the paper and put it into his briefcase.

"Shall we go?" he said.

Rosen was sniffing the air.

"What is it?" Grace asked.

"Something . . . some aroma. Are you wearing perfume?"

"No."

Jack said, "Must be my cologne—Triumph. Like it?"

They walked downstairs and out the door.

"Whew!" Jack said grinning. "It's almost as hot outside as it was in there." He offered his hand to Rosen. "By the way, very nice to meet you. You're from the Committee to Defend the Constitution?"

Rosen nodded.

"Wonderful organization by reputation. I know a few attorneys in the ACLU. I admire the civil-liberties work you all do."

"Seems you'll be doing some of it yourself."

"Defending Saul on his religious beliefs—right. Should be fun."

Grace grimaced. "You'll have to deal with Roy Huggins. I've never liked that man."

Jack laughed, then put his arm around her. Usually something like that embarrassed her, even when Steve had occasionally held her in public, but she didn't mind this time. She relaxed against him and smelled his cologne. She felt small and safe.

He said, "Don't worry about Huggins. I've dealt with men like him all my life. You know his type—a racquetball player. Stands in one place on the court, huffing over his sweating belly and trying to smash a little rubber ball to pieces against a wall. Any real challenge would kill him."

Rosen said, "I take it you prefer tennis."

"Love the game. Can't find too many here who play. Do you?"

71

"Sorry. What about Grace?"

"No, tennis is too tame for her. She's a champion reiner. You should see her ride."

Grace said, "I've been trying to get Jack on a horse."

He laughed. "No thank you."

Rosen said, "You strike me as the type to play the ponies, rather than ride them."

Jack's eyes narrowed slightly. "Do I? Well, back in L.A. I did go to the track with a client now and then. God, it was better than playing golf with them." To Grace, "You're still competing this Saturday?"

"I don't know. Father's in so much trouble."

"Oh, but you have to. And you'll come too, Mr. Rosen."

"Call me Nate." He checked his watch. "You'll excuse me now. Andi Wojecki's taking me up to the ridge. I want to look at the area where Gates was murdered."

"Of course. I would like to get together soon. It might be to our mutual advantage to collaborate."

"Sure. I'll see you both later."

Rosen walked across the street to the newspaper office.

His arm still around Grace's waist, Jack said, "I was going to ask you to lunch, but you must be tired. Poor thing, aren't you usually in bed at this hour?"

Nodding, Grace imagined him in bed beside her. She turned away for a moment, so he wouldn't see her face burning, and said, "I'm not tired at all. You know, I am kind of hungry."

Chapter 7

THURSDAY AFTERNOON

Just as some things were never discussed in the yeshiva, some words were never spoken. Rosen remembered, once in the prayer room, a boy saying the word *bamot* to an older student, who quickly hushed him and hurried away. Having never heard the word, Rosen later asked the rabbi what it meant.

Taking him aside, the old man stroked his long beard and half-whispered, "It means a high place. A place where people gathered before the Temple was built by Solomon."

"You mean Shiloh."

He shook his head. "Shiloh kept the Ark and was, therefore, sanctified. These other . . . *bamot* were not good. The people who prayed there fell to evil ways, even to the worship of Baal. Go back to your books. It's not good to dwell on such places of evil."

Rosen hadn't thought of that conversation for twenty-five years, but suddenly those words whispered in his ear, as Andi's car rumbled past True Sky's house up toward the ridge. The old Indian would be there, praying to the spirit of White Bear and calling to his gods, as the Canaanites might have called to their false deities three thousand years before. As the ridge loomed closer, Rosen's hand moved to brush a side-lock from his cheek, a sidelock he'd cut off twenty years before.

Andi parked behind a van, near a beehive-shaped hut. White with large blotches of rust, the van had been hand-lettered on the side, IKE'S FIX-IT. On the rear bumper was a faded sticker, McGovern for President.

Although the sun shone hard through a clear sky, a cool breeze blew across the tall grass. Ike walked up the other side of the ridge, his arms

73

carrying three or four logs, which he dumped onto a pile of wood near the entrance to the hut.

Dropping to his knees, the Indian motioned to Rosen. "I want to teach you something."

Rosen knelt beside Ike and watched him prepare a fire.

"First I put four logs facing east-west, to honor the winds that come from those directions. I crisscross them with four going north-south. Now I set these bigger pieces up straight, against each other, like I was making a tipi."

Rosen pointed toward the hut. "Is the pile supposed to look like that?"

"It does to the spirits. What you're pointing to ain't an ordinary tipi. It's an *oinikaga* tipi."

Andi stood over them. "It means a sweat lodge. He's preparing it for an *inipi*—a ceremonial sweat."

Ike smiled up at her. "You're a smart girl—not just all legs. I'm making ready to heat them." He nodded toward a pile of about two dozen stones near the sweat lodge.

Rosen walked to the stones and, picking one up, examined it carefully. "Wasn't a stone like this the murder weapon?"

Andi nodded. "It probably came from that pile. To your right are the Indian remains that Albert Gates and Saul were arguing over, the afternoon of the murder."

The skeleton was surrounded by a rope staked at four corners, each bearing an official seal. The grass within the cordon was matted and torn, probably from the police gathering evidence.

Andi said, "The cops took away Gates's digging box. It was over there, near the head. Guess everything else's like it was when the murder took place."

The skull stared back at him through empty sockets. The skeleton's shoulder blades and ribs were half-exposed, so that it appeared to be slowly rising from the ground after a hundred years of sleep. It was nothing, Rosen kept telling himself, just the earthly remains from which the soul had long since vanished. Yet he had been taught that the dead were resurrected in bodily form. If there was something of the body left, after all these years, had the soul really gone?

Andi shivered. "Lots of remains like this are around here from the 1870s and '80s. Think of him lying in the ground for over a hundred years."

Ducking under the rope, Rosen poked through the loose dirt near the skull, moved to the neck and shoulders, then along the ribs, several of which were broken. A thin leather package, the *wotawe*, lay half-buried against the third rib.

"Here's a wooden tip—probably from one of the picks Gates was using. What's this?"

He felt something brittle in the earth well below the third rib. It was a thin piece of oxidized iron, which crumbled in his fingers. Wiping his hands, he said, "Let's go over what happened. Will True Sky, Saul's son, discovered Gates's body near the skeleton."

"No, not here." Andi walked past the sweat lodge. "It was closer to here. From the marks made in the ground, the police figure that Gates was hit where you're standing but crawled over here and died. Have you seen Saul's vision pit?"

Rosen joined her and looked into a narrow trench about five feet deep, barren except for some dried evergreen twigs smelling faintly of cedar.

Andi said, "That's where Saul was when Gates was murdered."

"Not a very good place for him to be—a few feet from the dead man."

"I told you before," Saul True Sky said, coming up behind them, "I wasn't there." The Indian held a deer's antlers and a buffalo skull.

"Police Chief Cross Dog found you there in the pit."

"Most of the night I had traveled far away with White Bear. We visited our grandfathers and saw the buffalo run."

"You didn't see or hear anything involving Albert Gates's death."

"No. Here, this goes by the fire."

Rosen laid the antler beside Ike, who used a match to light the stacked logs. Returning to the sweat lodge, he watched True Sky place the buffalo skull near the entrance. The Indian tied offerings of sweet-smelling tobacco to the buffalo horns. Then he handed one of the stones to Rosen.

"Help me take these over to Ike."

Rosen looked at the green moss covering the stone. "Pretty."

"They're *sintkala waksu*—bird stones. My friends, the starlings, made these marks on them. My grandfather could read the future in these marks. These are good stones."

"The fire won't split them?"

"It's more than that. They're stone people that come from the earth. During the *inipi* they listen to our problems, clear away all our bad thoughts, and put us in touch with Tunkashila, the Creator. You know what *inyan* is?"

Rosen shook his head.

"It's rock like this, but it's more. *Inyan* was the first of all things. Everything else came from *inyan* and took a portion of its blood."

"Was this *inyan* a person?"

"Long ago, *Inyan Hoksi,* Stone Boy, made the first *inipi* and brought his dead uncles back to life. Some say that he sent his mother and uncles into the sky to be stars and that he made the buffalo girls into flowers."

"Yesterday, looking up at the ridge, Andi called Stevie 'Stone Boy.' "

"My grandson knows the story well, as all Lakota should. Stone Boy teaches us what to do, but also what not to do."

Rosen stared at the stone in his hands. "My people consider the Ten Commandments holy. They were written on two tablets of stone."

"Moses has a Lakota name. It's *Inyan Wasicun Wakan*—Holy White Stone Man. Come on, the fire's beginning to get hot."

It must have been several minutes before Rosen looked away from the stone; the pile had already gone down nearly a third, as True Sky trudged back and forth. Rosen loaded a half dozen in his arms, carrying them to the new pile near Ike.

Just as they were finishing, a tow truck drove up from the other side of the ridge. A young man stepped down from the driver's seat. He wore a mechanic's work clothes with the name "Will" stitched on the shirt.

"Sorry I'm late, Dad."

"Mr. Rosen, this is my son."

"I've been looking forward to meeting you. We have some things to talk about."

Will had a strong grip, but his eyes shifted away. The truck's passenger door opened, and Stevie jumped down. He held the door handle, as if ready to crawl back inside.

Will said, "Dad, I didn't know what to do. The school called Gracie, but she ain't been home all day."

"She's still in town. What do they say is wrong with the boy?"

Will ran a hand through his thick black hair. "He got into a fight with some of the other kids. Nobody knows what the hell it was about, but he's suspended for the rest of the day. Gracie's got to take him to school tomorrow morning and straighten it out. The boy's gonna have hell to pay, when she finds out." He suddenly flashed a smile. "Hello, Andi."

She nodded a reply but remained by the sweat lodge, gripping one of the tipi poles. Glancing at Rosen, she blushed.

Will looked her up and down and grinned.

True Sky said, "Remember why you're here. You must come in the right spirit."

"It's been a long time since I've done an *inipi*. Now with this problem with Stevie, maybe I'll just skip it."

"I made this *inipi* for Ike, to turn him away from drinking. I know your spirit is not right either, so you'll join us. It's good you brought the boy—he's old enough."

"I don't think that's such a good idea. Gracie'll raise hell as it is. You know how she feels about this kind of stuff. I'll just take him down to the house."

"You'll both do this."

True Sky motioned to Stevie, who came forward, head lowered, and stood before his grandfather. The old man lifted the boy's face and stared deep into his eyes.

Biting his lip, Stevie blurted, "It's the things they say. What they call us."

"It's not your fault. You're too young to understand what they say doesn't matter. I want you to go into the house and bring my *chanunpa*."

The boy's eyes grew wide.

"You know how to hold it?"

"Yes, Grandfather."

"Then go."

The boy ran down the ridge toward the house. Ike went to his van and returned with a stack of towels, a ladle, and a bucket filled with bundles of grass, sage, and cedar bark. He put everything down near the lodge's entrance, then emptied the bucket, which he handed to Will.

"Fill it at the stream. Make sure it's clear running water."

As Will angled to his left down the ridge, Rosen hurried after him.

"Can I ask you a few questions?"

"About what happened the night Gates was killed?"

"According to the police report, you found the body after coming home from work. That was about eleven o'clock."

"More like eleven fifteen. I went down to the house right away and called Gracie at the police station."

"Gates died around ten o'clock. Where were you at that time?"

They reached a brook that meandered snakelike down the ridge. Will filled the bucket with cold water.

"I usually close the station at ten, but not that night. Car came in with a busted hose, just as I was closing, and I stayed to fix it. There was a problem with the water pump, so I had to replace that as well. By the time I finished everything and washed up, it was about eleven."

"Not many people would find a mechanic willing to do so much work at closing time."

"Not many people whose car breaks down are Judge Whistler." When Rosen arched his eyebrows, Will laughed. "That's right. My alibi's a judge. Not that I had any reason to kill Albert Gates."

"The police found a bill of sale on his body. It had your signature on it and—"

"I already talked to Tom Cross Dog. So what if my old man wasn't going to honor the agreement and give Gates the *wotawe?*"

"You took the man's money. It might've been considered fraud."

Will snickered. "Listen, Gates's wife and my mother were real close. Belle woulda never let her husband get me in trouble. Besides, why would I want Gates dead? Wouldn't I want him to have his *wotawe,* so I could get the rest of my $500?"

"While working on the judge's car, did you see anyone drive down the highway from the ridge?"

"Nah. I was working on the car inside the garage, and my head was under the hood most of the time. Judge Whistler stood right next to me, making sure he wasn't getting cheated."

The two men started back. Halfway up the ridge, Rosen asked, "Could Stevie have seen anything that night?"

"You mean the murder? No way. The boy was in bed the whole time. He slept through everything—even the police sirens."

"He doesn't seem like the kind of boy who would sleep through any-thing."

"Well, he did. You just leave him alone. In fact . . . " Will looked away for a moment. "You could do us a favor—Gracie and me. She'll really flip out if Stevie does this *inipi.*"

"Why? It's just a sweat bath."

"Your mind starts playing games with itself. You start babbling all sorts of junk. With Stevie already edgy, I'd like to get him out of here. My old man won't listen to me, but maybe you can talk some sense into him. How about it?"

They were nearing the top of the ridge. Will had slowed his pace, as if giving Rosen time to answer. Maybe he should talk to True Sky, especially if the boy's condition was really that precarious. Yet, this might be the only way Stevie would speak about what happened the night of the murder. Rosen decided to trust True Sky—or was it just simpler that way?

The others were waiting for them. Stevie stood beside his grandfather, who held a ceremonial pipe with a long stem.

"This is my *chanunpa*," True Sky said. "You see the pipe bowl. It's made of bloodstone. My grandfather went east where the buffalo began and cut this from the ground. It was made from the buffalo's blood that seeped into the earth. Today you will smoke it with us."

"The fire's ready," Ike said.

Everyone placed the stones in the fire. Rosen watched as the moss—the spirit-writing—disappeared with the rising smoke and the stones turned white-hot. True Sky was right; none of them cracked.

Ike pulled off his T-shirt to reveal a chest brittle as a chicken's. "Come on, boys. You too, lawyer."

Rosen shook his head.

True Sky unbuttoned his shirt. "It will be good for you."

Rosen looked at the ground, feeling his cheeks grow warm and sensing that everyone was watching him. Wasn't this what he wanted—a chance to hear Stevie talk about what was troubling him? Yet to participate in such a ceremony—what would his rabbi and grandfather have said, let alone his father? It was apostasy, like the word *bamot* one shouldn't have spoken. Then he suddenly looked up and felt the trace of a smile. Wasn't he already an apostate in the eyes of his father? What would one more bit of backsliding matter? After all, it was for the case. There was always the case.

He removed his jacket and slowly unbuttoned his shirt.

Andi grinned. "Can I play too?"

Ike dropped his trousers. "The more the merrier."

"No!" Rosen swallowed hard. He couldn't undress in front of a woman, let alone sit naked with her.

"That's all right," Andi said, fishing a cigarette from her purse. "This sounds like one of those male-bonding things anyway. You'll all probably start hugging each other."

True Sky continued taking off his clothes, neatly folding and placing them in a pile. "Last year, a group of men came here from New York. They wanted to do an *inipi*. We took them into the sweat lodge, and they started to recite poetry and cry and say how good it was to be together. But as soon as the steam started to rise, they said it was too hot and ran outside."

"I think they were sissy boys," Ike said, also naked. "I saw them the next day in the hills, shooting each other with paint pellets. Do you want to get your camera, Andi, and take my picture? Maybe *Playgirl* will want it."

"I think you're more *National Geographic* material, but maybe another time."

"How about me?" Will asked, as he stripped down to his briefs.

Andi kept her eyes on Ike. "Give Nate a ride back to his motel afterwards." To Rosen, "Don't catch a chill. I'll see you tonight."

Walking quickly to her Mercury, Andi sped down the ridge. The broken muffler's rumbling stayed with them long after the car had disappeared into the distance.

When it was finally quiet, Ike said to Rosen, "We're waiting."

Everyone else stood naked. Taking a deep breath, he removed his clothes and put them in a pile next to True Sky's. Shivering, he scanned the horizon, half-expecting Andi to be taking pictures with a telephoto lens.

Ike handed out Holiday Inn towels. "I only use these on special occasions."

"Son," True Sky said, "pass the stones in to me."

As Will took the antler, Rosen lined up behind True Sky, Ike, and Stevie. Following their lead, he dropped to his knees. Holding his pipe in one hand, True Sky took the bundles of grass and cedar in the other, then crawled through a flap into the sweat lodge, ahead of Ike and Stevie. Rosen heard chanting and followed the others inside.

While groping in the darkness for a place against the wall, he smelled the aroma of cedar. Only when the flap was pulled aside and Will handed his father the antler holding five white-hot stones, did Rosen see the pit dug in the middle of the tipi. True Sky rolled one stone after the other into the pit.

"The first goes in the center for grandmother earth. Then west, north, east, and south." Handing back the antler, he waited for Will to return with more stones. "One on top for our grandfather the sky. Now we add the others." As Will left and the flap closed, True Sky asked, "Grandson, do you know why we carry the stones with an antler?"

Stevie's words floated through the darkness. "To remind us of our brothers, the four-leggeds." The boy spoke clearly, without any hesitation, the same way that Rosen, as the youngest in the family, had answered the Four Questions on Passover.

Again the flap opened, admitting Will and the antler filled with heated stones.

"That's enough," his father said, placing the stones in the pit.

Will brought in the ladle and pail of cold water. The flap closed, and, in the darkness, True Sky and Ike chanted in a singsong manner. Rosen remembered the men and boys swaying together in synagogue, their voices lifted to praise the Lord.

Suddenly he heard an angry sizzling, just before a blast of steam struck his face and filled his lungs. Coughing, he cupped his hands and sipped the warm air.

True Sky said, "This is the grandfather's breath. He's telling us the earth will listen to our problems and make us pure again. Take his breath in your hands and rub it on yourself. It's good medicine."

"The best," Ike agreed. "We open the flap four times, once after each time we smoke. If you can't take the heat, just call out, '*Mitakuye oyasin!*'—'All my relatives!' Then I'll let in some cool air."

"Here," Will said, handing Rosen something.

It was the *chanunpa,* True Sky's pipe. Rosen inhaled, coughed, and passed it to Stevie. He smelled the rich tobacco aroma and felt light-headed. Someone opened the flap just enough for the light to crawl halfway into the tipi. With it came a wisp of cool breeze, but, as suddenly, both were gone and the tipi again was plunged into darkness.

"I have a heavy heart," Ike said. "Like my prison counselor once said, I never lived up to my potential. I wanted to be an actor. If I had stuck with it, I might've been another Jay Silverheels, maybe even president. My friend Saul has said it's never too late, so I call on the spirits for help. I'm opening my heart to them. I'm sober now. I ask them to teach me to stay sober."

Ike continued to call on the spirits, as True Sky ladled water onto the heated rocks so that the steam engulfed them, and, as the sweat poured from Rosen's body, he inhaled the grandfather's breath. First it was searing, but gradually he grew accustomed to the heat, even welcomed it. After Ike, True Sky talked about the spirits' power—that they could do anything. Will said something about the need to get his life together, something boys always said to their fathers, lies before the words even left their lips. Did True Sky know his son was lying?

Only Stevie wouldn't speak. He did sing with the older men, his young voice as earnest as theirs. The chanting buzzing in his ears, Rosen remembered as a boy praying with his family, calling out to the God of Israel, the God of justice.

Rosen inhaled the *chanunpa,* watched the air grow ashen from the smoke and brief haze of light so that it resembled the skin of an old man . . . grandfather . . . his grandfather. Slowly the Indians' chanting grew intelligible; they sang in Hebrew. What Rosen was hearing had been his thoughts ever since his father had sent him away. But now they had become words, as the voices spoke to his grandfather.

"Why did you let him send me away—for asking questions? For not obeying blindly what he said I must do? Every Passover I had to answer the Four Questions, but they were easy. What about the questions I really wanted to ask—the ones he refused to hear? If we're in God's image, was the face my father showed me that day the true face of God?"

He didn't know if he was crying or if only more sweat was dripping from his face, but he felt good. When the flap was opened the fourth and final time, he smiled while, on his hands and knees, he followed the others outside.

He stood with them naked in the sun and rubbed his body dry with sage leaves. For the first time since childhood, he felt at peace. He knew the feeling would last only a little while, for all his fears and doubts still circled warily like coyotes in the distance. But for now they wouldn't dare come close, not as long as the tipi's fire blazed within him.

Chapter 8

THURSDAY EVENING

"You're really not gonna tell me, are you?" Andi glanced at Rosen from the driver's seat. "Well?"

He didn't feel like talking. The road ran smooth, the breeze pattered against his face, and day slowly dissolved into a twilight of clouds forming fantastic shapes across the sky. For the longest time he saw the face of an old Indian, like the head of a buffalo nickel, serenely watching the moon grow over the horizon. It might have been Saul True Sky, flying with his brothers the elk on a vision quest.

The breeze blew harder, as the face broke into pieces. Clouds drifted away, suddenly shifted, and merged once again, this time into an eagle. It grew nearly as big as the sky, descending toward him with wings outstretched and talons spread. Like its prey, Rosen sat frozen in place, hands gripping the car door, his eyes fixed on the eagle swooping closer and closer, its scream filling his ears.

"Jeez," Andi said, "are you gonna be like this all the way to Deadwood?"

He shut his eyes tightly, and when he looked back at the sky, the eagle had broken apart. Clouds hunched over him like curious bystanders, before slowly moving on.

"It's okay," she continued. "You were probably into all that man talk, like on those reruns of *My Three Sons*. Mike, Robbie, Uncle Charley—you know."

"No, I don't. I'd rather not talk about it."

"Maybe I should've insisted on joining you guys, though it probably was about as exciting as an American Legion square dance."

"You're forgetting Will was there."

As she gripped the steering wheel, her knuckles whitened. "That was a shit thing to say."

Rosen didn't reply. He knew she couldn't leave it alone.

"You've got no business messing into my personal life."

"I didn't realize your relationship with Will True Sky was so personal."

"Well, it's not."

"But you said . . . "

"Not anymore!"

"Oh." He looked out the window.

"We had something going, but that's over. Will's not the kind to be a one-woman man. There've been plenty others."

"Like Wendy, the dispatcher? Last night, in the station, you two were arguing over some man."

"Yeah. The problem with Wendy is that she just can't let go. She thinks I stole Will from her." Andi flashed a smile. "Well maybe so, but that's all ancient history."

"Did Will have anything to do with Albert Gates?"

"Ever since Will and Gracie were kids, they hung around the Gates's ranch—their mom and Belle were real tight. Will was always picking up a few bucks doing odd jobs for Albert—mowing hay, mucking out stables, running errands, even helping with the museum."

"Gates had a museum?"

"He had quite a collection of old Indian artifacts—arrowheads, clothing, even a few skeletons. It all started years ago, when he found some Indian remains on his ranch, just like the one you saw up on the ridge."

"White Bear."

Andi chuckled. "Yeah, that's what Saul calls his pile of bones. He and Gates sure didn't see eye to eye."

"And Will?"

"You mean about the bones and stuff like that? He could care less. He just likes to party."

"That document found on Gates's body—Will selling the *wotawe* to him. Would Gates have caused him trouble, because Saul refused to go through with the deal?"

"Albert Gates had a mean streak all right, but the hot air inside him could've filled the Goodyear blimp. Besides, Belle wouldn't have let him hurt Will. She cared too much about the family."

Rosen nodded; that was what Will had told him. "What about Judge

Whistler? Will said he was with the judge, working on his car, when the murder took place."

"That's a good one—Will and the judge. They don't exactly go round in the same circles. Calvin Whistler's used to seeing folks like Will at the back door. But Will couldn't have a much better alibi, if that's what you're getting at. The judge is straight as an arrow."

"So I hear. How about his wife?"

"I know what you're thinking—the judge's money and the difference in their age. Maybe she does run around, though in a town this small you'd think folks'd know. I'll tell you one thing—Pearl's got a brain among all those red curls. She's the biggest promoter of making Bear Coat the new Deadwood."

Rosen stretched his legs. "Speaking of Deadwood, how much longer?"

"Maybe ten minutes."

It was almost eight o'clock. Everything from Cadillacs to broken-down pickup trucks moved steadily toward town. It was the first time since his arrival that Rosen had experienced anything even resembling a traffic jam. Fast-food restaurants and motels grew thick as mushrooms along the side of the highway, which became Historic Main Street and continued into downtown Deadwood.

"How do you like it?" Andi asked.

On either side of the cobblestone street, illuminated by old-fashioned lights, were a series of buildings, all renovated to resemble a Wild West town. Filling the sidewalks, people kept moving from one spot to the next—old men leaning on their canes, women in straw hats and shapeless print dresses, families with little children trailing along like the tail of a kite. Rosen had been to hundreds of towns, but he'd never seen this type of restlessness.

There were bars and gaming halls like Calamity Jane's, Gold Dust, Midnight Star, Hickok's, and Silverado, but he glimpsed slot machines inside the burger joints as well.

Andi said, "The editor of one of the town papers calls this a bowler's Las Vegas. Everything's pretty much nickel-and-dime. And clean, just like Disneyland."

Rosen remembered, after being sent to live with an uncle, going with his cousins to Riverview, Chicago's old amusement park. It was dirty, smelled of sweat and vomit, and the rides clattered awkwardly along their tracks. The sideshows displayed bearded ladies, snake charmers, and others only slightly more bizarre than many of the customers. He'd been frightened by the whole experience but also excited, so much that, besides Wrigley Field, it had been his favorite place to go.

They'd torn Riverview down years ago, and now people drove to a new amusement park in the suburbs, with Bugs Bunny characters waving hello and an army of squeaky-clean teenagers picking up trash before it hit the ground. He'd taken Sarah and one of her friends there the previous summer, and it had seemed their fun was distributed in sterilized plastic bags. Looking up and down the street, he had the same sense about Deadwood.

Andi turned onto Pine Street and, after the VFW Hall, pointed to a solid, three-story brick building. Arches framed the first-floor windows, above which four Doric columns rose between the windows to buttress the second and third stories. Engraved above the columns were the words U.S. POST OFFICE AND COURT HOUSE.

"That's where the preliminary hearing's being held tomorrow."

She continued past the Lawrence County Sheriff's Office and parked in front of a small frame building with the sign Deadwood Tales.

"I thought you might like to meet an old family friend, Carrie Taggert. She edits one of the town papers. Better lock the car doors—I've got some camera equipment in the back seat." Looking up and down the street, she added, "This isn't Bear Coat."

The inside of the newspaper office was as modest as its exterior. Everything looked old and gray, except for the computers and monitors on the metal desks. There was no Western paraphernalia; a few framed front pages, going back to the forties, hung along the walls.

Someone sat behind a newspaper at one of the back desks.

Andi called, "Carrie?"

The paper dropped, and an old woman smiled. Wearing wire-rimmed glasses, her white hair in a bun, she could've been on the label of a pickle jar.

"About time you got over here for a visit. Come to see if I'm still breathing?"

As they approached her desk, Carrie stood. She was small and lithe and from a distance, wearing her UNLV sweatshirt and jeans, might have been mistaken for a girl.

Gripping Rosen's hand, she said, "You must be the lawyer Andi rustled from back East—Rosen, isn't it? Good luck—you're going to need it. In spite of his big mouth, Albert Gates had a lot of friends. I suppose you've already given Andi an exclusive on how you're planning True Sky's defense."

Rosen shrugged. "At this point, there's not much to say. I'll know more after the preliminary hearing tomorrow." He looked along the wall at the old headlines. "This town's got quite a history, and now it's come full circle, having gambling again. Andi tells me that Deadwood is what Bear Coat could look like."

"Yeah. It changes a place, that's for damn sure."

"For the better?"

"Depends who you talk to. Have you eaten dinner?" When he shook his head, she said, "Come on, you can see for yourself. Hand me my purse, will you—over there, on top of the file cabinet."

Her purse, a cloth bag with a drawstring, sagged as if filled with lead weights.

They walked back up Pine, then onto Main Street, which had grown even more congested. Carrie led them into one of the saloons. People played slot machines along the windows. To Rosen's left ran a long bar, behind which a man with a handlebar mustache served beer and pretzels. Above the shelves of liquor hung the portrait of a saloon girl, naked except for a feathered hat. A player piano banged out "Ragtime Cowboy Joe," sung almost in tune by a middle-aged woman layered in makeup, whose breasts threatened to pop over her bodice.

Past her, in a second room, men sat at felt-covered tables playing poker and blackjack. The room, smoky and smelling of stale beer, was much quieter than the bar. Nobody smiled or joked—there was only the patter of chips tossed upon the green tabletops.

Standing beside him, Carrie said, "It's all small stakes—just a way of passing time that's a little more exotic than bingo. A five-dollar limit on cards. Slot machines are nickel, quarter, and dollar."

"So no one gets hurt, is that it?"

"That's the way it was intended. Just enough money was supposed to be generated to give the town a shot in the arm and renovate Main Street for tourists. Back in '89, people thought there might be about a half-million spent in gambling the first year. Well, it turned out more like $20 million a month."

"Quite a shot in the arm."

"Yeah. Some real estate skyrocketed over a thousand percent, and a lot more jobs became available. Of course, most of the jobs are in places like this. And there's a helluva lot more crime, drunk driving, and child abuse. Having a gambling hall almost next to the elementary school didn't thrill too many parents."

They walked back through the bar, where Carrie paused before one of the slot machines. Reaching into her purse, she took out a handful of quarters which she inserted, one by one, into the machine, pressing a button and waiting just long enough for the three pictures to register before plunking in the next coin. It took perhaps two minutes to empty her hand.

They walked into another saloon, similar to the first, and while Carrie played the slot machine, Rosen and Andi continued into the back room. Andi suddenly pulled him into the shadows against the wall.

"Look over there in the corner."

Roy Huggins, the Bear Coat town council's attorney, slouched over the table, his tie loosened, one hand holding his cards while the other held a drink.

"See the guy beside him?"

She was referring to Chick Cantrell, the engineer. He wore a flannel shirt, the sleeves rolled above his thick forearms.

Rosen asked, "Did you know Cantrell and Huggins were friends?"

"No. Cantrell's from L.A. Been here only a few months. He's a big slob—can't keep his hands off women. He tried pawing me once, until I almost slapped that beard off his face. Definitely not the kind of guy Huggins would see on the golf course."

"Maybe their being together's just a coincidence."

"One thing that's not a coincidence is Huggins at the poker table. He's really bit by the gambling bug—takes those junkets to Las Vegas. Folks say he wants poker in Bear Coat just so he won't have to waste his betting time driving to and from Deadwood."

Rosen watched the two men playing cards. They didn't speak to one another, but neither did anyone at the table. Cantrell slammed his fist on the table when he lost, but chuckled like Santa Claus when he won. For Huggins, victory and defeat appeared the same; he stared at some imaginary spot in the middle of the table and silently sipped his drink, which extended like an appendage from his hand.

Ten minutes later, Andi tugged Rosen's sleeve. "We'd better go."

Back on the street, Carrie swung her half-empty purse with considerably more ease. She opened the door to a restaurant with a large picture window, above which was lettered, in script resembling branding irons, Della's Deli.

"What say we get some dinner?"

The restaurant, long and narrow, was divided into two rooms. Slot machines lined the walls of the front area, and a dozen square tables filled the back. Rosen and his two companions sat at the first table near a teller's cage, where a woman made change.

A man walked in, unkempt and in need of a shave. Three young boys tumbled after him. As if feeding a bird, the man carefully slipped quarters into the machine, while his children played tag up and down the aisle. They scurried among the machines until the teller, stepping from her cubicle, sat them at a table with three large Cokes and a huge basket of french fries.

Their father remained oblivious to his children and didn't even look up when the woman beside him screamed with delight, as a river of quarters cascaded from the machine into her sun hat.

Carrie said, "The half-breed in the teller's cage owns the place. It was just a dive, but once gambling came in and she got a license—you should see her house in the hills. Has a girl in law school. Speaking of lawyers," she asked Andi, "how's that handsome boss of yours?"

After the waiter brought their sandwiches and drinks, Andi replied, "He's real busy—what with running the newspaper and trying to help Saul True Sky hold onto his land."

"He made a pass yet, or is he too old for a young thing like you?"

"No."

"No, he's too old?"

"He hasn't made a pass at me." She narrowed her eyes. "He's not that old. I bet he's not much older than Nate here."

Leaning back, the old woman looked from Rosen to Andi. "No, I guess he's not. Maybe you two . . . "

"Who's that?" Rosen asked, nodding toward the window. "Wasn't that a Bear Coat police car?"

"I think so," Andi said. "Maybe it's come to give Roy Huggins a ride home."

Carrie shook her head sadly. "Sure as shootin', he can't drive himself. Why, they'd have to pour him into his car."

"I don't know why Belle and the rest of the town council put up with him."

89

Across the aisle, the youngest boy began wailing; his Coke had spilled over the fries. None of the gamblers turned to look, not even the children's father, who, like an automaton, continued working the slot machine.

"Let's get out of here," Rosen said.

Passing through the restaurant, he almost tripped over one of the boys, who started to cry while his brothers fell on the floor laughing.

Brightly lit, the street bustled with the same odd mixture of adults and children. Rosen wondered if anyone besides him noticed that, high above in a raven sky, the pale moon was full. He walked a few steps behind the two women, listening to them reminisce about Andi's father, until they reached the newspaper office. Again Carrie wished him luck and said goodnight.

Walking back, he and Andi noticed the Bear Coat police car parked in front of the sheriff's office.

She said, "I wonder what that's all about."

As if in response, the door of the building opened, and Tom Cross Dog walked down the steps with Stevie Jenkins. Hair matted and face dirty, the boy wore a jeans jacket over a torn Guns 'n' Roses T-shirt. Reaching for the passenger door, the policeman saw Andi and hesitated. She hurried to the boy, Rosen following after.

"What's wrong?" she asked Stevie, checking him for injuries.

"Nothing," he muttered, pushing her hands away.

"Tom?"

Sighing, Cross Dog sat heavily on the hood. "I got a call an hour ago from Sheriff Clarkson. Guess you'd call it a professional courtesy—he knows Gracie works at the station. Lucky it wasn't her shift when the call came in."

"What is it?"

"Looks like Stevie hitched a ride into Deadwood with a couple of his friends. The boys played some slot machines at one of the drugstores, until the owner kicked them out. Not before they did a little shoplifting. The other two got away, but Stevie wasn't so lucky. Tripped over a dog and got caught."

"Oh, God."

"Second time this year he's been arrested."

"How serious is it?"

The policeman shrugged. "I made good what was stolen, so the owner's not gonna press charges. Sheriff Clarkson's willing to forget about it—what the hell, Stevie's just another punk for him to process." He said the last words a little louder, so the boy was sure to hear.

Andi touched his arm. "You're a good friend, Tom. Gracie sure has been through enough not to need any more grief."

"Yeah. About Gracie." He leaned closer. "Look, she don't have to know anything about this."

"But she must be worried sick where he is."

"Call her now, and say you ran into Stevie in Deadwood. Let her know about the hitchhiking but nothing else. Then drive him home. Folks don't need to see the boy riding in a squad car. How about it?"

Andi smiled. "Okay. I'll go inside and phone her."

While waiting, Cross Dog absently kicked the tire with his heel. He cocked his head and, reaching out, pulled the boy to him.

"What happened tonight . . . your mother don't have to know. All right?"

Stevie looked away.

"Well?" Cross Dog grabbed the boy with both hands and lifted him from the ground. "You're not the only one who's had a rough time. Why don't you think about somebody else for a change?"

"Leave me alone!"

Stevie kicked at him, until Cross Dog let go. The boy stumbled, then quickly got up, clenching his fists as if ready to trade punches.

Andi hurried down the steps. "All set. Is everything okay?"

The policeman asked, "You didn't mention me, did you?"

"No."

"Good. See you around." Slamming the car door, Cross Dog drove away.

Andi put her arm around Stevie, who suddenly leaned against her like a little boy. He let her lead him to the car and, without a word, slid into the back seat.

Ten minutes outside Deadwood, traffic had thinned until all that Rosen could see in the darkness was a pair of tail lights twinkling in the distance below the stars. Shifting slightly, he tried to locate Stevie in the rear-view mirror. The boy curled against the rear door behind Andi.

"Gets really dark out here," Rosen said.

Andi nodded. "Easy to get lost, if you're not careful. It's a lot worse in the winter."

"I bet Saul's ridge gets dark as this. Isn't that so, Stevie?"

The boy didn't answer but raised his head.

"Of course, if you really knew the ridge, I bet you could find your way around in the dark without any trouble. Don't you think?" After a few seconds, he added, "Stevie?"

"I don't know."

"You like to wander around, don't you?"

No answer.

"Were you wandering around the ridge the night Albert Gates was murdered?"

Turning, Rosen watched the boy squirm against the door.

"You did see something. What was it?"

"Leave me alone!"

"That sweat in True Sky's lodge didn't last long for either of us, did it? A man must make his own peace. Stevie, you've got to talk to me sooner or later."

A muffled noise, maybe a sob, then the sudden rushing of air. The car swerved as Andi applied the brakes.

"Nate, stop him!"

Stevie was half out the car when, reaching over the seat, Rosen pulled the boy back inside. Rosen's left hand shivered; had it been struck by the closing door? Under the glimmering dashboard, he watched a thin line of blood slithering above his knuckles.

Turning back, he stared past the pocketknife, into the shadows that hid Stevie's eyes. No one spoke, no one moved—but in the stillness, Rosen heard the boy's breath quicken like the fluttering of a frightened bird.

Chapter 9

THURSDAY NIGHT

Grace pulled into her usual parking space behind Town Hall but waited, her fingers clicking the clasp of her purse. It was better going to work as usual; besides, what could she do at home? Stevie was in bed, and her father had promised to stay in the house with him. Had it come to this— taking turns guarding the boy like he was a prisoner? Sighing, she looked at the dashboard clock, just as it flashed 11:01. She was never late.

On her way into the police station, Grace passed Will's pickup truck. Her steps quickened. What was wrong now?

Will sat alone behind the control unit. Holding up a copy of *Cosmopolitan,* he flashed a smile.

"Not a bad job, Gracie, sitting here all night, looking at pictures of half-naked women and finding out how they think. Did you know that women find earth-tone bed sheets more romantic than all those hot colors? Surprised the hell outta me. Guess I'd better do some shopping tomorrow."

He gave the chair to Grace and, looking over her shoulder, continued flipping the magazine pages.

"It's Wendy's," she said.

"I know."

"That's why you're here. You two are back together."

Pointing to the advertisement of a woman slung over a man's shoulder, he said, "Guess I've got my needs like everybody else. She's in the ladies' room, prettying herself up for me."

Elroy walked from the cells, carrying a dinner tray. "Damn drunk thinks he's got room service." When Wendy rushed in from the hallway, he handed her the tray. "Drop this off at the diner—that is, if it don't

93

interfere too much with your plans for the evening. I'm already late for my shift."

"It's no trouble, Elroy. You know I always—" but the deputy had already walked out the door.

"What's his problem?" Will asked.

"Forget about him." She kissed Will on the cheek. "Come on, honey, I got my dancing shoes on. Bye, Gracie."

"You two have fun," she replied, forcing a smile.

The smile slowly melted as Tom walked into the station, just as the other two left. He sat heavily in Elroy's chair and swiveled to face her.

"Those two back together?"

"For tonight, at least."

"You all right?"

"Uh-huh. Why do you ask?"

He scratched his head. "No reason. The hearing tomorrow. If you want to leave a few hours early and get some sleep . . . "

"No, but thanks. Guess I am a little worried about tomorrow. I just wish Jack had taken the case. I guess Mr. Rosen will do a good job—he sure seems to know what he's doing, but it's not the same as somebody you know. I can tell you don't like him."

"Just like coyotes, one lawyer's the same as another."

"Jack's not like that."

Shifting in his chair, Tom asked, "You still planning to ride in the show on Saturday?"

She shrugged. "I don't know. Guess it depends on what happens tomorrow at the hearing. Don't feel much like doing it."

"You should. It'll be good for you, and you sure don't want to disappoint Curly. I've already got Cree Lansing taking your shift tomorrow, so you can get some rest and start off early in the morning."

"Will you be there?"

"I just might."

He turned back to the desk, and they lapsed into silence. It wasn't unusual for the two of them to be alone in the station deep into the night, without him saying a word. "That was the way of a Lakota warrior," her father would say. "Not to waste words, especially with a woman."

She liked Tom's silence, the way it always covered her soft and warm like a blanket. Even when they were kids, an Indian and a half-breed in a white man's school, Grace always felt protected. Reaching into the cubbyhole of her desk, she took out the turtle doll that had once protected her son.

Stroking the doll, she said, "Stevie got into trouble again." Knowing he wouldn't say anything until asked, she continued, "Andi called me earlier this evening from Deadwood. Stevie hitchhiked over there after school. She and Mr. Rosen brought him home about a half hour ago. I put him to bed and made Father stay in the house."

Tom looked down at his folded hands. "Did the boy say anything?"

"About what—you mean, what he was doing in Deadwood?"

"Yeah."

"We don't talk much anymore. Not since Steve died. Sometimes when I look into his eyes, there's nothing there. Like you could dive into them, and keep going and going forever. He scares me. You don't think he got in any trouble over there?"

Tom took a pen from his pocket and tapped it on the edge of the desk.

"Tom?"

"Stevie's just foolin' around like a hundred other kids in this town. Don't you remember when we was kids? Everybody acts a little crazy at that age."

"Not me."

"Well, I sure was."

"You?" Grace laughed.

"You remember how wild I used to get."

"Yeah—maybe about as wild as having old Two Feathers buy you a six-pack of beer. And you'd pass out after the third one."

"Now, Gracie, there was lots of times I used to cut loose with Ira, Billy High Horse, and—"

"Cut it out. Everybody said you were the nicest boy. Why do you think folks elected you police chief? Not 'cause you're so big and tough. It's 'cause they like you. Remember—I was seven or eight—when I fell off my first pony and it ran away? You chased after it. Must've taken you half the day to chase it down; Mother woke me to say you'd brought it back. You didn't even stick around for me to say thanks."

"That was a long time ago."

"People don't change. Father's always telling Ike that you would've been a great war chief, because men would've followed you."

Tom didn't reply, and for a long time Grace watched him study the pencil he held between his hands. She tried imagining him as a stranger might, like Nate Rosen. What did the lawyer see—just a big, tough cop with a stubborn streak? If Rosen got to know him better, he'd see the real Tom.

"Shouldn't you be on patrol?" Grace asked. She checked the schedule. "Wait a minute. You're not on this shift. What're you doing here so late?"

He tapped the pencil on the desk. "I was going out for a beer. Thought I'd check in for a minute."

"There've been lots of times Wendy or I can't get you on the radio. Elroy doesn't know where you've been going."

"Well, that ain't any of their business, is it?"

"People just get worried about you." She leaned over her desk and smiled. "Wendy thinks you've got a girl stashed somewhere."

"That sounds like Wendy."

"Well?"

He tossed the pencil on the desk. "Like I said before, ain't nobody else's business."

Grace nodded. "All right. Maybe you better go and get that beer."

"Yeah."

Tom stood but, instead of leaving the station, walked into his office. Through the half-open doorway, she saw the faint glow of his desk lamp and heard one of the drawers thump closed. Then the station settled once again into its late-night quiet.

For the next half hour, Grace typed some reports that, as usual, Wendy hadn't quite gotten to. She took a check-in call from the two patrol cars on duty; quiet as usual for a weeknight. She picked up the phone to call home, then lowered the receiver. It was almost midnight—her father would probably be sleeping. He needed his rest for the hearing. Besides, she told him to call her if there were any problems. She couldn't go on worrying about everybody else. Returning the turtle doll to its cubbyhole, Grace looked at the photo of her and Curly. Tom was right; come hell or high water, she needed to ride in Saturday's show.

She'd just finished filing the typed reports when the door swung open and Jack ran in. "Is everything all right?"

Startled, she didn't know what to say. Staring back at him, she saw that two buttons of his blue silk shirt were unclasped.

"Grace, are you all right?"

"Uh-huh."

"Where's Stevie?"

"Stevie? He's at home." Her heartbeat quickened. "Why, what's wrong?"

Jack lifted his hands. "I don't understand. I came home about an hour ago. I forgot to check my phone messages until just now, when I was getting ready for bed. There was a message—a man's voice, I don't know whose—saying Stevie was picked up by the Bear Coat police in Deadwood, and that the boy would probably need an attorney. I ran over here—but everything's all right?"

She nodded slowly, still trying to understand what he'd said.

"Then it was just a crank call?"

"Guess so. I mean, Stevie was in Deadwood earlier this evening, but Andi brought him home. She didn't mention anything about the police. You said Bear Coat police?"

Jack nodded.

"Tom!" she called, but he was already standing beside his door. "You know anything about this?"

"I got a call from Sheriff Clarkson about seven-thirty. He'd arrested Stevie for shoplifting."

"Oh, God!"

"Nothing for you to worry about."

"Nothing for me . . . !"

"I drove over there and took care of everything. The store owner dropped the charges. I even got Andi to drive him home, so that nobody'd know anything about it." He turned to Jack. "Almost nobody. I'd sure like to know who called you."

"As I said before, a stranger's voice."

Tom looked at him hard, then shook his head. "You're a liar."

"What?"

He took a step closer, the veins in his neck bulging. "You're a liar."

Jack almost smiled, and Grace sensed that Tom was about to grab him.

Striking her fist on the desk, she said, "You're the liar! You're the one who said everything was all right, when all along you knew—"

"I didn't want you to worry. I took care of everything."

"He's my son! I'm the one responsible for him, not you! Don't you think me not knowing gives Stevie something else to hide!"

Tom slouched like a bear and looked at her with his soft brown eyes.

97

Feeling the tears brimming, she looked away, wiping her eyes with her palms. "I gotta get out of here for a while."

"Sure, go ahead. I'll watch the dispatch."

As Grace came around the desk, Jack took her arm, then led her out the door.

The night air was cool but just as still as inside the station. A full moon hung perfect like a pearl in a black velvet sky. Grace's mother had worn a pearl necklace. Every time Grace saw a full moon, she thought of her mother bending to kiss her goodnight, felt the smooth pearl brush against her cheek, and smelled lavender soap. She liked taking long walks on such a night; it was as if her mother walked beside her, whispering in the breeze that everything would be all right.

"Would you like to go for a cup of coffee?" Jack asked. "We could drive over to the truck stop."

She shook her head.

"How about a drink?"

"It's after midnight. The bars are closed."

"I have some brandy in my office."

"I don't know."

"It'll do you good."

He was smiling, and his silk shirt felt soft against her arm. His cologne smelled so good.

"All right. Just for a few minutes."

They walked across the street into the newspaper office. The room was a square box, with a computer atop an old wooden desk in each corner. One corner displayed travel posters, another sports; Andi's walls were covered with her own gallery of photographs, entitled "Faces of Bear Coat." Grace was up there, with Curly nuzzling against her cheek.

Past a stairway leading to the second floor, the walls in Jack's corner were bare. He pulled a chair over for her, and she sat beside him behind his desk. Grace had been here a few times before, and she remembered how orderly his desktop was, and how handsome. A sterling-silver name-plate on mahogany, a leather cup for holding pencils, a padded stapler, and two intricately carved bookends resembling a dragon's head and tail. A half-dozen law books made up the dragon's body. A folded newspaper lay beside the stapler. Looking closer, she saw it was a racing form, with several horses circled and a series of numbers scribbled in the margin.

Jack also kept a liquor caddy in the corner. Setting two glasses on the desk, he poured them each a brandy.

"Cheers."

Grace sipped the drink slowly; at first it overpowered her, making her eyes water. Feeling the warmth spread through her body, she settled into the chair, her legs dangling like a puppet's. Maybe because she hadn't eaten supper, or because she was tired, or because Jack sat so close, Grace felt a little giddy. "This is nice."

He poured them each another drink. "Maybe it's none of my business, but don't you think you were a little rough on Cross Dog?"

"He should've told me about Stevie."

"Perhaps, but he was only thinking of you. He seems a decent guy."

"Guess you're right. I'll talk to him later. It's just, I get so worried about Stevie. It's so hard keeping tabs on him, especially when I've got Father to worry about too."

He leaned closer, holding the glass between his hands. She watched the brandy ebb and flow, and it made her a little drowsy. "Grace, you can't put the whole world on your shoulders. It's understandable that Stevie has some emotional problems, after all that's happened to your family. But he knows you love him, and he's getting professional help."

"I don't know how much that doctor's really doing for him. He just gives the boy something for his nerves."

"Maybe we should find a specialist, a psychiatrist who deals with children having Stevie's type of problem. There must be one in Rapid City or Sioux Falls. I'll make inquiries."

"A psychiatrist? We could never afford one."

"I . . . " He took a drink. "You wouldn't have to worry about any expenses."

"Oh, Jack, I couldn't let you do that."

"I'd like to see you happy, that's all. I can understand your worrying about Stevie. We can deal with that, but you must realize that your father's not your responsibility."

She shook her head, almost spilling her glass. "But the way he acts . . . "

"The way he acts is his own affair. He's not crazy—you, of all people, know he's not. His ways are just different. How often has he said, 'Why should an Indian eat merely because the clock strikes six?' "

"I know."

"Well, then, let it go. I'm taking care of the condemnation hearing, but that seems relatively minor at this point. Mr. Rosen's defending your father against the murder charge, and I have a strong feeling that Saul is in the best of hands. I had Mr. Rosen checked out. He's an excellent attorney. You shouldn't let this worry you."

"I'll try not to. Thanks, Jack. Seems all I ever do is say thanks."

"I care about you, Grace."

She sighed and, returning the glass to the desk, almost knocked it over. He reached to steady her hand, then held it. His touch was warm as the brandy, and suddenly she felt safe.

Grace wanted to tell him how safe she felt, but as she turned toward him, he kissed her. It was soft, natural as her next breath, and when he kissed her again, she let him pull her close. Her mouth opened to his, while the brandy kindled something she'd felt only with Steve, or alone in bed dreaming about him.

His hands were under her blouse; were those her own hands helping him? In the midst of their fumbling, she heard him as if far away.

"Upstairs."

She stood, her legs trembling, and let him lead her to the stairway. They kissed again, her blouse unbuttoned so that she felt the softness of his silk shirt against her skin. She held him tightly, when suddenly he pulled away.

Looking up at him, she saw her own look of surprise reflected in his eyes.

"No," he said softly, "not like this. You're a little tipsy. I don't think you know what you're doing."

Shutting her eyes, she leaned forward, as if she were galloping Curly, running him as fast as she could, until his legs blurred and her heartbeat raced with him. She wrapped her legs tightly around him, and it was Jack holding her, kissing her and carrying her upstairs.

In the soft darkness that must have been his bed, she didn't know if her eyes were open or closed, only that she saw nobody—not Stevie, her father, Tom, or even Jack. Only herself, moaning under his touch, moving her body for herself, then drifting alone down an endless stream black and silent as the night.

Chapter 10

Rosen knew he should be paying more attention. Assistant District Attorney Ernest Reedy, a redheaded young man with woodpecker persistence, was examining Will True Sky.

"So you found the victim, Albert Gates, a little after eleven p.m."

"Yes, sir."

"He was lying on the ground, with the back of his head bashed in."

"Uh-huh."

"And you saw nobody in the vicinity at or near that time, except for your father, Saul True Sky."

"Well—guess that's right."

Reedy pointed his index finger at the witness. "A simple yes or no, Mr. True Sky."

"I guess it'd have to be yes." He smiled good-naturedly.

"Don't guess. The answer is yes."

The assistant D.A. was shamelessly leading the witness. Reedy's awkward prosecution demonstrated inexperience, nervousness, or, worse, needless showboating. Of course, Saul True Sky would have to stand trial; there was too much evidence for any judge to dismiss the charges. But this preliminary hearing wouldn't be a total loss.

Besides having the opportunity to preview the state's witnesses and evidence, Rosen always used such a hearing to evaluate his opponent. That was something he'd learned as a boy, listening to the radio as one of his heroes, Floyd Patterson, fought Sonny Liston. At the weigh-in, the announcer mentioned how Patterson had been transfixed by Liston's glare, like a mouse before a cobra. The fight, which didn't last a round, ended before it had begun—when Patterson first looked into the cobra's eyes. Rosen remembered and, in all his cases, made sure those eyes were his.

Finishing his examination with a self-satisfied nod, Reedy strutted to the prosecutor's table.

"Mr. Rosen?" Judge Whistler inquired.

Instead of replying, he glanced over his shoulder. Although the court-room was filled, the two people he most wanted to see were missing.

"Counselor?"

The judge arched his eyebrows, bringing the slightest blush to his pallid cheeks. With its patrician features and snow-white hair curling softly like fleece, Whistler's head could have adorned a Roman coin.

"Just a few questions, Your Honor."

Rosen didn't bother to leave his chair. "Mr. True Sky, you say that you discovered the body of Albert Gates a little after eleven."

"Yes, sir."

"How did you know he was dead?"

"Huh?"

"How did you know that Albert Gates was dead and not uncon-scious?"

"Well . . . the body was cold. I checked for a pulse and there wasn't any. He was dead, all right."

Rosen paused to reread a section of the police report. "According to Chief Cross Dog's report, your flashlight was found about halfway between the victim and the Indian remains, where Gates was struck. If you bent over the dead man, then left the flashlight there when you went for help, perhaps he crawled . . . "

"Oh, I see what you're getting at." Will half-closed his eyes, as if try-ing to remember. "What happened was, I started to go for help, then thought I'd better leave the flashlight there, so I put it down. That's what happened."

Rosen stared at Will, until the young man looked down at his hands. "Doesn't the gas station where you work normally close at ten?"

"Uh-huh, but that night I was working on a car and didn't finish till after eleven. Then I closed up and went home. That's when I found Gates's body."

"And you have someone to verify your presence in the station until eleven?"

Scratching his head, Will glanced at Judge Whistler. "Sure I do. You can just ask . . . "

"Objection," Reedy said, rising to his feet. "There's no need for Mr. True Sky to establish an alibi . . . Will True Sky, that is."

The judge nodded. "However, this does raise a delicate issue. Mr. Rosen, surely you know that I'm the owner of the car and can establish Will True Sky's alibi. If that's going to be a problem either at this hearing or in the case of a subsequent trial, I'll recuse myself."

Rosen looked from the witness to the judge. By any standard, the two men couldn't be more opposite, which in itself lent credibility to Will's alibi.

"Mr. Rosen?"

"I have no objection to Your Honor trying the case."

"Very well. You may proceed."

"Mr. True Sky, I understand that a contract was found on the victim. According to this agreement, you sold Albert Gates the right to—"

"Again I must object." Reedy jumped to his feet, his index finger jabbing the point home. "At a preliminary hearing, we need only establish enough evidence to warrant—"

"Yes, I believe this court knows what a preliminary hearing entails. Mr. Rosen, we're investigating the culpability of the elder Mr. True Sky, not his son. You understand that?"

"Yes, Your Honor. I have no further questions for the witness."

Will stepped from the witness stand and passed the defendant's table without once glancing at his father. Saul True Sky, in turn, stared straight ahead. Wearing an old brown suit, shiny at the knees, and a turquoise string tie, he seemed from another era, like Rosen's people with their long black caftans and hats. Like them, he displayed the great dignity that moral certitude brings.

Next, the prosecutor called Tom Cross Dog. While the police chief recounted his discovery of the body—all of which was included in the police report, Rosen again looked over his shoulder. Andi still wasn't in court. He had assumed she would drive him into Deadwood for the hearing, but she hadn't come for him or answered her phone. Finally he'd called Grace for a ride. Maybe Andi had been sent on another assignment by Jack Keeshin, who sat beside Grace taking notes.

Stevie Jenkins was another matter. Of course, the boy would be in school—that is, if he hadn't run away again. Rosen was certain Stevie knew something about the murder, something he refused to tell. Why?

"Does the defense have any questions?"

Rosen rubbed his eyes. "Yes, Your Honor. Chief Cross Dog, where did you discover Mr. True Sky?"

"He was in a ditch, what's called a vision pit, a few feet from the victim."

"If Mr. True Sky did kill Albert Gates, isn't it odd that he would remain at the scene of the crime for the police to find him?"

"Once again, I object," Reedy said, popping up and shaking his head in disbelief. "Counsel is asking the witness for a conclusion."

"I don't mind answering," Cross Dog said. "Saul True Sky's full of crazy ideas. Don't forget, he's been drunk and killed once before."

The judge rapped his gavel. "The objection's well stated. Chief Cross Dog, you know better than to proceed before my ruling."

Rosen asked the witness, "Did you test Saul True Sky to see if he'd been drinking?"

"No."

"Did you find any evidence of liquor on the premises—liquor bottles, the smell of whiskey on his breath or clothing?"

Cross Dog shook his head.

Reading through the policeman's report, Rosen continued, "You found something clutched in the victim's fist."

"Yes."

"Do you know what it was?"

"No. Some dirt and an old piece of metal. Just something he grabbed from the ground while dying, I guess."

"Has it been tested to determine its identity?"

Taking a ball-point pen from his shirt pocket, the policeman clicked it nervously. "We . . . uh . . . couldn't test it."

Rosen leaned forward, suddenly alert.

"Why not?"

Cross Dog's big shoulders shrugged. "We misplaced it. But it couldn't be anything important."

"Misplaced? You mean, you've lost this important piece of evidence?"

Reedy's face grew flush. "Your Honor, it's unfortunate that this piece of evidence has been misplaced—we're sure only temporarily. It really has no bearing on the case."

For the first time that morning, Judge Whistler almost smiled. "How can you be certain of that without first examining the evidence?"

"Indeed," Rosen said. "Even if it's found, one can certainly question the chain of evidence. And if the prosecution has been so sloppy with one piece of evidence, might we not suspect how the murder weapon—the stone—has been safeguarded?"

Once again Reedy stood. "As Dr. Gustafson will testify, there are absolutely no improprieties regarding our handling of the stone. I resent the defense counsel's attempts to indicate otherwise."

Rosen shook his head sadly. "And I resent the prosecutor popping up every few minutes like a jack-in-the-box to object to legitimate lines of questioning."

Blushing more violently, Reedy sunk into his chair.

Judge Whistler rapped his gavel. "That's enough, Mr. Rosen. I suggest that Mr. Reedy and Chief Cross Dog do everything in their power to locate the missing evidence. Any other questions?"

"No, Your Honor."

The prosecution's final witness was the medical examiner, Dr. Iver Gustafson, a hatchet-faced Swede who answered every question a little too loudly, as if his comments needed translating for the hearing-impaired. Gustafson confirmed the time of death at about ten o'clock, "give or take a half hour," and that the blood found both on the stone used as the murder weapon and on True Sky's sleeve was the same type as the victim's.

Rosen said, "Chief Cross Dog has admitted 'misplacing' whatever was in the victim's hand. Did you examine the hand and take any scrapings from it for analysis?"

"No. I examined the wound that killed him, and that was on the back of his skull, not his hand."

"I see. Have you examined other murder victims before?"

"Thirteen. This makes fourteen. If you're questioning my competency—"

"No, quite the contrary. As the prosecution has already stipulated, I believe fourteen murder examinations does indeed make you an expert. As an expert, how would you characterize this particular crime?"

The medical examiner shifted in his seat. "I don't know what you mean."

"Would you say that this murder was premeditated or perhaps occurred spur-of-the-moment?"

"No way to say for sure."

"Did you examine Albert Gates for any marks or wounds, besides those that killed him?"

"Sure did. Didn't find any."

"No signs of a struggle?"

"No."

"As if the murderer snuck up behind Albert Gates and struck him."

"Sure could've happened that way."

"In your experience, did you ever know a man who, in such a calculated manner, murdered someone and then waited, with the victim's blood on his sleeve and the murder weapon nearby, for the police to arrive?"

Reedy began to rise, then returned to his chair. His voice was softer, more tentative. "Objection. This calls for a conclusion."

Rosen said, "Mr. Reedy has already stipulated this witness as an expert. All I'm doing is asking his expert opinion."

"Sure would seem stupid for True Sky to hang around," the doctor agreed.

Judge Whistler thumped his gavel. "Objection sustained."

"I have one more question for the witness. Dr. Gustafson, I ask you again, and please think carefully. Did you find any other wounds on the deceased?"

"No . . . least ways, not connected to the murder."

"There was something else."

"Well, Gates had a bandaged cut on his right hand, just above the knuckles."

"Could you determine what made the wound?"

The doctor stroked his chin. "I suppose any type of thin blade. A razor or penknife, for example. To tell the truth, I didn't really pay much attention to the cut, because it obviously happened another time."

"But recently . . . the same day perhaps?"

"Umm . . . maybe."

"Thank you. No further questions."

Rosen scratched the bandage on his left hand, where Stevie had cut him the night before.

After the doctor left the witness stand, Reedy shuffled through his notes. "Your Honor, the prosecution believes not only that a murder has occurred, but that there's probable cause to bind over the accused, Saul True Sky, for the crime."

Whistler turned to Rosen. "Your response, Counselor?"

"The defense has shown how unlikely it would've been for Saul True Sky to have committed the crime. In addition, at least part of the evidence has been tainted—we feel irreparably."

The judge nodded. "Since this is a preliminary hearing, the court feels that the prosecution has established sufficient evidence to bind the defendant over. Let's schedule—" he flipped a page in his calendar, "—next Wednesday for the arraignment. Your client can make his formal plea then, Mr. Rosen. If there's nothing further from either of you gentlemen, court is adjourned."

Above the din of the courtroom behind him, Rosen heard Judge Whistler calling his name. They met at the witness stand.

"A moment of your time, Counselor."

Whistler's jaw tightened, and, for the second time that morning, his pallid cheeks blushed. A judge always looked different once he stepped down from the bench, more common and occasionally even coarse. However, remarkably thin and delicate, Whistler displayed a gentility that reminded Rosen of a flower pressed between the pages of an old book.

"I wanted to talk to you, not about the case—that would be improper—but about the young assistant district attorney."

"Reedy?"

"Yes, Blake Reedy. I understand you're from back East. New York?"

"Washington."

"Just as bad, I suppose. I'm talking about manners, what folks around here call common decency."

"I don't understand."

Gripping the witness stand, Judge Whistler rose to his full height, almost as tall as Rosen. "You have the right to use every legitimate means to defend your client, especially when faced with a murder charge. But don't kill the messenger because of the message."

"I still don't understand."

"Blake Reedy is an inexperienced trial lawyer who's never argued anything of this importance. The district attorney, Ted Benton, has pneumonia, and his staff's shorthanded at the moment. You were rough on the boy, rougher than you had to be."

"I didn't know."

The judge nodded curtly. "I'll accept that. If your client pleads not guilty at Wednesday's arraignment, I'm setting the trial date for January.

That will allow both sides sufficient time to develop their cases, as well as let Ted Benton recuperate before taking over from the young Mr. Reedy. Now, if anything I've said makes you want to move for my recusal, I'll grant the motion."

The two men stared at each other. Rosen had felt the weight of many judges' eyes; most were cold as gunmetal. Whistler was different. It was difficult to guess his age—somewhere in his fifties or sixties. But his eyes, bright and innocent, belonged to a young man.

Rosen found himself shaking his head. "No, Your Honor, the defense is satisfied trying the case in your court."

For a moment Whistler's eyes widened. Then, looking away, he coughed softly.

"Cal?"

Rosen turned to see Pearl Whistler standing behind him. She wore a royal-blue dress with sheer blue stockings, which made her red hair even more striking.

"Cal, dear, is there anything wrong?"

"Not at all. Mr. Rosen and I were just discussing a point of law. We're finished."

"Well, then, come along. We do have that luncheon engagement in fifteen minutes."

"Of course." He reached for her hand. "Such soft white skin, like a dove resting in the branch of a gnarled oak."

Laughing, she gently tugged his arm, and he followed her into chambers.

Rosen inhaled a fragrance that somehow seemed familiar. As he took his briefcase from the defense table, he felt a hand upon his shoulder.

"Well done," Keeshin said with a broad smile.

Grace stood beside him. "Jack said there wasn't any hope of winning the preliminary hearing, but you were real good."

Keeshin continued, "The prosecutor looked like a boy scout out to win a merit badge. Andi certainly picked the right man for the job."

Rosen scanned the courtroom. "Where is Andi?"

"I thought she'd be here, not just to cover the story, but as Grace's friend. Perhaps she assumed that I'd write the article—she couldn't take any photographs in the courtroom anyway. You were expecting her?"

Rosen shrugged.

"Don't worry about Andi. I've found that she's the proverbial free spirit. If you need a lift, I'd be happy to oblige. I do have a few errands to run here in Deadwood first."

Glancing at Keeshin, Grace said, "I'll be busy for awhile too. But if you're willing to wait . . . "

"Thanks," Rosen said, "but I've already asked Ike if he could take me back along with Saul."

"Ike?" Keeshin laughed. "You'll be traveling in the lap of luxury, all right. Maybe you'd better wait for me. I can spot Ike twenty minutes and still beat him home."

"Thanks anyway." To Grace, "Are you still planning to ride tomorrow morning?"

"Uh-huh."

"Good. I've never seen a reining competition before. See you then."

Rosen walked from the courthouse and met the two Indians by Ike's old van.

Ike slid the side door open. "Sit in back. You've got the longest legs, and I don't want Saul getting his best suit dirty."

The van was filled with long wooden boxes of carpentry tools, as well as pipes and plumbing fixtures. Leaning against the back of Saul's seat, Rosen stretched between an old kitchen sink and a large wooden box of assorted nails.

"Here." Ike handed him a Diet Pepsi. "I've sworn off the sauce. Saul says the spirits will help me find the good Indian path. He looks sharp wearing that tie, don't you think?"

"Yes."

"You did a good job in there. I liked the way you handled the prosecutor. It reminded me of 'Perry Mason.' I really like the detective Paul Drake more, because he does all the work, while Perry sits on his fat ass and shows off. But you do your own legwork—that's what they say on TV—so I guess you're okay."

Shifting his weight to the back of the seat, Rosen knocked against the wooden box of nails. He idly ran his hand through them, then took out a single iron nail, long and black and tapered to a point. There was something about its shape. Turning halfway, he handed the nail to Ike.

"That's pretty odd-looking."

"It's an old one—the kind the blacksmith made before there were store-bought ones. He'd break off a piece from a thin iron bar, put it through a hole in his forge and hammer the end."

"That's why the head's so thick."

"Yeah. Folks used to call them Jesus nails, because they looked like what people thought was used to crucify Christ. A blacksmith named Carl Elton used to make them. He settled here around the time that mare of Little White Man gave birth to two foals at once, around 1910. He rented a room in Owen Manderson's house, where Saul lives, and set up his forge on the ridge. We're always finding his nails and other odd pieces of iron up there." Ike returned the nail to Rosen. "You take it. White man's metal don't do us spiritual Indians no good."

Rosen held the nailhead between his thumb and index finger. "Does Andi live right in Bear Coat?"

"On the edge of town, just off Main Street."

"Drop me there."

Settling back, Rosen closed his eyes. The next thing he felt was someone jostling his shoulder.

Ike leaned in from the van's open door. "Wake up—we're here. Andi lives in her father's house, at the end of the block. I thought you could use the walk."

Putting the nail in his shirt pocket, Rosen crawled from the van and stretched his legs. He reached for his briefcase.

"Thanks for the lift. See you later."

The street was lined with two-story frame houses, old but well kept, with front-porch swings and potted plants decorating the steps. At the last house on the right, Andi's Mercury stretched like an old tomcat across the driveway. Her home, white with green trim, was as neat as the others. Red roses bloomed in a series of flower boxes on the porch railing.

Climbing the stairs, Rosen paused to look at the flowers. His mother had loved roses. They were always his birthday present to her and, after she'd died, what he'd laid on her grave. Not quite seventeen, he'd been away two years by then, living with his uncle, and could see her only in snatches of time, when she was shopping or walking to a friend's. Never at home; his father wouldn't allow it. Rosen hadn't even known she was seriously ill, and not being able to say goodbye . . . another reason not to forgive his father. But he saw her smile in every rose, like these.

Swallowing hard, he knocked on the door. No answer, but the door was unlocked. Stepping inside, he called Andi's name. Again there was no answer, no sound at all.

He stepped into the living room, filled with old furniture and a dozen framed photographs—more of Andi's work. Returning to the hallway, past the stairs, he paused at a darkened corridor. To his left, something long and thin stuck out from a doorway. His stomach tightened. Flicking on the hall light, he saw Andi's naked leg.

Clad only in a T-shirt and panties, she lay sprawled across the bathroom floor. Kneeling, he checked her pulse, which was normal. He felt a bump on the back of her head.

Turning on the light, he saw that the wall to the next room had been removed to create a large darkroom. He ran some cold water over a towel, then dabbed her face. "Andi?"

She stirred slightly, and her eyes blinked open.

"Don't move. I'm calling the paramedics."

As he started to rise, her hand stopped him. "I'm all right." She sat up slowly. "Ooh, my head. There, that's better. What happened?"

"Don't you know?"

She glanced at his watch. "Is that one in the afternoon? I've missed the hearing?"

"Andi, tell me what happened."

"Yeah, well . . . I was up early this morning, working in the darkroom. It must've been around six. I heard a noise, stepped into the hall and was hit from behind. That's all I remember."

"You didn't see who did it?"

"No."

Andi drew her long legs into the lotus position. They were beautiful, her legs, and he could see her nipples through the T-shirt.

"Whoever hit you didn't . . . hurt you?"

She rubbed the back of her head. "What do you think . . . oh, Jesus. No, I don't think so. Say, you didn't take advantage of me, did you?"

"I think that knock on the head scrambled your brains."

"Maybe I should be offended—here I am lying half-naked, and the thought never crossed your mind."

She grinned, and Rosen realized how much he liked the firm line of her jaw. She put a hand on his shoulder, drawing him close, and they kissed. He put his arms around her.

"Oww!" She'd hit her head against the sink's cabinet.

"Sorry."

She giggled, bending toward him.

"No."

"You're not married, are you?"

"I used to be."

"Still hung up on her?"

"I don't know. Maybe the idea of being married. It's like having your leg amputated and still feeling it afterward."

She patted his leg. "As long as that's the only appendage cut off, you'll be okay. Well, guess I better get dressed and straighten the place up. Why anybody would break in here . . . Oh, my God!"

Struggling to her feet, Andi pushed past him and stumbled into the darkroom. She turned on the overhead light, then opened a large metal cabinet.

"It's here, thank God!"

Reaching inside, she removed a small, squarish camera. She caressed it, her hands trembling.

"My Hasselblad. It's what I take my best portraits with. Half my portfolio . . . God, if I'd lost it."

Beside the cabinet ran a long counter with an enlarger and boxes of various chemicals. Two file cabinets stood against the wall in the corner.

Rosen looked over the counter. "Nothing's missing?"

Staring down at her camera, eyes half-closed, she didn't seem to hear him.

"Andi, is anything missing? Andi?"

Blinking hard, she looked at the counter. "No . . . wait a minute. I'd left out the file with the negatives of Gates's murder. It was the last big project I'd worked on. It's gone." She ran a hand across the counter. "The whole file's gone. Why would somebody steal it? The police and D.A. have copies."

"Not copies of everything. Did you ever take a photo of what was in Gates's hand?"

"I shot one picture at the murder scene . . . Tom was holding whatever it was. I never printed the photo, 'cause Tom didn't think it was important. It's one of the negatives that're missing. Why?"

"Whatever was in Gates's hand is also missing." Taking out the nail Ike had given him, Rosen laid it on the counter. "Think back to the night of Albert Gates's death, when you photographed that small, discolored, squarish piece of metal."

She nodded.

"Now look at this iron nail. Suppose it'd been in the ground eighty or ninety years. The shaft, rusted and brittle, would be ready to crumble apart, maybe into a grayish powder. Remember, I found a thin piece of oxidized metal by the Indian remains. But the nailhead, with its thicker mass, might keep its shape—the same squarish shape it once had when the blacksmith pounded it on his forge. Could what you saw have once been a nail like this?"

"Wait a minute." Flipping up the Hasselblad's viewer, she aimed the camera at the nail and took a long look.

"Well?"

"Don't rush me, I'm an artist."

Finally putting down the camera, Andi said, "That's it. Gee, I like it when you smile."

"At least that's one mystery solved."

"Is it really important? I mean, maybe Gates just picked it up by accident."

Rosen shook his head. "Then why's it missing, and why were your photographs stolen? At least it's something."

"Hell, yes."

"I'm going to get some ice."

She grinned. "For a celebration?"

"No, for that thick skull of yours."

Chapter 11

SATURDAY MORNING

As Andi's Mercury rumbled up the dirt road of the Double G Ranch, Rosen blinked from the sun and adjusted his Chicago Cubs cap. They had both dressed for a hot summer day, she in a tank top and cut-offs, he in his Bill of Rights bicentennial T-shirt, jeans, and sneakers.

Andi said, "With that cap, you almost look like one of us natives."

"What else do I need?"

"Shit-kicking boots, and maybe my pack of cigarettes rolled up in your shirtsleeve. And, of course, talk in fewer syllables. Got it?"

"Yup."

Laughing, she rubbed the back of her head gingerly.

"Sure you're all right?"

"I don't know why you're so worried, after dragging me to the medical center. The doc said everything's okay. I swear, you're one of those Jewish fathers."

"It's 'Jewish mothers,' and I still think you should be home in bed."

"Why, Nate, is that a proposition? I was beginning to lose faith in you."

Shaking his head, he turned to look out the window. They were about a quarter mile from the ranch house, a rambling frame building that had been added onto a time or two. The field to their right was filled with rows of cars, pickups, and horse trailers. Andi parked behind a jeep with a gun rack and bumper sticker: "Guns don't kill people / People kill people."

Slinging the camera case over her shoulder, she waved to an old couple leaving their Cadillac.

The man tapped his forehead. "Good thing you're as hardheaded as

115

your old man, God rest his soul. Got a bodyguard, or is this young fella your new boyfriend?"

Grinning, Andi led Rosen through the parking lot.

He said, "I suppose, by now, the whole town knows what happened to you."

"Word travels pretty fast around here. Sometimes I wonder why Bear Coat even bothers to have a newspaper. 'Course, now the Hendersons can scoop everybody about me having a new boyfriend. You won't be too hurt, honey, if I leave you to take some photos for the paper?"

"Not if they're from under a horse at full gallop."

They walked under a banner stretched between two tall spruces: "Double G Reining Championships." It seemed like a company picnic for the entire town of Bear Coat. Hundreds of people strolled across an open field, while boys chased each other back and forth, yapping dogs nipping at their heels. Lemonade stands gave away free lemonade, popcorn stands popped free bags of popcorn, and cotton-candy machines swirled pinkish clouds that babies reached for in wonder. In the center of the field lay a deep trench.

"A vision pit?" Rosen asked.

"If you're Porky Pig. This afternoon, Elroy Baker's making his famous Carolina barbecue. He roasts a couple of pigs, adds his special sauce—it's really something. I think he waits all year just for this event."

Between the pit and the arena, a dozen horses were tethered, each animal being groomed like a little girl before her birthday party.

Andi pointed a few yards along the fence. "Doesn't Curly look great!"

Grace wore a cowboy hat, Western shirt with a thin ribbon at the neck, new blue jeans, and flat-toed boots. Her hair, ebony smooth, was tied in a single long braid. Brow furrowed and lips tight, she brushed Curly's long mane with quick strokes, while Jack Keeshin currycombed the horse's back. Raising Curly's left hind leg, Stevie cleaned the inside hoof with a metal pick. The boy looked freshly scrubbed; even his Motley Crue T-shirt was clean.

Glancing at Andi, Grace frowned. "Shouldn't you be in bed? I heard you took a real nasty knock on the head."

"Don't you start babying me too."

Keeshin asked, "Do the police have any leads?"

"No. Weren't any fingerprints, and nobody in the neighborhood saw anything. It was pretty early in the morning. Hold him just like that, Gracie."

Andi began taking pictures. As the camera clicked near the animal's face, Curly suddenly spooked and kicked his leg free.

"Easy, fella," Grace said. "Stevie, you know better than to let him do that. Lean into his rump and hold his leg tight."

"My fault," Andi said.

"No, the boy's been around horses enough to know better. All I need is for Curly to come up lame on me." Her strokes on the horse's mane quickened.

Keeshin said softly, "I think you're a little nervous."

"Damn right I'm nervous."

"And maybe a little hard on Stevie."

She stopped in midstroke and looked at her son. "I'm sorry. With everything that's gone on, you know how much this means to me."

As the boy reached for Curly's hoof,. Rosen extended his left hand to hold the horse's rump steady. Stevie stared at the bandage on Rosen's hand, where he had cut him two days before. The boy's eyes widened, then he quickly finished cleaning the hoof. Dropping the pick, he raced into the crowd.

Grace shouted, "Where the hell . . . !"

"Let him go," Keeshin said, putting his hand over hers. "Just tell me what to do. You know, putting on all of this tack isn't exactly like stringing a tennis racket."

She smiled, almost hiding her face in Curly's mane. "Hand me the bridle. Right—that one."

Snapping another picture, Andi said, "I've got to circulate. Don't want the paper to show any favoritism in next week's photo spread. Good luck."

Rosen nodded. "I'd better be off too." He checked his watch—almost ten. "Belle Gates said she'd see me for a few minutes. Do you know where she is?"

"Probably with the judges," Keeshin said. "They're in a box along the arena fence, just off to your left. More questions about the case, I take it."

"I want to find out more about her late husband." To Grace, "I'm looking forward to seeing you ride. Good luck."

He followed Andi toward the fence. She suddenly grabbed his arm, as Will and Wendy strolled toward them.

Wendy said, "Hi, Andi. We were just talking about you. Sure hope you're all right."

"I'm fine."

"Yeah, we was just lazying around this morning . . . together, and our thoughts naturally went out to you."

"Thanks, but I'm fine. Nate's taking good care of me. He's been really sweet and so attentive, in spite of all the important calls he's had to make to Washington. That's the Washington with the president, not the one with all the rain and big trees."

Rosen said, "I really need to see Belle Gates. If you'll excuse me."

"And I've got work to do. Meet you back here in an hour, honey. That's when Gracie's scheduled to ride." She kissed him hard on the lips, touched his cheek, then hurried into the crowd.

The judges' box, decorated with a floral horseshoe and red bunting, was only a few yards away. Belle Gates sat with her back to Rosen, talking to two well-dressed men and a woman. Chick Cantrell, the engineer, snug in a red polo shirt, stood beside her.

Rosen started forward, then stopped. He still felt Andi's kiss upon his lips, and his cheek burned where she'd touched him. It was silly to feel embarrassed, considering what men and women did in public. But he remembered what his rabbi had said in yeshiva about the proper decorum between the sexes. What would the rabbi have thought of Andi?

"Rosen, you wanted to see me?"

Belle Gates stood beside him. Unlike the other women, who wore Western skirts or jeans, she had on a simple gray dress. Less than a week had passed since her husband's death.

"You know Chick Cantrell," she said. "He was at our council meeting the other day."

Cantrell stepped forward and, bicep bulging, gripped Rosen's hand. "Nice seeing you again."

Rosen said, "Actually, I saw you Thursday evening in Deadwood, playing poker with Mr. Huggins."

Cantrell scratched his beard. "Yeah? You should've sat in—maybe you could've brought him some luck."

Belle glanced at her watch. "I can spare you about twenty minutes."

"Fine. I'm flying back to Washington in a few days. This was our only opportunity to talk about your late husband."

"Well, best place for that is in Albert's museum. Chick, Elroy Baker should be here any minute to start that pig roast."

"Don't you worry. I'll get it all set up."

The smile between Cantrell and Belle lingered. Taking Rosen's hand, she led him through the crowd to her house. Despite her limp, she moved quickly.

A loudspeaker announced, "Our first rider is Peggy Tolliver, from the Clearwater Ranch, riding White Lightning!"

They walked to the end of the house, where a room had been added on. Above the door a sign read "Double G Western Heritage Museum."

The room was long and narrow. On either side of the aisle were a series of glass-enclosed exhibits. Across the left wall were the words GATES FAMILY, and, across the right, GARDNER FAMILY. The exhibits encased a variety of Old West paraphernalia—clothes; pots and pans; rifles and pistols; playing cards; gold-mining equipment, including panning plates and a rocker for separating nuggets from gravel; and assorted historical documents, such as bills of sale, deeds, surveys, and letters. The Gates side included a model grist mill and old burlap bags lettered "Cap Gates Flour." The Gardner side displayed lassos, chaps, and horse tack, as well as a series of photos of ranch life during the past hundred years.

Belle said, "You can see that both our families go back to when South Dakota was a territory."

Rosen nodded. How long had you been married?"

"Only ten years. Albert was twice a widower—lost one wife to cancer and one in a car accident."

"And you?"

She hesitated a moment. "Never married, but when I was seventeen, I got pregnant. The guy joined the Army and was killed overseas. I had twins, a son and daughter living out East now."

"Were they at the funeral?"

"No. I didn't tell them until after Albert was buried. They never particularly cared for him, and I didn't want no crocodile tears shed at his funeral. I know why you're here, to find out the kind of man Albert was. Well, he was a bigmouth and schemer, but he had a good heart, and he made me laugh. For me that was enough."

"And for other people?"

She shrugged. "Everybody around here knew Albert's bark was a lot worse than his bite. There was that one customer, about eight years ago, who tried to shoot him, but hell, that comes with selling used cars. I swear, Mr. Rosen, you won't find anybody in these parts who'd want my husband dead."

At the end of the aisle stood one final exhibit, a small gold nugget, inside a glass case. Above the case, a series of panels told the story of "The Salted Stream."

Belle chuckled. "You know what salting a stream meant?"

"Wasn't that putting gold into a stream or mine to make the claim appear valuable?"

"Yes, indeed. My granddad Salty Gardner salted a stream with gold nuggets, sold it to Albert's granddad, and used the money to start this ranch. Old Cap Gates didn't do so badly. The stream didn't have any gold, but he used the running water to start a grist mill. Albert often said it was the last time any Gates ever got swindled, and I believe it was. How Albert loved to tell the story of his granddad and old Salty Gardner."

They walked into an adjoining room, "Indians of the Dakotas." More glass cases containing Native American clothing, a case of painted rawhide decorated with feathers, pipes with tobacco pouches, various weapons, and a buffalo skull.

On a shelf at the end of the aisle, a half dozen human skulls watched Rosen approach. Below them lay the remains of four bodies, like those of White Bear. The bones of White Bear hadn't bothered Rosen, perhaps because they seemed to belong on True Sky's ridge. But this was different; it was like a charnel house. He remembered the Torah's strictures against touching a corpse; it was an impurity that took seven days and a secret potion to make clean. He took a step back.

"Creepy, ain't it?" Belle said. "In our ten years of marriage, this was the one thing Albert and I fought over. I never felt it was right."

Rosen pulled his gaze from the bones. "Some museums have returned Indian remains for reburial."

"That's what I wanted to do. But Albert believed this museum was his legacy to the West, maybe to make up for the children he never had. Funny, thinking of these old bones as his children. Some of them, up on that ridge, got him killed." She held her arms, as if shivering. "Let's get the hell out of here."

Leaving the building, they heard the crowd around the arena cheering.

Rosen asked, "Do you think that Saul True Sky killed your husband?"

"When I got pregnant, my old man was so mad he threw me out of the house for a month. Eleanor True Sky, Gracie's mother, took me in.

She was the best person I've ever known. Now, Saul's a different story. Maybe he's found God or the Great Spirit or whatever, but he used to be a crazy son of a bitch." She shook her head. "Bad enough I've lost Albert. I'd hate to believe that Eleanor's husband could've killed mine."

As they walked toward the arena, Rosen said, "Mr. Cantrell seems quite taken with you."

She smiled. "It does appear that way. Can't say I'm not just a bit tickled by the attention. Does that shock you, my Albert barely cold in the ground?"

"I try not to make a habit of judging people."

"You're too good a lawyer to really believe that. Anyway, Chick's got some rascal in him, like Albert did. But I seen Chick's eyes follow lots of the gals, all a lot younger and prettier than me. You don't think his infatuation might have anything to do with him working for the town and me being mayor?" She winked.

More cheering could be heard from the arena as Belle and Rosen joined the crowd. The loudspeaker reported one rider's score, then announced the next contestant.

Rosen said, "People get pretty excited at these events."

"You don't know anything about a reining competition, do you? Folks are expected to cheer. They say that judges keep their eyes on the rider and their ears on the audience. Gracie's up next."

They passed the barbecue pit. Deputy Elroy Baker was inside, spreading the bottom of the pit with charcoal, wood, and a mixture of leaves and herbs. Crawling out, he lit a rolled newspaper, leaned over the edge, and started the fire. Several people applauded, and Baker shook their hands enthusiastically.

Rosen said, "Looks like he's running for something."

"Police chief, maybe?"

"People wouldn't seriously vote for him over Tom Cross Dog."

"Tom's a good cop, but he's still an Indian. If it turns out that Saul True Sky did kill Albert . . . well, that's not gonna make voters feel kinder toward any Indian. Look, I've got to go over to the judge's box. See you later."

After watching Baker work the crowd, Rosen stared into the pit, not so different in size and shape from the one where True Sky had sat as Albert Gates was being murdered.

"Now Grace Jenkins on Curly!" the loudspeaker announced.

Rosen heard a few boos from the crowd, with the words "True Sky" and "murderer." He leaned against the arena's fence beside Keeshin; further down stood Wendy and Will, whose arm rested on Stevie's shoulder.

Grace spurred her horse, so that it dashed toward the other end of the arena. Nearing the fence, she suddenly pulled on the reins, and Curly's hind legs slid as the front legs churned forward to a perfect stop. Quickly turning the horse, she leaned forward in the saddle, running him the way they'd come, and executed a pattern of circles, again sliding to a stop. Curly ran forward, stopped, and spun, pivoting on his back leg, then again was off and running.

All the while the horse's mane flowed beautifully, as did the two reins Grace held in her hands. Rosen noticed that she didn't use the reins to guide Curly; everything was done with her legs and the subtle shifts of her body. It was like gliding on ice, the horse and rider blending into a singular body of power and grace.

The crowd along the fence remained quiet; it seemed that only Will, Wendy, and Keeshin whooped their support. As Grace ran Curly through the course, a few more people cheered, which only seemed to punctuate the silence. Even Stevie, hugging the fence post, said nothing.

When she'd finished, Grace received scattered applause, and the judges announced her score.

"Is that good?" Rosen asked.

Will spat on the ground. "She deserved better. People are blaming her for what they say Dad did. It ain't fair."

The boy bolted from the fence.

Rosen followed Will, who caught up with Stevie in the parking lot. Will said a few words, then ran to his truck, returning with a bat, ball, and two fielder's gloves. He and the boy walked past a bunkhouse toward the open field.

Rosen was about to call to them, when Gil McCracken, Belle Gates's foreman, stepped from the bunkhouse. He carried a toolbox.

Approaching Will, the foreman said, "I heard your sister's name on the loudspeaker and figured you'd be by the arena. Here." He dropped the toolbox at Will's feet.

"What's this for?"

"We almost lost two horses through the fence you was supposed to fix for Mr. Gates last weekend. You remember that, don't you, breed? That was two days before your old man killed Mr. Gates."

Will handed the baseball equipment to Stevie. "I've had enough of your big mouth."

"Fine with me."

Fists clenched, Will took a step forward.

Rosen grabbed his arm. "Not in front of the boy." To McCracken, "Mrs. Gates wouldn't like this, not with everyone having such a good time."

"Everyone except Mr. Gates lying six feet under."

Rosen picked up the toolbox. "Come on, Will. Let's get Stevie away from here."

Will's eyes locked on McCracken's, then he nodded and walked into the field.

After a half mile, they came to within fifty yards of a barbed-wire fence.

Will handed Rosen a glove. "Play the outfield. I'll pitch to the boy. This is about the only thing that settles him down."

Trotting toward the fence, Rosen saw what McCracken had been talking about. One of the posts tilted almost to the ground, and the top strands of wire had broken loose.

"Come in more!" Will shouted, then pitched the ball to Stevie.

After dribbling a few grounders, the boy got his rhythm and hit several line drives, even lifting a fly ball almost over Rosen's head. He reached up and speared it with one hand. He loved the game, even if it only meant shagging fly balls. He had never played baseball as a kid, and his daughter, Sarah, had only tolerated playing catch, until she sprained a finger and couldn't practice the piano for a month.

When Stevie and Will switched positions, Rosen stepped back. Will peppered the ball through the infield, hit a few bloopers, then connected, arcing a long fly toward the fence. Rosen ran, glove upraised, imagining himself as Billy Williams plucking the ball from the ivy at Wrigley Field. Suddenly his right foot stepped on something soft, and he tumbled to the ground.

He lay on his back, eyes closed, listening to the crickets chirping, the sun strong against his face.

A shadow blocked the sun, and Will asked, "You okay?"

"I think so. Nice hit."

Will helped him up, and nothing hurt until he shifted his weight to his right leg.

He took a minced step. "Twisted my foot. Just a sprain, but I think this puts me on the disabled list for today. What did I trip over?" He examined the ground. "It's all soft over here, like someone's been working the soil."

Will shrugged. "Sometimes gets like this when a horse kicks up his heels or rolls around. Maybe seeing the fence down got 'im all excited. Here, lean on me. I'll walk you back."

"You've got that fence to mend. Stevie can help me back."

He put his right arm around the boy's shoulder. Glancing at Rosen's bandaged hand, Stevie stiffened as if being touched by a spider. They slowly walked away, Rosen limping gingerly beside the boy.

"Sorry to take you away from your uncle. You two seem pretty close."

No reply.

"You also seem pretty close to your grandfather. You've been hearing a lot of bad things about him. They must hurt, especially since we both know your grandfather didn't kill Albert Gates."

The boy tried to break free, but Rosen held him tightly. "You know something about the murder, and it's eating you up inside. You've got to tell the truth, Stevie, and not just for your grandfather's sake."

The boy jerked free and faced Rosen. "My grandfather's sake!" Tears rimmed his eyes. "What the fuck do you know? What the fuck does anybody know!"

Turning, the boy ran toward the arena. Rosen let him go—what else could he do?

He walked a few steps, then rested, shifting his weight to his good foot. Wiping his forehead, he adjusted his baseball cap and stared into the sun, just as a starling landed nearby.

The bird looked up at him curiously, as if to ask, "You call this a scarecrow?" then pecked at his heels all the way back to the arena.

Chapter 12

MONDAY MORNING

George Manderson had built the old Pyramid Theater in the center of Tin Town during the heyday of the mine. When the mine closed, some local entrepreneurs had the theater moved to the edge of Bear Coat. It sure was one of a kind. Its tall columns, on either side of the doorway, were topped with replicas of the Great Pyramid. Inside, atop more columns along the walls, stood plaster pharaohs, each one bearing the likeness of Manderson himself.

As a child, Grace had gone there Saturdays with the other kids to watch Doris Day, Elvis, and those teenage beach movies. She used to dream about Frankie Avalon, but even in her dreams she couldn't imagine herself as Annette. That was somebody like Pearl, not a half-breed. It had never occurred to Grace then, that the man who had built the theater was her great-grandfather, and that the pharaohs' faces resembled hers far more than they did Pearl's.

The theater had long ago stopped showing movies and was now used for high school plays, summer stock, town meetings, and an occasional court hearing. Today Judge Ted O'Hara would decide whether a road would be built through her father's property.

In contrast to the hot morning sun, the building's interior felt cool and dark like a church. Townsfolk filed down the center aisle, nearly everybody sitting on the right. A dozen rows were filled with businessmen and ranchers supporting the town council's plan. Only one row on the left was occupied. Grace sat between her father and Nate Rosen, with Andi, Will, and Ike taking the remaining seats.

In front of the first aisle, three tables were arranged in a triangle. At the corners, Jack, representing Saul True Sky, and Roy Huggins, representing the town council, faced Judge O'Hara. A stenographer sat on the judge's right, and on his left stood a witness chair.

Judge O'Hara, a small man with russet hair and a brush mustache, was known for his impish grin. Schools tacked on their walls one of his sayings: "Doing right is easy, if you don't think about doing wrong." O'Hara didn't need to tap his gavel. Everybody was so quiet, his first words seemed to crackle in the air.

"We're holding this hearing in Bear Coat, rather than Deadwood, because it's more convenient for the parties involved, as well as this court. Everybody knows why we're here. Mr. Huggins, you have some witnesses to call."

Huggins was dressed in a crisp blue suit, which seemed a little tight around the waist. He coughed hard, then unbuttoned his coat. "To begin, I'd like to remind the court that both U.S. and state constitutions give Bear Coat the right of eminent domain and, therefore, the power to condemn private property when such condemnation will benefit the public. We will show there's no question the town needs this land and that it is willing to pay Mr. True Sky more than the market price. If I may just cite *U.S.A. v. Welch,* which states that—"

"Cut the applesauce, Mr. Huggins. I've read your citations. Let's get on with your witnesses."

Huggins reddened but kept his temper. "Mayor Belle Gates."

Belle limped to the witness stand, and the judge swore her in. Hunched over the table, Huggins led the mayor through her testimony, the same arguments she'd given to Grace the week before.

She concluded, "I can't see how Bear Coat will make it much longer without this development."

Unlike Huggins, Jack walked around the table for his cross-examination. He wore a light-brown suit that tapered from his broad shoulders to his narrow waist. His suit, the color of sand, his tan and muscular body— it suddenly occurred to Grace that Jack could've been in those beach movies. He was the kind of guy she'd dreamed of as a teenager, and she'd already lain in his arms.

"Mayor Gates, how do you define 'making it'?"

"I don't understand your question."

"You said that Bear Coat wouldn't make it without this plan to bring in gambling."

"That's right. We need this development to save the town."

Reaching behind him, Jack picked up a large blueprint, which he unrolled like a proclamation. Belle fidgeted in her chair.

Jack said, "These are the proposed plans for Wild West World, which include a gambling strip and other activities—panning for gold, a shooting gallery and such."

"Those are just some ideas, nothing definite. Besides, helping our economy will also restore Tin Town to what it once was. Just like Deadwood."

"Come now, Mayor." Grace sensed Jack smiling, while Belle blushed like a schoolgirl. "This plan would no more make Tin Town look like it once was, than Disney's Pirates of the Caribbean resembles a den of real pirates." He glanced at Huggins. "The truth is, you're exploiting the land to make a gambling strip and cheap amusement park."

"That's not true."

"You're right—I apologize. There's nothing cheap about it. This plan will generate millions, and several people sitting in this hearing will be the beneficiaries." He looked at the plans. "I see here a riding stable. That's your ranch, isn't it?"

Huggins banged his fist on the table. "I resent this attempt to impugn Mayor Gates's character!"

"I withdraw the question and have nothing further to ask Mayor Gates."

Huggins next called the engineer, Chick Cantrell, who wore his suit as uncomfortably as Paul Bunyan. He testified that the most direct route from the highway into Bear Coat was through Tin Town "and the True Sky ridge." He added that the road would alter the landscape as little as possible.

After Huggins finished, Jack asked, "What about the plans for Wild West World? Won't they inflict serious damage to the landscape?"

"I guess it all depends how you define 'damage.' The way I see it, anything would improve the eyesore that Tin Town's become."

"The road you propose building through Saul True Sky's ridge. Won't that affect the spiritual setting so important for his religious beliefs?"

Huggins shook his head. "Mr. Cantrell is an engineer, hardly an expert in religion."

"That's my point. People who know nothing about Mr. True Sky's religion are trying to . . . "

"True Sky's religion is no reason to stop this project!"

"It is precisely the reason the road and the entire project should be stopped."

"The Supreme Court has already—"

Judge O'Hara tapped his gavel. "No doubt we'll have the opportunity to consider the relevance of Mr. True Sky's religion, when he testifies. Move along, Mr. Keeshin."

"Mr. Cantrell, have you heard of Bixby Engineering of Sioux City, South Dakota?"

"No, I'm from Los Angeles myself."

Opening a folder on his desk, Jack continued, "I asked Bixby to do an independent survey of the area between the highway and Bear Coat. According to their findings, a road could be constructed into Bear Coat that would swing around the ridge, leaving Mr. True Sky's property alone. Do you agree that such a road could be built?"

"Sure, but it'd cost more money, be less direct, and wouldn't go through a renovated Tin Town, which is key to the project."

Huggins said, "Your Honor, I need only refer to the case of *Trans Continental G.P.L. Corp. v. Borough of Milltown* to remind Mr. Keeshin that a municipality doesn't have to justify a particular route, so long as the condemnation itself is valid."

"Your point's well taken," O'Hara said. "Anything else, Mr. Keeshin?"

"No, Your Honor."

Huggins called Pearl, who sat primly on the witness chair. Wearing a white blouse with a high collar and puffy sleeves, she resembled a turn-of-the-century cameo, her thick red hair tied back with a tortoise-shell comb. Her legs looked smooth as ivory against a tan skirt.

"We've had five independent realtors from the Rapid City area assess the land," she said in that voice that was almost a whisper. "Remember, we're only discussing Tin Town and an access road. Mr. True Sky would still be able to keep his house—it's set far enough from the proposed road. We're offering him the highest assessment, $105,000."

When Jack had his opportunity to cross-examine Pearl, he hesitated. For a moment, Grace wondered if he was falling for her too, like all the men did.

Finally he asked, "As a realtor, can you tell us what will happen to property values if this project goes through?"

"I suspect they'll rise."

"If Deadwood is any example, won't they skyrocket?"

"It's quite possible."

"I understand that you and your husband own considerable property in Bear Coat. In fact, over the past year you've purchased several properties in the downtown area. Wouldn't this project—"

"For Chrissakes!" Huggins bellowed. "Now, he's not only questioning the integrity of this witness but also her husband, a respected member of the bench."

Judge O'Hara stroked his chin. "Mr. Keeshin, you may have gone a bit too far."

"Besides," Huggins continued, "there's nothing wrong with private interests benefiting from a condemnation, as long as it's for the public good. I need only cite *Re Chicago & N.W.R. Co.* to prove . . . "

"You've made your point. Mr. Keeshin?"

"No more questions."

As Pearl returned to her seat, Huggins said, "We have nothing to add, Your Honor."

O'Hara turned to Jack, who nodded. "Just one witness. Mr. Saul True Sky."

Grace's father walked slowly to the witness stand, while the townsfolk behind Huggins muttered to one another. He had on his old brown suit and turquoise string tie. His long hair fell loose, except for the small elk hoop he always wore above his right ear.

Jack asked, "Does the reason you don't want to sell your land have anything to do with the price the town's offered?"

Her father shook his head.

"Is it because you have a grievance against its residents?"

Again, a shake of the head.

"Perhaps you're against the idea of gambling and, therefore, oppose the project."

"I see what gambling does to people, leading them to crime and drinking. But it's not for me to say what others should or shouldn't do."

"Why won't you sell the land?"

"Since my people can remember, it has been a holy place. My grandfather would go up to the ridge and talk to those who've gone before us. He used to cry for a dream and would fly with the starlings to meet our ancestors—to hunt the buffalo with them."

Jack asked, "Have you personally had such experiences?"

"When I was younger, I'd drink and get into fights. I went to prison.

When I got out, my grandfather took me into his sweat lodge. He puri-fied me, then took me up to the ridge. Together we dug a vision pit, and I sat there alone with my *chanunpa* for three days, crying for a dream. On the third day, the sun suddenly grew dark, and from the east came a wind with the sound of hooves. It was then that I saw the elk. They came striking the ground like lightning and made me their brother. They taught me their secrets."

"What kind of secrets?"

"How to care for those who are helpless, especially women, just as the elk protects his females."

"You can heal people?"

"Those who are brothers to the elk have good power to help sick women."

That was true. Grace had seen him cure women with coughing and fainting fits, even white women who came to him. She herself had gotten over a bad fever with the tea he'd brewed.

"Anything else?" Jack asked.

"An elk dreamer can make a *siyotanka,* a love flute. When a woman hears a man play it, she'll come to him."

"The remains of a Lakota has been discovered on the ridge."

"White Bear."

"I understand that yesterday you reburied these remains and put up a marker, which you yourself carved."

"Yes, but I've talked to his *wanagi.* It's still restless."

"Is White Bear's ghost restless because the road might be built through the ridge?"

Her father shook his head. "There's something else troubling him. I don't know what, but it's something else."

Jack sat back in his chair and studied his notes. He seemed confused, then asked quickly, "What will happen if the road is built through the ridge?"

"The spirits will go away."

"No further questions."

Judge O'Hara signaled to Huggins, who for a long time shook his head sadly.

"So, this religion of yours helps you do all sorts of mumbo jumbo. Why can't you just keep doing it, once the road's built? It's not like the whole area'd be torn up."

"The spirits will be disturbed. They'll leave."

"Let's suppose the spirits do leave. Does that mean the end of your religion? In other words, won't you still be this elk holy man?"

Sitting beside Grace, Rosen shook his head and whispered, "The *Lyng* case." Taking out a notepad, he scribbled something and, leaning forward, handed it to Jack.

Meanwhile, Grace's father said, "Where would you have me go? All our sacred land is vanishing. Bear Butte, our most sacred place, is filled with new roads and parking lots. The tourists come and take pictures while we do our ceremonies."

Huggins thumped his hand on the table. "But you still do your ceremonies. That's the point. Progress goes on, and so does your religion. Thank you, Mr. True Sky."

"Any closing comments, Mr. Huggins?" Judge O'Hara asked.

"We've shown the public need for such a road and that the town's monetary offer to Mr. True Sky is more than fair. As for Mr. True Sky's religious objections, I need only cite the U.S. Supreme Court decision of *Lyng v. Northwest Indian Cemetery Protective Association,* which ruled that the U.S. Forest Service could build a road through an area claimed to be of religious importance to an Indian tribe. The inconvenience the Indians faced trying to practice their religion was not allowed to stop progress. We've got exactly the same case here, Your Honor, and all we ask for is the same ruling. Thank you."

"Mr. Keeshin?"

"I think this case hinges on how one might interpret the *Lyng* case. I'd like to defer to a colleague who is an expert on constitutional law. Mr. Nate Rosen."

Rosen's eyes narrowed. He hesitated, then walked down the aisle to join Jack.

Huggins shook his head like a bear. "What's this, a hearing or a relay race?"

Judge O'Hara said, "I don't see the harm in it. Mr. Rosen?"

Rosen was conferring with Jack, who pointed to the judge, then sat down.

"Counselor?"

"Excuse me, Your Honor," Rosen said. He paused a moment, rubbing his eyes. "*Lyng* dealt with land already owned by the government. This deals with private property."

"Same principle," Huggins said. "And we've got the Supreme Court's decision."

"Citing the majority opinion in *Lyng* is but one interpretation."

"What other interpretation than the Supreme Court's is there?"

"Both the original court and appellate court found in favor of the Indians. Even the Park Service's own anthropologist . . ."

"But the Supreme Court—"

" 'Indeed, you are the voice of the people, and wisdom will die with you!' " Rosen's eyes flashed at the other man. Then he looked away, and Grace could barely hear him finish, " 'But I, like you, have a mind, and am not less than you.' "

"Huh?"

For the first time that morning, Judge O'Hara grinned. "The Bible, if I'm not mistaken."

"The Book of Job, Your Honor," Rosen said.

Huggins clicked his tongue. "Kind of strange for an Indian's lawyer to quote a Christian Bible to prove his case. I'm sure this Court could use a bit more substantial evidence."

Rosen stared at Huggins, then said, "What about two hundred years of precedent cases that support a person's right to the free exercise of his religion? As Justice Brennan pointed out in his dissent of *Lyng,* by not interesting itself in the effect a public road will have on the Indians' religion, the Court virtually destroyed their form of worship."

"You don't expect Judge O'Hara to challenge the Supreme Court?"

"Why not? No court is infallible. The point is to do what's right. If there were a Catholic church on the ridge, and Mr. True Sky's name was Ryan or Gleason, would the town be so quick to condemn the land? Yet, the land is even more sacred for the Indian, who finds holiness in the earth itself."

"Come on," Huggins said. "Spirits in a rock—isn't that a little ridiculous?"

Rosen looked at Judge O'Hara. "Is it any more ridiculous than believing the body of Christ is in a communion wafer? Why should an Indian's religion be held to a higher scrutiny than anyone else's? What's fair for one citizen should be fair for all."

The judge slowly folded his hands together. "Anything else?" When Rosen shook his head, O'Hara started to say something, then hesitated. For several minutes he paged through a stack of papers, drumming his fingers on the table. The drumming was the only sound in the room, and Grace felt it like her own heartbeat.

Finally he said, "The history of this state is the struggle for land. My great-grandfather came here and, I guess, fought some of Mr. True Sky's ancestors for the right to raise cattle. All he asked was to be left alone. That's what most folks around here want—to be left alone." He shook his head. "Taking away a man's land is sometimes necessary, but it's got to be for a damn good reason. The cases cited by Mr. Huggins only emphasize how important the public good must be. Taking into account Mr. True Sky's religious beliefs and how they're tied up in his land, I believe Mr. Rosen has a point. What's fair for one citizen's got to be fair for another. I see no cause to order the condemnation of this land and, therefore, find for Mr. True Sky. Court is adjourned."

For a long time, nobody moved. People mulled the words over as if they hadn't quite heard right. Then came, not sound, but a smell—the strong odor of a cheap cigar. Arms folded, Ike was puffing contentedly.

"I had to wait sixty years to see some real justice, but then, my father never saw any. I guess that's progress."

Jack walked over, and Grace suddenly grabbed him, kissing him hard. Pulling back for a moment, she looked into his eyes, felt his strong hands on her waist, and smiled. She didn't care who saw. Nor did she mind what the people said, across the aisle, as they left the theater. She kept staring into Jack's eyes.

Finally a camera flashed, and she blinked. Andi was taking pictures. Cigar jutting from the corner of his mouth, Ike stood beside her father, whose face remained smooth as a stone. Will had left. She wondered if her brother was happy with the decision; he never seemed to care one way or the other.

Jack shook Rosen's hand. "Well done, Counselor. The *coup de grace,* so to speak."

"I didn't intend to interfere. The note was just a suggestion on how to handle Lyng."

"Nonsense. I'm grateful for your help." He hugged Grace. "We both are."

"You know, Huggins will appeal."

Grace asked, "You mean, Father may still lose his land?"

"It's quite possible. Next time you may not get a judge as enlightened as O'Hara."

Jack laughed. "Comparing Indian spirits to a communion wafer," he broke into a brogue, "for a God-fearing Irishman like Judge O'Hara himself. Damn clever."

Grace said, "But next time?"

"It's a game," Jack insisted. "The law's a game. That's what makes it so exciting. Don't you agree, Nate?"

Rosen shook his head. "It's finding the truth, and right now, I'm far more concerned with finding Albert Gates's murderer than how this land is disposed of."

"Of course. Still, it was rather like scoring an ace, wasn't it?"

Grace followed the two attorneys from the theater and blinked in the bright sunlight. Tom was leaning against his squad car, as if waiting for somebody. She turned back to see Andi, then Ike and her father, step through the doorway.

Suddenly she heard a loud crack, and the brick beside her father splintered. Andi pushed the two old men back inside, while Grace was dragged to the pavement. Tom held her wrist tightly against the squad car while he opened the passenger door and pulled out a rifle.

"What is it?" she half-whispered.

"Sniper up in the feedstore across the street. You stay down." He patched himself through to Elroy, who was on patrol.

"Yeah, I heard the shot," Elroy's voice crackled through the receiver. "I'm a half-block away. What's that?"

"Elroy!" Tom shouted into the receiver, then looked over the hood. When Grace tried to join him, he shoved her down roughly.

The line came alive. "I'm coming up to the side entrance of the feedstore. There's a pickup—looks familiar. Why, it's—"

Again silence. Then, through the speaker, "Bam!" followed by another gunshot, only softer. A few seconds passed, and Grace heard a third shot just as soft.

"Tom?" she began, but he was already on his feet, running toward the feedstore.

He flattened himself against the building, then edged around the corner. Grace hugged the car door, eyes closed, expecting more shots.

"Tom," she whispered.

There weren't any more shots, and, opening her eyes, she watched Rosen run across the street. Then she was running too, ignoring the voices calling her to stop. She turned the corner just as Jack caught up with her.

The two policemen stood with Rosen near the side entrance of the feedstore. Tom's foot rested on the rear bumper of an old pickup. Elroy's squad car was parked across the street, the driver's door wide open. Gripping Jack's hand, Grace walked toward them.

"Tom?"

He looked over his shoulder and frowned. "You shouldn't be here."

He moved toward her, revealing Gil McCracken slumped against the building's door, a rifle lying a few feet away. McCracken's shirt was matted with blood, and blood had also collected into a pool alongside the body. She felt her knees buckle, but Jack held one arm while Tom grabbed the other.

"I'm . . . all right."

Tom looked hard at Jack. "Why'd you let her see this?"

"I can assure you that I had—"

"Don't either of you baby me." She shook loose of both men. "McCracken tried to kill my father. Isn't that what happened?"

Tom said, "Looks that way, though I never got a chance to ask. Elroy took care of that."

Elroy nodded. "He shot at me as soon as he came running down the stairs."

"So McCracken shot first?" Tom stared at Grace. What was he trying to tell her?

"Hell yes, he shot first, then I got in my two. Lucky his aim wasn't as good as mine."

A siren sounded down Main Street, growing steadily louder.

"Paramedics," Tom said. "Another wasted trip."

Walking over to Elroy, Jack asked him several questions, jotting the answers into a notepad, probably for the newspaper. Meanwhile, she followed Rosen and Tom back to the corner.

Rosen said, "You're not satisfied with this, are you, Chief?"

"Doesn't look like there's anything irregular."

"Sure. Elroy's quite the hero."

"What's this to you?"

"Grace is right—McCracken was trying to kill Saul True Sky. The question is, why?"

135

"You tell me."

"Maybe he thought Saul had murdered his boss, or maybe it was something else."

Grace said, "Maybe McCracken was the one who killed Albert Gates."

Tom shook his head. "Why would McCracken murder Gates?"

"You're the police. You find out."

"The state has its murderer."

"My father didn't do it!"

"Look, I'm not . . . " Then, striking fist into palm, he added, "Why doesn't your lawyer here find out who did?"

Rosen smiled. "I could use a little help. I'll be leaving town in a few days. Of course I'll continue to stay in touch with Grace and her father until the trial. I could use anything you find out."

"About Gates's murder?"

"That and what happened here today. I know something's bothering you about the shooting. See you both later."

They watched Rosen walk across the street.

"I still don't like him," Tom said. Glancing at Jack, the policeman added, "But he could be worse."

December 8

Dear Nate,

I was going to drive into Rapid City to get a Hanukkah card for you, but there was a bitchin' snowstorm yesterday that put the highway out of commission. We got lots of snow already, so be sure to bring plenty of winter gear when you come out next month for the trial. Dakota wind's gonna freeze the cherry blossoms off you!

Haven't heard from you in over a month. Are you too busy to answer my last letter, or does it just hurt too much to think of us so far apart? You know, I called your office. They said you were on the road with some case. Who is she?

Nothing much new to report. Romance is kind of in the air. Jack and Grace are a thing. He's been taking her and Stevie to Sioux Falls to see some psychiatrist. Grace says the doctor seems to be helping Stevie. Belle's been spending a lot of time with that engineer Chick Cantrell. Will and Wendy broke up, then got back together, then broke up again. He's been going through the women around here faster than a box of Kleenex (don't worry, as Paula Abdul says, I'm forever your girl).

I saw Ike in town last week. He says hello and wants you to bring him a Washington Redskins jersey. He says he wants to wear it this summer, when he goes up on Mount Rushmore and pees down George Washington's nose as a protest against white injustice. That's what he says anyway—no, he wasn't drunk. I haven't seen much of Saul. He keeps to himself up on the ridge. Grace says he's okay.

Better go now—got film in the developer. Can't wait to see you. You know, I sent my resume everywhere, including the Washington Post—I used you as a reference. Wouldn't it be seriously cool if we wound up in the same town? You'd be like that fat guy Perry Mason on TV and I'd be your assistant, what's her name—Della Reese. You let me know when you're due to arrive in Rapid City, and I'll come get you like last summer. Can't wait!

XXXXXXX.

Andi

P.S. Rumor is that Elroy the Dork Baker is going to run against Tom Cross Dog in next year's election for police chief.

January

Chapter 13

SUNDAY AFTERNOON

"We're beginning our descent into Rapid City," the pilot said over the intercom. "Hope you brought your thermal underwear. The temperature at 3:37 is *minus* five degrees, with a wind chill of twenty-three below. We should be on the ground in about ten minutes, right on time."

Fastening his seat belt, Rosen looked out the window and shivered, despite his wool sweater. Far below stretched the broad, snow-covered plains of South Dakota, as desolate as Siberia. As the plane descended, he saw a few ranch houses and the outline of fences, but no signs of life. Only the bare branches of the trees swayed mournfully, battered by the wind. He hoped his lined topcoat would be enough.

No one seemed eager to leave the warm cabin. Returning the True Sky file to his briefcase, he put on his coat and followed the last passenger into the terminal. He shielded his eyes, waiting for the camera flash that would certainly come.

It didn't. Looking around for Andi, Rosen checked his watch; it was nearly four. He walked through a long corridor to get his suitcases. They puttered down the conveyor a few minutes later, and he wondered what to do next. Get a room, rent a car, and drive tomorrow into Deadwood for the trial? He really should see Saul True Sky to review the case, although there was nothing new to discuss. He sat on a bench near the exit, hunching his shoulders every time the wind whipped through the sliding doors.

Ten minutes later, he walked to the hotel directory and picked up a phone. He had punched two numbers when a hand pulled the receiver from him, hanging it up. Andi's lips were cold against his but warmed quickly. She had pushed back the hood of her coat, and its fur lining, icy along the edges, prickled his cheek. It was good having someone meet him and he liked kissing her, so he kept holding onto her, until finally she pulled away, gasping for breath.

"Whew!" She unzipped her parka and fanned herself. "You brought some of that warm weather from D.C."

He felt his cheeks burning. "I'm sorry. I—"

"Now that you're here, maybe I won't have to worry so much about keeping warm—you're even cuter when your face turns red. Sorry I'm late. I had to drop something off in Rapid City, then get some gas."

"You're not still driving that old Mercury?"

"Unlike several men I've known, it's never let me down."

Seeing her grin, Rosen wanted to kiss her again. Instead he asked, "No camera? You look naked . . . I'm not used to seeing you without it."

"No time. I've been in the darkroom all night." She yawned and rubbed her eyes. This is a big story, Nate. The biggest."

"Did some woman in Bear Coat win the Pillsbury Bake-Off?"

"Wouldn't you like to know."

"Well?"

"Sorry, I promised Jack I wouldn't tell anybody. Come over here and see what I brought you."

She had draped a hooded parka over his two suitcases.

"Belonged to my dad. It may be a little short, but it's a lot warmer than what you've got on. Wind could sneeze that off you. Here."

The coat was down-insulated, and inside its deep pockets were a pair of heavy leather gloves. She tied his hood.

"Now you stand a chance of not turning into a Popsicle. We'd better get you some boots tomorrow before the trial." She took one of his suitcases. "Let's get going—I left the car running."

Following her outside, he asked, "Such a classic—you aren't afraid of somebody stealing it?"

He lost her reply in the bitter wind. Grabbing his arm, Andi led him across the street. After throwing his briefcase and luggage in back, he settled into the front seat as the warm air streaming through the vents clouded the windows. He loosened his hood, then, taking a deep breath, coughed hard.

"What's wrong?" she asked.

"Car smells like an ashtray."

Andi drove through the parking lot, the Mercury rumbling as if also clearing its throat. "If you don't start on my smoking, I won't light up till we get home."

"Deal." He looked out the window. "This reminds me of Chicago, when I was a boy."

"This ain't nothing like it can get. The Black Hills usually shelter Bear Coat from the worst weather, but they're saying not this year. We already got a couple feet of snow, and it's been ball-bustin' cold."

"Wonderful."

"So how was your holiday season? I called your office—they said you were on a case."

"Small town in Maryland. Otherwise, I would've been here a few days earlier. I was helping an atheist try to remove a Nativity scene from his town square."

"Bet that really put you in the holiday spirit. They must've thought you were the Grinch. Know who the Grinch is?"

Rosen nodded. "I used to read Dr. Seuss to my daughter."

"How is she? Get a chance to see her when you made your Chicago connection?"

"No, but I attended her fall recital. She's doing fine."

"And your ex-wife? Oh, hell."

The Mercury's engine suddenly died; the car cruised onto the shoulder and stopped. Andi cut the lights, and through the twilight Rosen gazed across a plain hard and smooth as slate. Beside the road stood a mound shoulder-high, mottled where the snow had been blown away—one of the old hay rolls left rotting in the field.

Reaching across to the glove compartment, Andi took out a small plastic bottle. "De-icer. Some water must've got in the gas line when I filled up on the way to the airport." She opened the car door, and the wind froze her breath.

Following her outside, Rosen sheltered her while she poured de-icer into the gas tank. Wind whistled across a cold, dark void, as if Rosen were in the middle of a nightmare. A few of the passing cars slowed, but Andi waved them on.

Rosen asked, "Don't you think . . . ?"

Andi patted the tail fin, and they went back inside. She let the motor run for a few minutes, put the car in gear, and the Mercury crept back onto the highway, seemed to stretch its long body, then roared ahead.

Rosen closed his eyes and let the sweat slide down the back of his neck.

"You all right?"

He swallowed hard.

"Nate?"

"When I was about five, I went shopping with my mother. Somehow on the walk home, we were separated. It was winter, cold and dark like this . . . I think it was the darkness more than the cold that frightened me. I was probably only a few blocks from my house, but what did I know? One of the neighbor kids found me and brought me home. I got home before my mother. She was searching everywhere, half out of her mind—two boys had been kidnapped and killed in Chicago a few years before. How she hugged me—she wouldn't let go. She covered me tight in my blanket and slept with me that night, stroking my hair until I fell asleep. I was never so scared, and I never felt safer." He closed his eyes, imagining his mother's hand upon his forehead.

Neither of them spoke for the next ten minutes. The long flight, the car's movement, and the warmth of his parka coat made Rosen drowsy. Andi could've easily driven the rest of the way with him asleep, but he didn't want to appear so vulnerable.

Stiffling a yawn, he asked, "What's this big news story you mentioned before?"

"I can't tell. I promised Jack."

"Pulitzer Prize material, no doubt."

"I know you're teasing me, but don't be surprised if this doesn't win some big journalism award. Even better"—she squeezed his arm—"this is gonna get me what I been dreaming about all my life. My ticket outta here. I've already talked to this old couple on the block, whose daughter just got married. She's willing to rent my house, so there's nothing holding me here once those job offers come rolling in."

"Maybe you'd better not—"

"You think I'm dizzy, but you'll see." She giggled. "Maybe I did promise Jack not to tell, but that doesn't mean I can't show you. Just wait till we get home."

Forty minutes later they arrived in Bear Coat. Pulling up her driveway, she said, "Better take your luggage in. You don't want to have to thaw out your pajamas tonight."

"You're not dropping me at the hotel?"

"Remember, I've got something inside to show you."

"Your etchings?"

"Huh? Hell, it's cold!"

Grabbing a suitcase, Andi ran ahead of him into the house. Tossing her coat over a living room chair, she pushed up the sleeves of her turtleneck.

"Leave your stuff in the hallway." She pointed to a pile of wood stacked near the fireplace. "We can get cozy later on."

"You were going to tell me about this big story."

"Show you. C'mere."

She led him into the bathroom and, closing the door, kissed him in the darkness. Her lips lingered on his for a long time, but before he could consider the implications, she switched on the light.

"Just wanted to remind you what you've been missing." Sitting on the sink, she wrapped her legs around him. "Promise you won't tell anybody till the paper comes out tomorrow afternoon?"

"Sure."

Her breath upon his cheek, she whispered, "The mob's trying to take over Bear Coat."

"What?"

"Uh-huh. It's been trying to take over the Tin Town development, 'cause with all the gambling that could come in, like in Deadwood, these crooks probably figured it'd be easy to take over, with them starting slow and kind of worming their way in, when all of a sudden . . . "

"Wait a minute."

" 'Cause Jack says if we hadn't caught them right away, no telling how things might've ended up, with lots of folks getting—"

"Hold it." He shook her gently.

"But the F.B.I . . . "

"The F.B.I.? Maybe we'd better back up a bit."

"Sorry. Here, look."

Strung across the bathtub were two clotheslines, from which hung about a dozen black-and-white photographs.

"Mind you, I took my best shots to the printer in Rapid City this afternoon. Jack's getting a special edition ready for tomorrow, before anybody else breaks the story. Gonna deliver it in Rapid City and Deadwood, as well as Bear Coat. We've got the scoop, and it's my byline on all the photos!"

In the first row, Rosen saw a photograph of Belle Gates, one of Huggins, Pearl Whistler, Elroy Baker, and Jack Keeshin. All the photos had one thing in common: Each subject was standing with the project engineer, Chick Cantrell.

"You mean, Cantrell's—"

"He's what you call the mob's advance man—that's what Jack says. I never thought much about it—guess nobody did, but Cantrell was always kind of sucking up to people. Always going over plans with Pearl, out gambling with Huggins, courting Belle the minute after Albert Gates was put in the ground. It was just his way of finding a weak link. And he found it." She pointed at Belle Gates.

Rosen shook his head. "Not—"

"Oh, no. Belle got suspicious when Cantrell started romancing her and then kept pressuring her to get him a gambling license as part of his engineer's fee. Also said he had friends with lots of money to invest in the development. Then she found out that he also held some heavy markers of Huggins's. Well, she talked to Jack—figured with his background and experience, he'd know what to do. Jack hired a detective in Los Angeles to check on Cantrell's background. I started following Cantrell around. Look what I came up with."

She took down the photo of Cantrell with Elroy Baker. The two men stood, as if strangers, on a busy street corner.

Rosen asked, "Where was this taken?"

"In Deadwood about six weeks ago. Look at their hands. Kind of blurry . . . You see anything?"

"Hard to tell."

"Here." She took down three more photos, each one enlarging the men's hands.

"It's money."

"That's right. Here's another photo of Elroy putting it in his pocket. Maybe Cantrell was setting up Elroy to be the new police chief. Nothing like having the top cop in your hip pocket when the gambling comes in. At least that's what Jack thinks."

"You mentioned the F.B.I."

"They contacted the paper about a month ago, after talking to Belle. Seems they were conducting their own investigation and didn't want us to mess anything up. Now that they're about to make their arrests, we're running the story."

"How did the F.B.I. find out?"

"I think Tom got suspicious and called them in. I'm not sure—you'll have to talk to Jack."

Leaning against the wall, Rosen studied the photographs, then stared at Elroy Baker's face. It was as if he'd struggled for months over a puzzle, only to find that the missing piece had been in front of his eyes all along. It was so simple, maybe . . .

Andi squeezed his arm. "Isn't this some big-time story!"

"I need to talk to Tom Cross Dog."

"Sure. Tomorrow after the paper comes out—"

"I need to talk to him now. Don't you see, Baker could be the key to Saul True Sky's trial. What if Baker killed Albert Gates to frame Saul, the only man standing in the way of bringing gambling into Tin Town? Baker had access to all the evidence—he could've taken the rusted nail clutched in Gates's hand."

"What does that nail have to do with anything?"

"I don't know yet, but somehow it's involved. I still think you were robbed for photographs of that nail."

"Hold on. Then maybe Elroy was somehow connected with Gil McCracken."

"Sure. When Saul won his hearing, McCracken tried to murder him. When McCracken failed, Baker gunned him down, maybe to cover his own involvement. Now do you understand why I have to see Cross Dog? Lend me your car for a few hours."

When Rosen turned to go, Andi's grip tightened. "You can't see Tom today."

"Why not?"

"I promised not to tell anybody. Jack'd get awful mad. Besides, Tom and the F.B.I. don't know we're running the story. We may be jumping the gun on them a day or two, but we don't want anybody scooping us. We worked too hard on this. Please, Nate."

He looked into her eyes. "All right, but I'm talking to Cross Dog and Keeshin tomorrow afternoon." Her grin made him smile back. "What's for supper?"

"I thought we'd order a pizza."

"You're not going to prepare a home-cooked meal?"

"I didn't want to spoil you. Besides, us modern women aren't into being chained to the microwave. I suppose you cook for yourself."

"When I'm not on the road. What do you have in the kitchen?"

She shrugged. "Refrigerator Surprise. Oh, there're some eggs, pota-toes. If this were breakfast . . . "

"I'll take care of dinner."

"Get real."

He walked her down the hallway, saying, "Be a modern woman—go into the living room and start the fire."

It was a handsome kitchen, with old oak cabinets and a large pantry next to the refrigerator. On a small table lay a cereal bowl with some-thing purple floating in the milk, and an ashtray filled with cigarette butts. He found eggs in the refrigerator; potatoes, onions, flour, and oil in the pantry; a bowl and an old grater in a drawer. There was already a large skillet on the stove. Thinking about his mother an hour before—he wanted to keep the feeling for awhile. Potato latkes was one way he always could.

His mother used to grate the potatoes by hand, then the onions, which made her eyes tear even while they laughed together. Maybe because he was the youngest and his brothers were always busy with his father, he liked following her around. Even when he was supposed to be studying, he would watch her cook and listen to stories of his grandparents in Russia. Now, holding up a hand, he smelled the onion, which would stay on his skin for days, no matter how often he washed. That was all right. Some people inhaled a certain perfume or spice and thought of their mother; with him it was always the smell of onion.

Wiping his eyes, he stirred the ingredients in a bowl, then dolloped the mixture into the sizzling oil, waiting until one side of each latke was golden brown before turning it over.

"Ooh, that smells good!" Andi stood behind him smoking a cigarette.

"Put that out. I want your taste buds sharp as they can be. Get the table ready. These have to be eaten hot."

Setting a plateful of latkes between them, he took a carton of sour cream from the refrigerator. "The perfect touch!"

"I wouldn't open that, Nate. Last time I looked it was kinda green."

"I think that's how they discovered penicillin. Do you have any apple-sauce?"

"I haven't checked the fruit bin lately. By now, maybe some of the apples have turned—"

"Never mind. I suppose we'll have to eat them plain." He shook his head. "It's not going to be the same."

"Wait a minute." She went to the refrigerator, returning with something red in a preserve jar. "Homemade raspberry jam the next-door neighbors gave me over the holidays."

"Raspberry jam with potato latkes? There are some traditions that shouldn't be . . . ."

"Mmm," she said between mouthfuls. "Shut up and eat them while they're hot. Say, Nate?"

"What?"

"You can cook for me anytime. Want a beer?"

They both ate greedily for the next fifteen minutes, and he resisted the impulse to wipe the jam from her mouth. He liked sitting across from her eating dinner, with the smell of oil and onion lingering over them. Not feeling the need to talk. Later, he'd wash the dishes while she dried. Over the last few months, he'd come to realize that, next to Sarah, what he missed most about no longer being married wasn't Bess. It was having someone at home to eat dinner with; someone to help clean up afterwards.

"You're thinking about your ex-wife," Andi said.

"Really?"

"Yeah, I know the look. I've seen lots of guys in bars, after a few beers, start mooning over their ex-wives. They have this look kinda like babies get with gas. So—what about her?"

He hesitated. "Just that she always insisted on using an electric blender to grate the potatoes. Never tasted as good as doing them by hand."

"I suppose that's why the two of you split up."

He shrugged her off.

"Or was it something juicier? Was she cheating on you?"

"No."

"You sure?"

"Yes," he said a little too loud. "It was something else."

She swallowed hard. "Pretty stupid of me, having this romantic dinner with a guy, then asking about his ex-wife. Sorry."

"That's all right. I shouldn't be so sensitive. It happened a long time ago."

"How about some dessert? I'll put on some coffee . . . no, you'd rather have tea. You like Christmas cookies?"

"That depends—what year?" .

Ten minutes later, backs against the couch, they stretched before the fireplace, a plate of cookies between them. While sipping his tea, Rosen listened to Andi talk of the True Skys, Keeshin, and members of the town council, most of whom he already knew from her letters and his phone calls to Grace. Maybe it wouldn't be necessary to see Saul that evening.

Opening day in court was nothing special. Both sides would go over the ground rules, then the prosecutor might call a few witnesses to establish the nature of the crime—maybe Cross Dog and the medical examiner. He'd have to see Cross Dog tomorrow, whether Andi liked it or not. There could be a connection between Cantrell's involvement with the mob and Albert Gates's death. And Elroy Baker might somehow . . .

"More tea?" Andi asked.

Backlit by the fire, her hair was golden, and the shadows shimmered across her face like a veil. He wanted to draw away the veil and kiss her.

"Nate?"

"No thanks. You're lucky, living in a place where your neighbor makes you a jar of preserves for Christmas."

"Try living here your whole life." She yawned. "Told you, this story's gonna be my big break. New York, Chicago—anywhere but Bear Coat." She scooted forward, resting her head on the rug. Her hand held his. "This is nice. You're nice."

Her face turned toward him for a moment—lashes fluttered—then moved back into the shadows. Her legs stirred languidly, and he remembered how she'd looked last summer in shorts and a T-shirt. Putting down the tea, he rubbed his eyes; his head felt heavy, as if he'd been drinking. There were things he should be thinking about—questions to ask, warnings—but all that mattered to him at that moment was Andi.

Pushing aside the tray, he touched her shoulder, feeling her body gently undulate. He moved her face toward his and kissed her lips.

As Andi pulled off her turtleneck, Rosen said, "It's been a long time."

"Don't worry; it's like riding a bike. You never forget. Here." From her jeans pocket she handed him a foil packet. "Just like the Scouts: 'Be prepared.' "

Her lips were on his, her hands helping him with his clothes. The windows rattled from the cold wind, and for a moment he shivered. He kissed her breasts, feeling her heartbeat quicken and feeling the heat radiate between them. A heat that drew them closer, fused them as one, consuming everything else. Only Andi, her legs wrapped around him, her breath whispering his name. Only Andi.

Afterward, she smiled and, closing her eyes, fell into a deep sleep. He wanted to smile too, but something was wrong. Again he shivered.

Leaning against the couch, Rosen watched the fire crackle. He added a log, which caught instantly; the flames oozed and puddled through the wood, poured over the side, then suddenly rose together like two hands in prayer. Without thinking, he whispered the evening prayers he'd said as a boy. His own hands smelled of onion, just as his mother's had while tucking him into bed. The fire was warm as a blanket, and, lying beside Andi, he yawned once before closing his eyes.

Chapter 14

MONDAY AFTERNOON

"You made no attempt to converse with your father, after shining the flashlight into his vision pit?" Rosen asked from his seat at the defense table.

Will shook his head.

"So as far as you could tell, your father didn't know about Albert Gates's death."

"Yes, sir."

"That would explain why he remained in the pit until the police arrived. I'm finished with the witness."

Judge Whistler asked, "Anything more from you, Mr. Benton?"

The district attorney peered into his papers, like a chicken about to peck corn. Looking up, he ran a hand through his shock of white hair, curled a thumb around each red suspender, and smiled. "Just one question. Will . . . Mr. True Sky, couldn't the defendant have just come from murdering Albert Gates?"

"I don't understand."

"I think you do. Despite what Mr. Rosen wants you to say, you don't know from Adam what your father was doing before you arrived at the murder scene. Isn't that right?"

"Uh . . . yes, sir."

"Thank you. I'd like to call Police Chief Tom Cross Dog."

Rosen felt a slight queasiness in his stomach. This wasn't like the preliminary hearing last summer, with that young assistant D.A. who couldn't handle himself, let alone a murder trial. Ted Benton was a "good old country lawyer"—cuddly as a teddy bear, but with razor-sharp claws. At least Rosen had waived the right to a jury trial. He'd rather trust the verdict to Judge Whistler, not the kind of man to be impressed by red suspenders.

Benton guided Tom Cross Dog as if the witness were telling an old family story. The prosecutor asked a simple question in a soft, earnest voice; an occasional follow-up for clarification; an interruption, almost apologetic, to keep the witness on track—but never leading too far or putting words into the policeman's mouth. Like Will, Cross Dog said nothing new.

Standing at the defense table, Rosen asked a few questions clarifying the time the body was found and its location. The police chief seemed more relaxed than he had been during the preliminary hearing last summer.

Rosen approached the witness box. "When you examined Albert Gates's body, did you find anything clutched in his hand?"

Without blinking an eye, Cross Dog said, "There was something in his left hand."

" 'Something.' Could you be more specific?"

"I'm not sure what it was. Maybe a clump of dirt."

"Or a piece of metal?"

"Maybe. Can't say for sure."

"Why not?"

"As you know, my department misplaced the evidence before the preliminary hearing. We never found it."

"You're not concerned that whatever was in Gates's hand might be important evidence?"

"No."

"Your Honor," Benton said, scratching his head, "the prosecution regrets the loss of this dirt or piece of metal or whatever, but we'd hardly call it evidence. Dr. Ericson will testify that a blow to the back of the head killed Albert Gates and that a stone found nearby was the murder weapon."

Rosen replied, "The object might have belonged to the real murderer or could be a clue to his identity."

"Can the defense give any reason why it thinks the material in Gates's hand was anything other than just something he grabbed blindly on the ground in the agony of his death?"

Rosen had anticipated the question, just as he knew what his answer had to be. "It was the police's job to secure the evidence, so that the defense would have the chance to pursue this line of investigation."

He could have told them the evidence was an old nail, but what of it? He still hadn't been able to connect the nail in Gates's hand to the murder.

Judge Whistler said, "Technically, Mr. Rosen has a point, although I can't see how the prosecution's case is jeopardized by this missing object, in and of itself. Any other questions?"

"Chief Cross Dog, you found the defendant in his vision pit, the exact same place his son Will has testified seeing him an hour earlier."

"That's right."

"Isn't it unusual for a murderer to remain at the scene of the crime, waiting for the police?"

"No."

"What?"

Glancing at Benton, who nodded slowly, the policeman said, "I remember back about twelve years ago, when we arrested Bobby Howard."

There were gasps and a loud murmuring in the courtroom, as Judge Whistler tapped his gavel.

"Howard was a peculiar fella," Cross Dog continued. "He lived by himself up in the hills and came to believe God was talking to him. Told him to stop this car and take a mother and daughter with him up to his cabin. We found him a few hours later just sitting there, the two women dead. They were . . . well, no need to go into all that. Point is, he was waiting there, in some kind of trance. Just like True Sky over there."

"Objection," Rosen heard himself say, and though he was sustained, the damage had been done. Benton leaned back in his chair, stifling a smile, thumbs hooked around his suspenders.

Looking down, Rosen noticed that his own hands, resting on the railing of the witness stand, were damp. He brushed them against his coat. "No further questions."

"It's after four," the judge said, "and I have an appointment. I understand that Dr. Gustafson is the next prosecution witness. We'll resume at nine o'clock tomorrow morning. Court is adjourned."

Looking across the room, Rosen didn't recognize Grace at first; the charcoal-gray knit dress, high heels, and hair pinned up made her look much older. That and the way she moved, in small, deliberate steps with her hands clutching one another. She walked toward the prosecution table, passing Cross Dog, and spoke directly to Benton. The prosecutor replied while patting her shoulder. After a few minutes, she turned and quickly left the courtroom.

"What was that all about?" Rosen asked True Sky.

"I don't know. She doesn't talk to me much anymore."

"You don't have any idea?"

"You worry too much."

"I'm your lawyer."

"Be a man, not a lawyer. Every man has a straight path, but he needs clear eyes to see it."

Rosen shook his head. "My eyes weren't too good today. Maybe I should've arrived in town last week and reviewed the case with you and Grace. Still, I don't see how anything would've changed. Benton's just very slick."

"It's nothing to worry about. There are more important things in a man's life."

"Like what?"

From an old paper bag, Saul took out a long wooden flute, which he gave Rosen. One end of the instrument had been carved to resemble a bird with an open beak.

"This is for helping me, and because you need it."

"It's beautiful, thank you. Is this what you were whittling from the branch last summer?"

The old Indian nodded. "A courting flute. We call it *siyotanka*—great prairie chicken. When you blow into it, the flute makes the same noise, *siyo,* as a prairie chicken. I put into it the power my brothers the elk have over women. You seem to be lonely. This will get you a woman."

Rosen couldn't help but smile. "Does it really work?"

"Learn to play, and you'll see."

Putting on his parka, Rosen carefully laid the flute diagonally inside his briefcase, then followed True Sky downstairs through the doorway. It was bitter cold, but Rosen enjoyed breathing the crisp air. Across the street, Ike sat in his van with the motor running. The van had snow tires and chains.

"You need a ride back to Bear Coat?" True Sky asked.

"No thanks. Andi's meeting me here at five for dinner." Just then, he caught sight of Jack Keeshin talking to the driver of a delivery truck. "Excuse me."

He ran a half block up Pine Street, as Keeshin waved goodbye to the truck. With the same motion, the editor shook his hand. Even though they both wore gloves, the other man's grip was like iron. His face had the same California tan as it had the previous summer.

"Afternoon, Nate. I saw you in court. Benton scored a few aces, but the match is far from over. Wish I could help."

"Maybe you can."

As if he hadn't heard, Keeshin unfolded the newspaper that had been under his arm. "Special edition of the *Bearcoat Chronicle*."

The headline read: MOB RULE?

"Not too literary, is it?" Keeshin asked. "You know—the pun on 'mob'."

Below the headline, Andi's photo, four columns wide, showed Cantrell and Baker together on a Deadwood street corner. The rest of the page was divided between two stories, both with Keeshin's byline: ENGINEER SOUGHT BY POLICE and ELROY BAKER ARRESTED. Rosen skimmed both articles, which detailed what Andi had told him the previous evening.

"Is Cantrell still at large?"

Keeshin nodded. "He could be out of the country by now. Elroy Baker wasn't so lucky. He was arrested at his home early this morning. I understand he was in his pajamas."

"This connection between Cantrell and Baker—"

"It's too cold to talk out here. I'll buy you a cup of coffee."

They ducked into a small snack shop and sat at the counter. It was warm and, smelling of grease and grilled onions, reminded Rosen of the night before. Unzipping his coat, he ordered hot tea and lemon.

Keeshin opened the newspaper as carefully as if it were a bolt of silk. "Beautiful, isn't it?"

"Congratulations. You must've spent a great deal of time and money putting this story together. Andi's hoping for a Pulitzer Prize. I don't think it's out of the question."

"That's not why I ran the story. Six months ago, when I arrived here, it would've been." He stared into the steam rising from his coffee. "Coming to Bear Coat, I wondered if I could really give up the life I'd led back in L.A.—you know how fast it can be."

"Like a good tennis court."

"Exactly. You're a pretty perceptive guy—maybe you know how I feel about Grace. She's different from any woman I've ever met. We've driven to Sioux Falls several times with Stevie, to get the boy psychiatric help. Taking her out to places I once frequented, comparing her to the kind of women I was used to . . . Grace has a deep sense of values, like she's anchored and no matter what her troubles, she can ride them out. Maybe it's an Indian perspective she gets from her father, but I find it incredibly appealing. No, it's more than that." He shook his head. "Guess what I'm really saying is that I love her."

Rosen sipped his tea, not quite knowing what to say. Was it really so strange? Did Keeshin want anything more than Rosen—a family and a sense of roots? "I guess congratulations are in order a second time, but what does this have to do with the newspaper story?"

Keeshin's smile was so infectious, Rosen had to force himself not to smile back.

"It was a kind of test . . . for me. At first, when Belle mentioned her suspicions concerning Chick Cantrell, I saw it the way most lawyers would. You know."

"Sure—another game."

"That's right. A chance to uncover some dirt and add to your reputation. But I've changed, Nate. I want to clean out the garbage like Cantrell and Baker, because this is Grace's town and decent like her." He laughed. "It was such a simple concept, I had a difficult time understanding it. It felt good keeping this town clean for Grace and Stevie. So good that I'm going to ask Grace to marry me."

Rosen furrowed his brow but said nothing. Why was Keeshin telling him all this?

As if in response, the other man continued, "There's really no one else here I can talk to. Andi speaks about you often, and I get the sense that we're alike in many ways—from big cities, traveled a lot, don't really have the kind of roots found in Bear Coat. It's presumptuous for me to think of us as friends, but I felt the need to talk to somebody. I hope you don't mind."

When Rosen didn't answer, Keeshin asked, "Something wrong?"

"I find it hard to reconcile your newfound righteousness with the way the newspaper's being promoted. A special edition, not only in Bear Coat, but also here in Deadwood."

"It's not what it seems. Carrie Taggert, who runs one of the newspapers here, helped me set up today—gave me the use of her news boxes and so forth."

"I've met her. She's a good friend of Andi's."

"That's the point. This is all for Andi. You know how much she wants to leave Bear Coat. If the story gets picked up by any of the news services, they'll reprint her photos. It'll be wonderful for her resume." He hesitated, then added, "There is another reason. I'm thinking of selling the *Chronicle,* and this publicity can't hurt the selling price. I've had enough fun being an editor, and how often does a story like this come along for a small-town paper—once in a lifetime? If Grace says yes, I'm buying her a ranch; we'll settle down and raise horses, maybe even a kid or two."

"When are you going to ask her?"

Keeshin lifted his hands. "I've never been this close to marriage before. I don't know when's the right moment—now or after the murder trial, or once the town council's appeal's been heard on the condemnation. Then there's Stevie . . . "

"Wait a minute. You mean the town's still going ahead with its plans to bring gambling into Bear Coat?"

"Oh yes. Despite what Cantrell tried to do, Belle says the development's as necessary as ever for the town's economy."

Rosen poured a second cup of tea. "What about this connection between Cantrell and Baker?"

"You want to know if Cantrell might be behind Albert Gates's murder. I suppose it's only natural for Saul's lawyer to look for other suspects. Interesting scenario: Cantrell framed Saul for murder and, when Saul won his condemnation hearing, wanted a quicker way to get rid of the old man, paying Gil McCracken to kill him. Sort of like the JFK conspiracy theory—fascinating, but no proof. The private investigator I hired couldn't find any evidence linking Cantrell to the two deaths."

"I'd like to talk to this investigator."

"Of course. His number's in my office. I doubt if Tom Cross Dog or the F.B.I. have discovered anything either. Maybe once Cantrell is found, if that ever happens. My guess is that he's lying on some Caribbean beach right now."

Rosen checked his watch. "I'd better get back to the courthouse. I'm meeting Andi for dinner. When we get to Bear Coat, I'll visit Baker in jail. Maybe he can tell me something."

"Didn't you know? Baker's being held here in Deadwood; it's the county seat. Jail's in the courthouse basement."

"I still have a few minutes. I better get over there now. Thanks for the tea and conversation."

Both men stood, Keeshin taking out a gold money clip inlaid with a silver tennis racket. He dropped a five-dollar bill on the counter. "The pleasure was all mine. See you tomorrow at the trial. Remember"—he swung his hand in a wide arc—"the match is a long way from over."

The sky had darkened, as Rosen hurried down the street. He maneuvered past dozens of people who, hunched against the wind, were leaving the courthouse for the day. Inside, he reached the elevator just as Tom Cross Dog and an older policeman stepped through the open door into the corridor.

"Going down?" the older man asked.

Rosen replied, "It looked that way in court today, didn't it?"

Cross Dog introduced Rosen to Sheriff Clarkson, who, with his round face and wire-rimmed glasses, looked more like a professor than a policeman.

"I'd like to see Elroy Baker," Rosen said.

"What for?" Cross Dog asked.

"I want to ask him a few questions concerning the Albert Gates murder."

"You really are in trouble, if you need Elroy's help."

"Won't he cooperate?"

"He don't know a damn thing about Gates. He may be a crooked cop, but he ain't no murderer. At least . . . " He stopped suddenly.

Sheriff Clarkson touched his arm. "Why don't you take him downstairs? That unfinished business you have with Elroy—best get it off your chest. I'll see you over at the restaurant. Nice meeting you, Mr. Rosen."

The two men stood at opposite corners in the elevator.

"Glad I caught you," Rosen said. "What made you call in the F.B.I.?"

Cross Dog shrugged. "Something never was right about Cantrell, the way he was always sucking up to people and throwing his money around."

"You made a smart move."

"Cantrell wasn't the only one I checked up on. He just was the only one we found dirty."

"Who else did you investigate?"

"It don't matter."

The way the policeman grimaced answered Rosen. It must've been

160

Jack Keeshin. He wondered if Cross Dog knew how involved Keeshin and Grace really were.

As the elevator door opened, Rosen said, "Too bad you didn't get Cantrell. Think you will?"

"The F.B.I. monitored his calls. He's linked with organized crime out in L.A. They've picked up the man Cantrell's been calling—maybe he'll give us a lead, though I doubt it."

"So Elroy's left holding the bag."

Cross Dog grunted and pushed past Rosen, who followed him into the jail's processing area. The small room was painted a green that had faded to fish-belly gray. Behind a counter sat a policeman, leaning back against the wall and reading a wrestling magazine.

"Forget something, Tom?"

"I'm taking this man in to see Baker."

Cross Dog checked his gun, while the policeman patted down Rosen. Then the two men walked past the counter and through a heavy steel door.

The cellblock, smelling of sweat and urine, reminded Rosen of a zoo. The smell, the iron bars, but mostly the prisoners with their listlessness and furtive eyes. The Torah said that man was made in God's image. Looking at these brutish creatures half-hidden in shadows, Rosen fought against the question that had troubled him ever since his father had sent him away. What kind of God sat on His throne in heaven?

Cross Dog opened the door to the third cell on the right. Dressed in prison-green, the man slumped over the bunk seemed a stranger, not the cocky, glad-handing policeman Rosen had known. Baker's mouth twitched as if he were unable to speak.

Rosen stopped just inside the cell door. "Hello, Elroy."

Cross Dog said, "You remember True Sky's lawyer. He wants to ask you some questions. You don't have to answer, or if you want me to call your lawyer . . . "

"No, that's all right. I want you both to know I didn't do nothing wrong. I mean, nothing serious. You and me go back a long way, Tom."

Rosen sat on the bunk next to Baker, who smelled from layers of sweat. The prisoner kept staring at the floor.

Rosen asked Cross Dog, "What's he been charged with?"

"Accepting bribes."

"That's all," Baker said, stepping on an ant, then grinding it into the floor. "I was a fool, Tom. They ain't gonna put me away just for taking a few hundred bucks."

"What happened?" Rosen asked.

Baker shrugged like a schoolboy caught cheating. "Wasn't my fault. I mean, he was so nice to me. 'Pals,' he said."

"Cantrell?"

"Uh-huh. At first it was just going for pizza and beer. I mean, he was always out with Huggins, Pearl Whistler, and Belle Gates. None of them ever paid any attention to me. Why should they pay any attention to the deputy chief of an eight-man police department?"

"So Cantrell bought you a couple of beers. What else?"

"He said somebody with my experience shouldn't have to settle for second best, especially to an Indian—sorry, Tom. Said there wasn't any reason why I shouldn't be chief of police. Said he'd be willing to finance my campaign. He gave me a hundred-dollar bill right then. I ain't ever known anybody who could peel off a hundred-dollar bill, just like that."

"And all he wanted from you was a little information now and then. What kind of information?"

"Nothing special. Just whatever crossed Tom's desk. Cantrell said he had some friends who'd like to invest in Bear Coat but wanted to be sure it was a safe, quiet town."

Cross Dog sighed. "You believed him?"

"Yeah . . . I don't . . . hell, Tom!" He looked up, tears running from his pale eyes. "You didn't hear the way he could talk. It all sounded so natural. 'Just business,' he said." Baker shook his head hard, his tears scattering upon the floor. " 'Just business.' "

Rosen persisted. "What kind of information?"

"I told you—anything. Like drunk-and-disorderlies."

"Did he ask about the Gates murder investigation?"

"I guess so."

"What did he want to know?"

"How it was going. Did we have enough evidence to convict True Sky."

"Did you tamper with the evidence?"

"Huh?"

"What was found in Gates's hand—did you take it?"

Again Baker shook his head. "No way. Tom, I swear it!"

162

Rosen continued, "Couldn't Cantrell have framed True Sky, then hired McCracken to kill him?"

"I . . . I suppose so."

"And you killed McCracken. A nice cover-up."

"No I didn't!"

Cross Dog said, "You lie once about any of this, and the D.A. will bury you."

"All right. What I meant was, I didn't kill McCracken for any cover-up. I . . . uh . . . was just . . . " His voice trailed off.

"He was just a little quick on the trigger," Cross Dog said softly.

Baker looked up and wiped his eyes. "You knew?"

"Yeah. That morning McCracken took a shot at True Sky, I raised you on the radio. You told me you saw McCracken's car by the side door of the feedstore. Then three shots were fired. You said McCracken fired first, then you returned two rounds in self-defense. You lied."

"How'd you know?"

"I heard three shots over the radio, the first one loud, then two softer ones. You shot first—the bullet's sound practically exploded into the speaker. You must've caught McCracken coming out the door. Man probably didn't even see what hit him. He must've got a round off wild before he hit the ground, and you went over to finish him. Just like a horse with a broken leg."

"I shoulda warned him to stop, but I was scared. He was a real badass."

"Sure," Rosen said. "Gunning him down at high noon made you quite a hero, and maybe the next police chief of Bear Coat. The question remains, did Cantrell order you to do it, so that McCracken wouldn't talk?"

"No!" Baker tried to grab Rosen's arm, but his hand was so sweaty it slipped.

Rosen, in turn, gripped Baker. "Cantrell did hire you, didn't he?"

"No!"

"They're going to bury you in here."

"That's enough," Cross Dog said, pushing the cell door wide open.

Baker cowered on the corner of his bunk and started to sob. Rosen took a step toward the prisoner, but Cross Dog pulled him into the corridor, closing the door behind them. They walked silently through the cell-

RONALD LEVITSKY

block, past the policeman still reading his magazine, and into the elevator.

Rosen said, "I wanted to apologize to Baker. I got a little carried
away."

"You believe him?"

"What's more interesting is that you do."

"I've known Elroy a long time. He may be a lot of things, but he's no
cold-blooded murderer."

"How long have you known Saul True Sky?"

Cross Dog grimaced.

"Don't you think you're letting what happened to your uncle poison
your mind against True Sky? I think you and Grace . . . " Rosen stopped
suddenly, remembering Keeshin's intentions. As the elevator doors
opened, Cross Dog held him back.

"What about me and Grace?"

"Oh, nothing," Rosen said, checking his watch. He'd kept Andi waiting twenty-five minutes. That was enough trouble for one day.

Chapter 15

TUESDAY MORNING

Grace looked at the clock on the courtroom wall, then checked her watch. 9:03. Where was the judge . . . Why couldn't they get on with it! She sat between Stevie and Jack in the first row behind the prosecutor, her son's hand warm in hers. It would be all right. What else could she do, after Stevie woke up from that nightmare and told her? Jack had agreed, last night on their way to pick up Dr. Hartrey from the airport. What else could she do?

People around her were getting to their feet. She joined them as Judge Whistler stepped up to the bench. Stevie looked so grown-up, wearing the blue dress shirt they'd bought that morning and his father's best tie. He looked like his father, tall and wiry with that one cowlick that never would stay in place. Only the smile was missing, but he'd be smiling soon—the doctor'd said so. He was doing real well, and this would help make him better.

As they sat, Grace glanced at her father at the defense table. She looked away quickly and, cheeks burning, clutched her purse until her knuckles whitened. Damn it, *he* should be ashamed, not her!

"Good morning," Judge Whistler said. He looked tired and much older than he had the summer before, at the preliminary hearing. "Mr. Benton, would you like to call your first witness? I believe it's Dr. Gustafson."

The district attorney leaned over the table, shuffling through a stack of papers. "If it please the court," he said, looking up, "I'd like to reschedule Dr. Gustafson's testimony for this afternoon. The prosecution has a new witness to call—that is, actually, two who are not listed."

"I don't like such irregularities. They strike me as playing games with this court."

165

"Not at all, Your Honor. I myself only became aware of these witnesses yesterday, after court had adjourned, and didn't meet with them until last night."

Judge Whistler frowned. "Very well. Call your witnesses, with the stipulation that Mr. Rosen must have sufficient time to prepare his cross-examination."

"Thank you. I call Dr. Karen Hartrey."

She'd been sitting in the second row, and, as she walked down the aisle, her perfume scented the air. She carried a leather slipcase. Dr. Hartrey took the oath and sat very straight in the witness stand. Grace had never realized how pretty the woman was. She wore a brown turtleneck with a plaid vest and matching pleated skirt of hunter green. Her hair was short, black with red highlights, and her green eyes sparkled when she smiled, which was often. It was easy to see why people trusted her. Grace felt a little better, now that she was here.

Benton folded his hands on the table. "Would you please state your name, occupation, and current residence for the record."

"Karen Hartrey, doctor of psychiatry. I have my own practice and am attached to the staff of St. Theresa's Hospital in Sioux Falls. That's also where I live."

"I understand that you specialize in the psychiatric problems of children."

"That's correct."

Benton looked at Judge Whistler. "Dr. Hartrey needs to lay the foundation for my next witness, whose testimony is crucial for the State's case. Now, Dr. Hartrey, when did you first see Stevie Jenkins as a patient?"

From the slipcase she removed and opened a manila folder. "On August 2 of last year."

"Under what circumstances?"

"I was contacted by Mr. Jack Keeshin, a resident of Bear Coat. Mr. Keeshin brought Stevie and his mother to see me regarding a program of therapy for the boy."

"What sort of therapy?"

Again Dr. Hartrey consulted her notes. "Of course, you understand that, although a child, Stevie has the same right to privacy as any adult. I'll only touch upon what's relevant to the proceedings in this courtroom and, more importantly, what Stevie and his mother both have permitted me to share."

"We understand that. We only need to establish, in general terms, why Mrs. Jenkins sought your help for her son."

"To put it as simply as possible, Stevie Jenkins had gone through some traumatic experiences within the last few years—most significantly, his father's sudden death in a highway accident, and, more recently, his grandfather's arrest for murder. These were the two most important men in Stevie's life."

"So the boy had sort of an identity crisis."

Dr. Hartrey smiled. "Yes, but the cause went far deeper, having to do with Stevie's background. He's one-quarter Sioux—Lakota—and, growing up, had been very close to his grandfather."

"We're talking about the defendant, Saul True Sky."

"Yes. Remember, Stevie's father was a truck driver and on the road a great deal, and his mother worked nights. The boy was often alone with his grandfather, who believes very deeply in the traditional Lakota religion. This belief was not shared by Stevie's mother, who, in fact, discouraged her son's involvement with his grandfather. She wanted him to grow up, to use her own words, 'white like his father.' Indeed, Stevie was taunted in school by classmates and even by one teacher, who found his grandfather's 'Injun' ways odd. You could see the dilemma the boy was in. He loved his grandfather and the old customs and rituals, but the rest of the world, including his mother, was telling him he was wrong."

Dr. Hartrey spoke softly and so earnestly, like one of those women on a morning talk show. It seemed to Grace that this was like TV, that the people being spoken about publicly were somebody else, not her family.

Benton nodded his head gravely. "What was your treatment for the boy?"

"A combination of therapy and medication. Since August, Stevie's seen me eight times."

"With his mother, Mrs. Jenkins?"

Dr. Hartrey consulted her notes. "On three occasions we had a family session. Otherwise, I saw him alone."

"You mentioned medication."

"I've prescribed a medication which is often used to calm a child and keep him on task. One of Stevie's symptoms was restlessness—he had difficulty sleeping, paying attention in school, and doing his homework."

Benton paused to look at Rosen, who leaned back in his chair, apparently unconcerned. Then the prosecutor returned to Dr. Hartrey. "I'm going to anticipate a question by the defense. Could this medication impair the boy's memory, make him think he's seen or heard things that weren't there?"

"Absolutely not. I've prescribed this medication to dozens of children. It doesn't challenge reality. Quite the contrary. It helps the child see reality for what it is."

" 'For what it is.' Well stated, doctor. Now let's get to the reason why you're here."

"Mrs. Jenkins called me Sunday night or, to be more accurate, about one a.m. Monday morning. Stevie had woken from a nightmare involving the murder of Albert Gates—the nightmare was probably triggered by his grandfather's trial, which was to begin later that day. Stevie told his mother things he had seen and heard the night of Gates's murder. These were the same things he'd told me in confidence at a session we'd had last month. After I talked to Stevie on the phone, the three of us agreed it would be best if he testified in court."

"'Best' in what way?"

Dr. Hartrey looked past the prosecutor to Grace and Stevie. "As a doctor, I take a far greater interest in my patient's recovery than in the outcome of this criminal proceeding. Stevie has tried to keep the events of that night, the night of the murder, buried. The resultant stress of that decision has only exacerbated his psychological problem. Fortunately, one value shared by his Lakota grandfather, his mother, and the Judeo-Christian institutions of white society, like his school, is a respect for the truth. It is this common respect for the truth that has allowed Stevie to state publicly what happened the night of Albert Gates's murder."

Benton paused to let the weight of her words sink in. Half-bowing, he said, "I'd like to thank you for flying in from Sioux Falls. I know you must have a busy schedule. No further questions."

Judge Whistler turned to the defense. "Any questions for the witness?"

Rosen shook his head. "Not at this time. However, I reserve the right to cross-examine Dr. Hartrey after we've heard the prosecution's next witness."

"Very well. Mr. Benton?"

"The state calls Stevie Jenkins."

Stevie stood, untangled his fingers from Grace's hand, and walked toward the witness stand. As he passed Dr. Hartrey, she squeezed his shoulder and whispered something to him. He took the oath a little too loudly and sat straight in the chair without touching the back rest. He looked so grown-up, and yet Grace couldn't help feeling he was a frightened little boy. She wanted to put her arms around him, but couldn't. Reaching into her purse, she gripped Stevie's turtle doll.

Walking to the witness stand, Benton rested one arm on the railing. "You're Stevie Jenkins, grandson of the defendant, Saul True Sky?"

"Uh-huh."

"How're you feeling this morning? Not nervous, I hope."

"I'm okay."

"You just heard Dr. Hartrey testify about how she's trying to help you. Would you say she was accurate about the problems you've been having?"

"I been pretty messed-up. I been fighting, screwing up in school, making my mom miserable."

"And now?"

Stevie shrugged. "Better, I guess. I'm not screwing up as much."

"Why do you think that is?"

"Talking to Dr. Hartrey helps. That and the stuff she gives me."

"The medication?"

"I take it three times a day—once in the morning, once at school, and before going to bed. It gets me kinda zonked sometimes, but otherwise it's okay."

Pursing his lips, Benton nodded. "By 'okay' you mean it doesn't affect your memory."

"Yeah."

"And you don't see or hear things that aren't there."

"You mean like the *heyoka?*"

"Excuse me?"

"The *heyoka*—people who see visions of the Thunder Beings, and then they do exactly the opposite of what they say. Like if now I was to tell you we're not really talking, or that you're a woman and not a man. Like that?" Stevie paused, and when the prosecutor scratched his head, added, "No. I don't see or hear what's not there."

"Good. That *heyoka* thing . . . you learn that from your grandfather?"

"Uh-huh."

Benton waited, maybe to see how Stevie would react to his grandfather being mentioned. Grace, feeling a deep longing at the sound of the Lakota word, remembering the funny stories her father used to tell about the *heyoka,* tightened her grip on the turtle doll. If Stevie felt the same way, he didn't show it. His face was like her father's when talking to a white man—smooth as a stone.

The prosecutor continued, "Let's talk about the night Albert Gates was murdered. All right?"

For a second, Grace watched the old Stevie bite his lower lip, while the boy's hands shuffled along his thighs.

"Would you like a glass of water?"

He shook his head defiantly. "What do you wanna know?"

Benton returned to his desk and skimmed a few pages in a file. "What time did you go to bed that night?"

"I went up to my room about ten o'clock, but I didn't go to sleep. Sometimes I didn't go to sleep for hours."

"Did anything unusual happen after you went upstairs?"

"The light."

"What light?"

"There was a light up on Grandfather's ridge. I saw it from my window. I knew Grandfather was up there crying for a dream. I knew he wouldn't be using any light."

"What did you do?"

Stevie closed his eyes a moment, as if once again seeing the light from his window. "I went out of the house and up to the ridge."

"About what time was that?"

"Ten-thirty or so, I guess. Just after my mom left for work."

"Did you carry a flashlight?"

"No need. I know my way around the ridge with my eyes closed, and there were enough stars out. Ever since I was a little boy, Grandfather and me . . . " He stopped suddenly, looking down at his hands.

"That's all right. Take your time."

Stevie spoke more softly. "You know that Stone Boy sent his mother and uncles into the sky to be stars for the Lakota?"

"Yes, yes," Benton said, trying to hide his impatience. "What happened when you went up to the ridge?"

"I walked up toward the light. It was by the bones of White Bear."

"Didn't your grandfather and Albert Gates argue over the remains that very afternoon?"

"Yes."

"Go on."

"I saw Mr. Gates's tool kit near White Bear. Then I heard something make a sound. At first I thought it was White Bear—it scared me real bad. But it was coming from the other direction, not far from Grandfather's vision pit. I walked toward the sound. It was Mr. Gates."

"So he wasn't dead."

Grace heard several people gasp, then mutter to one another.

Again Stevie shook his head hard. "He was lying stretched out not far from the pit, moaning real soft. I almost ran away but didn't. I walked around and knelt in front of him. The back of his head was all bloody, real bad."

"What did you do?"

"I thought maybe I should go for help, maybe call to Grandfather in his vision pit."

"Did you see anybody else? Hear anybody else on or near the ridge?"

"No. Anyways, I just kinda froze. My knees wouldn't let me stand. I think I called Mr. Gates's name. Maybe I did, because he sorta moved his head and looked up at me."

Closing his eyes, Stevie wiped his forehead with the back of his arm. Grace felt like taking him from the stand, taking him right home. If Dr. Hartrey hadn't said Stevie's testimony would help him get better . . .

"What happened next?" Benton asked more insistently. When Stevie hesitated, the prosecutor added, "We're almost finished, son."

"I'm not your son!" Lips trembling, he looked past Benton to Grace. She started to rise, but he shook his head. "All right. Gates looked up at me, his eyes real glassy like he wasn't seeing anything. Then . . . I think he knew who I was. He pushed out his fist, hit me with it, and . . . " Stevie's voice trailed off.

"What did he say? What did Albert Gates say?"

"He said, 'Saul T . . . ,' then he collapsed."

There was a moment of absolute silence, as if the court rested within the eye of a tornado. Then all hell broke loose. People shouting, reporters running up the aisle and out the door, and Judge Whistler banging his gavel again and again, like the blood pounding inside Grace's head.

Finally the courtroom grew quiet. Benton took a deep breath, then sighed, as if a burden had been lifted from him as well.

"One last question. I can understand why you waited so long to tell the truth—because of the horror that you saw, as well as your affection for your grandfather. Why did you come forward?"

Stevie looked at his shoes, not replying.

"Was it because of what Dr. Hartrey said earlier? It's important for you to tell the truth?"

He shrugged. "Yeah, I . . . had to tell the truth."

"You did the right thing. Thank you." Returning to his chair, Benton added, "Your Honor, I suggest a short recess before Mr. Rosen's cross-examination to let the boy collect himself."

"Of course. In fact, if defense counsel wishes, we'll adjourn until tomorrow to give him a chance to prepare questions for both Stevie Jenkins and Dr. Hartrey. Mr. Rosen?"

Grace was afraid to look at the defense table, afraid to look into her father's eyes. Glancing in that direction, she saw her father smiling at Stevie. Rosen leaned forward so still, so collected, he reminded Grace of a coyote catching the scent of its prey in the air.

"Mr. Rosen?" Judge Whistler repeated.

"I only have a few questions for the boy. Stevie, you feel up to answering a few more questions?"

He shrugged.

"Good. Now, I want you to remember as clearly as possible what happened up on the ridge with Albert Gates."

"I told you what happened. Can't I get outta here?"

"Very soon." Rosen walked to the witness stand and stood very close to Stevie. "Think about exactly how things happened. For instance, what did Albert Gates do when he saw you?"

"Told you, he hit me with his fist."

"Which way was his fist?"

"Huh?"

"Was it this way," Rosen jabbed with his right fist palm down, "or like this?" He jabbed with his left fist palm up.

"That way." Stevie pointed to Rosen's left fist.

"Which fist did he shove at you?"

Stevie thought for a second. "The same one, his left."

"You're sure?"

"Yes, sir."

Rosen looked at his fist slowly opening. "About what you thought you heard Gates say—"

"Objection!" Benton said.

"I'll rephrase my question. What did you hear Gates say?"

Stevie swallowed hard. "He said, 'Saul T . . . ,' then he collapsed."

"How soon after he finished speaking did he collapse?"

"I don't know."

"Think carefully. It's important."

"I don't . . . " Stevie shook his head. "Maybe a couple seconds, that's all."

"You're sure?"

"I must object again," Benton said, standing. "Mr. Rosen is badgering the boy about a rather trivial point."

Judge Whistler nodded. "I'm going to sustain the objection. Mr. Rosen, you'll kindly refrain . . . Counselor?"

Rosen was no longer looking at Stevie or the judge. Grace watched him scan the courtroom behind her. She saw her brother Will, Andi, Ike, Huggins, Belle, Tom, Pearl, Dr. Hartrey—was he looking for one of them?

"Sorry, Your Honor," Rosen said. Once again he seemed lost in thought. "Uh . . . I have no further questions for the witness today. I may continue my questioning tomorrow. If it please the court, I would like that recess you offered, to prepare my cross-examination."

"For both Stevie Jenkins and Dr. Hartrey?"

He hesitated, then replied, "I have no questions for Dr. Hartrey."

Judge Whistler frowned. "Indeed. Very well, court is adjourned until nine o'clock tomorrow morning."

Before the judge could gavel adjournment, Grace hurried toward her son. She passed Rosen, who walked just as quickly in the opposite direction. As Stevie stepped from the witness stand, she held him tightly and kissed his damp forehead.

"It's all right," she murmured. "It's all right."

Jack stood beside her, then Will and Dr. Hartrey. Grace's eyes blurred, and she dabbed them with a handkerchief.

Patting Stevie's shoulder, Dr. Hartrey said, "I know how difficult that was, but nobody should have to bear the burden you've had. What you did today is for the best."

The four of them walked from the witness stand. In a far corner of the room, Rosen was talking to Belle. He seemed excited, far more than when questioning Stevie. Belle nodded a few times, then they left the courtroom together. Grace was about to ask Jack what he thought of that, when suddenly she found her father standing before them.

He smiled at Stevie. "I don't like the medicine this doctor puts into you, but I'm glad you told the truth."

Stevie reddened, as he looked at his shoes.

"After all this is over, we'll throw that medicine away. You're old enough to cry for your own dream."

Pushing Stevie behind her, Grace glared at her father. "Isn't it bad enough what you've already done to him?"

His smile faded slowly. "Daughter, you don't know what you're saying."

"Get away—just get away from me!"

Her legs wobbled, and she leaned against Jack. As they walked away from her father, Grace heard him say, "*Ohan*—All right." Just as when he talked to the spirits.

Returning the handkerchief to her purse, she felt Stevie's turtle doll. Grabbing it, she felt the word form on her lips—"*Ohan*."

Chapter 16

TUESDAY NOON

Stamping the snow from her boots, Grace walked into the Bear Coat Motel, followed by her son and Dr. Hartrey. Greg Castor, the owner's son-in-law, nodded from behind the registration desk and reached for Dr. Hartrey's key.

"You can wait on that," Grace said. "We're gonna have lunch in the coffee shop."

Greg smiled at Dr. Hartrey, who wore a full-length mink coat, as well as a fur muff which covered her hands. Grace had never known anybody who owned a muff. It seemed not only of a different place but of a different time as well, like the elegant ladies her white grandfather might have visited in San Francisco.

Despite her warm coat, Dr. Hartrey was still shivering. "I could use a cup of hot coffee. It's too darn cold, even for January." As they walked through the lobby, she continued, "Thanks for showing me around town. The landscape is positively breathtaking. Nothing like it in the eastern part of the state."

Grace said, "We figured to let you rest for a few hours after lunch. Then Jack's taking us all into Deadwood for an early dinner."

"Fine. I should get back to the hotel by seven or so. I've several calls to make and some reports to write up."

Fancier than the Village Diner, the coffee shop displayed a series of historic maps and photographs along its sand-colored walls. Dark-brown booths lined three of the walls, and the counter, to their left, was gray slate cut from the Black Hills. The shop had always been special to Grace. As children, she and Will had swiveled recklessly on the counter stools while drinking milk shakes overflowing from their metal canisters. In high school she and Molly McGaffey, the owner's daughter, watched

175

the tourists with their cameras and crazy clothes, imagining going back with them to New York or Florida or anyplace far from quiet little Bear Coat.

But seeing the place as Dr. Hartrey probably did, Grace noticed the spider-cracks in the wall and the taped cushions that Mr. McGaffey never quite got around to replacing. He was getting old, like the motel and just about everything else in town.

The place was empty, except for an old man drinking coffee at the counter and Molly, like a plump chicken in her waitress uniform, chatting with her father behind the register. Grace walked straight ahead to the long wall with a view of the foothills, then slid into the middle booth. Stevie sat beside her, across from Dr. Hartrey.

Grace said, "You can hang your coat up over there . . . Well, maybe it is too expensive to just put anyplace."

Dr. Hartrey laughed that gentle laugh of hers. "I'm still a little cold. You didn't think this was real?" She pulled the tag from an inside coat pocket. "See, man-made. My friends would skin *me* alive, if I wore a real fur coat."

"Why?"

"Because of the needless cruelty. Why inflict pain on an animal unnecessarily just to flatter your ego, when an imitation fur is just as nice?"

Molly came over and took their order.

After she'd gone, Dr. Hartrey continued, "I suppose, with all the rifles and hunting, most people around here wouldn't agree."

Stevie sat very tall and still. "Grandfather says we're allowed to take the animal's fur, if we first ask permission and treat the animal with respect. That's how the Lakota were able to live, ever since White Buffalo-Calf Maiden brought the *chanunpa* to our people."

"*Chanunpa?*"

"Sacred pipe," Grace explained. She looked down at her hands for a moment, embarrassed that her son went on so, speaking what her father had taught him—had taught them both.

"I understand what you're saying," Dr. Hartrey said to Stevie. "I can even accept the reason your grandfather gives for killing animals."

"And me?" he asked.

"Yes, if you also believe."

Grace clicked her tongue. "It's no good setting the boy back on those ways. Not after what his grandfather did to him."

"You mean, your father."

"Same thing."

"Is it?" Dr. Hartrey put her hand over Grace's. "No one's all good or all bad. Your father may have killed Albert Gates for whatever reason, but that doesn't negate the goodness of his faith or how it can help Stevie."

"Help Stevie? How can you, a doctor, say all that mumbo jumbo is any good? It just confuses the boy."

"I think Stevie's quite clear in his attitude toward his grandfather's faith, and in my opinion it's done the boy good. People make the mistake of trying to find some *one* to believe in. That someone often turns out to have feet of clay, I suppose like your father. Better to believe in some *thing,* like the faith of your father. If you don't mind my saying so, Grace, you could use a little of that faith."

Grace didn't know what to say. Stevie was getting better. That's what was important, she kept telling herself, trying not to think of her father. Of how he looked at her in the courtroom, his face smooth as a stone, as if he were dealing with a stranger, a white woman. That didn't matter, she almost said aloud, squeezing her hot eyes shut. Stevie was who counted.

Blinking hard, she saw Nate Rosen walk into the coffee shop and take the second booth on his right, along the wall perpendicular to them. He laid his briefcase on the seat beside him, then gave his order to Molly. Grace felt her stomach tighten and grabbed Stevie's hand under the table, as she had held it before his testimony earlier that morning. So what if Rosen was here; after all, he was staying at the motel. He didn't seem to notice them, but how couldn't he?

A few minutes later, Molly brought their lunch.

"Your hamburgers look good," Dr. Hartrey said. "Of course, this is cattle country."

"How's your tuna salad?" Grace asked.

She raised an eyebrow. "I don't think they raised this on a tuna ranch. I don't eat meat—that wouldn't be too consistent with my opinion on fur coats, would it? Besides, I need to watch my cholesterol. I really should exercise more but never seem to find the time." She looked out the window. "Not that you have to worry about keeping fit, what with riding and hiking and all this clean, crisp air. I can see why Jack likes Bear Coat so much."

At the mention of Jack's name, Grace's eyes narrowed. Dr. Hartrey wore a wedding ring, and on the desk in her office was a family photo with her husband and son. Still, she was beautiful, and Grace had always wondered if there was anything between the woman and Jack. It wasn't something you'd talk about, especially in the woman's office, but this was Bear Coat. Somehow Grace felt that gave her more of a right to know.

"I didn't realize you and Jack were . . . friends."

Dr. Hartrey pushed aside the rest of her lunch. "We're not, really. He's just called the office regularly to see how Stevie was doing. Didn't you know?"

"No."

"Hmm. He cares very much about the boy. And you."

Grace glanced away, a little ashamed but relieved even more. She shouldn't doubt Jack; he'd done everything, been everything she could've wanted. Shaking her head, she promised herself: no more doubts.

"Stevie, how about some of Molly's mud pie? Think you can work through all that chocolate?"

Head cocked, her son was listening to something at the other end of the room. A sound soft and low. Dr. Hartrey turned, and both women followed the boy's gaze.

"What's Mr. Rosen trying to play?" Dr. Hartrey asked.

"A *siyotanka*," Stevie said.

Grace explained, "A Lakota courting flute, but where'd he get it? Of course . . . "

"Grandfather must've carved it. He's a brother to the elk. They gave him the power."

"What power?" Dr. Hartrey asked.

"The power to make a woman fall in love with you."

"Really? I wonder if Warren Beatty has one. No, I shouldn't be making fun of your grandfather's beliefs. I'm sorry."

The boy didn't seem to hear. He said, "That's not the way to play it," then slid from the booth and walked across the room toward Rosen.

"That man," Grace said, and was about to go after her son when Dr. Hartrey put a hand on her arm.

"You've got to stop feeling afraid for the boy. He's tougher than you think."

"It's just . . . " But she let Dr. Hartrey draw her back into her seat.

For a minute Stevie stood over Rosen, watching him try to play the *siy-*

otanka. After they exchanged a few words, the lawyer laid his briefcase on the floor, and Stevie sat down. Taking the courting flute, he tested the sounds. There was a pause, then the music came soft and sweet, so sweet. Closing her eyes, Grace remembered as a little girl lying in bed, while downstairs in the kitchen her father played the same wondrous music for her mother, until suddenly the music would stop and the house grow silent, except for the whispering between them that rippled up the stairs.

"May I join you?"

The music had stopped. Opening her eyes, Grace saw Stevie, fingering the *siyotanka,* beside her again. But it wasn't the boy who'd spoken. Holding a cup of tea, Rosen stood over her.

"Please," Dr. Hartrey said, scooting over. He sat beside her, and she continued, "We haven't been formally introduced. I'm Karen Hartrey."

"Happy to meet you. Excuse me." He signaled Molly. "More hot tea, please."

"I see you had your first music lesson."

"Yes. It's a present from Stevie's grandfather. I didn't realize how wonderful it could sound."

Dr. Hartrey sipped her second cup of coffee. "Grace tells me the instrument is a courting flute. You're a lucky man."

"I need all the luck I can get, especially with what happened in court this morning."

"I didn't mean to bring up—"

"I'm glad you did."

Grace set her jaw tight, not wanting to let the words begin, knowing how they'd taste of anger and fear. But Rosen stared at her; he wasn't going to let Stevie alone.

"What's the matter, Grace?"

Shaking her head, she finally said, "Why don't you leave the boy alone?"

"I'm not bothering him. As a matter of fact, we have many things in common. We're both interested in baseball, music, and other traditions. And we both like his grandfather very much."

"He told the truth in court this morning. Can't you leave him alone? What his grandfather did has nothing to do with the boy."

Dr. Hartrey nodded in agreement. "Stevie is telling the truth."

Rosen said, "Why don't we let the boy speak for himself?"

Stevie put the *siyotanka* to his lips and began playing. The music was no longer sweet, but low and mournful—something, Grace knew, that shouldn't be coming from a courting flute. No one spoke, even after he'd finished the melody.

Finally, Stevie lowered the flute. "That was a song for the dead, to help a restless spirit on its journey. Maybe it will help Mr. Gates's spirit." He looked across the table to Rosen. "I didn't lie. I told everybody what I heard Mr. Gates say. I wish he hadn't told me, but he did."

"There, you see?" Grace said. "Now will you leave us alone?"

Slowly, Rosen put his left hand on the table and rolled back the cuff to reveal a small scar. Grace shuddered. It looked so much like . . . No, it couldn't be.

"Remember this, Stevie?" Rosen asked.

The boy nodded. He spoke in the same detached way he'd been speaking ever since taking that medication. "I didn't mean it. I just got scared. I used to be scared all the time."

"That's all right. I think I understand." To Grace, "The night Andi and I brought Stevie home from Deadwood, he cut me."

She was too afraid to speak, but Dr. Hartrey said, "Stevie told me about the incident. He was very confused at the time. It was a blind reaction, as he said, based on fear. He was afraid you'd get him to tell the truth, because of what might happen to his grandfather."

Rosen nodded, then used the index finger of his right hand to lightly trace the scar. "When I was a boy, before morning services I used to wrap the tefillin, a leather strap, around my hand and arm. It had a leather box with passages of the Torah inside to keep one's thoughts on God." Again he traced the scar. "One of the straps went right there. I think the courting flute is something like that—it keeps your thoughts on God. It reminds you what it means to be an honorable man."

For a minute everyone stared at the scar on Rosen's wrist. Grace knew where he was going but didn't know how to stop him.

He said, "When the medical examiner looked at Gates's body, besides the blow to the back of the head, he found a cut on Gates's wrist. It had been bandaged but could've been made earlier that same day. Did you do that, Stevie? Did you cut Albert Gates with your knife?"

Stevie fingered the courting flute. "Uh-huh."

"Gates poked my father with one of his digging picks," Grace said. "Stevie was just protecting his grandfather. You said yourself how much the boy loves him."

"How close was Saul, when Stevie cut Gates?"

"He was right there. He stopped Stevie and took away his knife. It was self-defense. Anybody who'd seen it would've said the same thing."

"The wound bled?"

Grace furrowed her brow. "Bled? Yeah . . . sure."

"Could Gates's blood have gotten onto your father's sleeve?"

"I guess so."

Dr. Hartrey asked, "Are you suggesting that's how the victim's blood got onto Saul's sleeve?"

Rosen nodded.

Grace wasn't sure how to react. She wanted desperately to believe that her father was innocent, but not if that meant her son was guilty. Is that what Rosen was getting at?

Rosen leaned back and said to Stevie, "This place looks like it has a great soda fountain. Why don't you go over there and have something on me?"

"You want to talk to my mom about me in private. That's okay." Handing Rosen the *siyotanka,* he slid from the booth and walked to a stool at the far end of the counter.

Dr Hartrey asked, "Do you still have suspicions about the boy? Because in my professional opinion, he's telling the truth. Of course, experts who testify in court are often labeled as hired guns, so I doubt you'll take my word for it."

"On the contrary, I believe you. I admit that after court adjourned, I called Sioux Falls to check your credentials. They're very impressive. But I didn't need you to confirm his honesty." Rosen picked up the *siyotanka*. "I believe Stevie isn't the kind of person to lie—not about this or anything else. I like to think we're similar in that way, bound by the strength of our beliefs."

"Then why these questions?"

He shrugged. "I don't think he could lie, but I wasn't sure if he could kill somebody."

"That's crazy," Grace said. "You see how he is. He couldn't—"

"How he is wasn't the way he was last summer, before seeing a psychiatrist. Dr. Hartrey, can you honestly say that Stevie was incapable of the murder?"

She hesitated, searching for the right words. "I think he was in an extremely sensitive state and, if threatened, might have lashed out at his attacker." She shook her head. "But the way the attack on Gates was described . . . "

"Exactly. If Gates was struck on the back of the head, how could he be physically threatening his assailant? No, Stevie isn't the murderer."

Grace relaxed against the cushion. The words came out without her thinking. "Thank God."

Dr. Hartrey asked, "Then why all these questions about the blood? If you believe Stevie, doesn't that make his grandfather the murderer?"

Rosen turned the *siyotanka* in his hands, as if the answer were written somewhere on the instrument. "I'm sure you know, doctor, there are usually several ways of seeing something."

"Like a Rorschach test?"

"Sure, or the *chanunpa*—the sacred pipe Stevie and I smoked in Saul's sweat lodge. To most people the pipe bowl is just an old piece of red stone. But to the Lakota it's something quite different, isn't it, Grace?"

She nodded, remembering what she'd so often been told by her father. "It's the blood of the buffalo that gave their lives, so our people could exist. It seeped into the ground and turned to stone. For our people, it's the blood of life."

"The blood of life." He paused for a moment, deep in thought, then slowly stood, one arm cradling the *siyotanka*. He laid a twenty-dollar bill on the table. "Lunch is on me, ladies, as is the dessert Stevie seems to be enjoying. You've helped me not only to understand the boy but perhaps to clear Saul, as well."

"Saul?" Grace repeated. "My father?"

Before she could ask him more, Rosen had picked up his briefcase from the other table and left the coffee shop. She looked at Dr. Hartrey.

The other woman shrugged. "I understand as little as you what he meant. But it sounds like good news, doesn't it?"

"I . . . suppose so. Yes."

Dr. Hartrey patted Grace's hand and flashed one of her warmest smiles. "Well then, to hell with the cholesterol. Let's have a piece of that delicious mud pie you were talking about."

Chapter 17

Rosen spent the next few hours in his motel room. Andi promised him the use of her car later in the afternoon. Just as well; he needed time to think things through. He was almost certain what really happened to Albert Gates. Almost.

Lying back in bed, he blew gently into the courting flute while drifting in and out of sleep. As in an absurdist play, the people of Bear Coat passed through his mind. Saul and Ike sitting naked in the sweat lodge, while Judge Whistler rapped his gavel from inside the circular pit of heated stones. The stones glowing the same color as Pearl Whistler's hair and giving off an aroma far stronger than cedar. Grace galloping her horse through a Tin Town bustling as it had a hundred years before. Will, Huggins, Cantrell, and Tom Cross Dog walking from the tin mine with a hundred other workers directly into a gambling casino, where Saul's sweat lodge stood in the middle of the floor. Will's hand opening to reveal a single nugget of gold. Instead of a band playing, the sweet, sad music of the courting flute filling the room. Stevie, standing on a balcony above them all, playing the *siyotanka*.

The boy had the same look as when he'd played the flute in the restaurant. Trying to hide his emotions, Stevie didn't realize the music made more obvious the pain he felt for his grandfather. The pain and the love, and suddenly Rosen remembered seeing that same look on his own daughter's face as, soon after his divorce, she sat at the piano. He should've taken the boy aside at lunch, but now that would have to wait. No, he couldn't see Stevie, but at least he could talk to Sarah.

It was four o'clock. He liked calling her that time of day, five p.m. Chicago time, because usually she was home and Bess wasn't. Sure enough, Sarah answered the phone.

183

"Nothing special," Rosen said, "I just wanted to hear the sound of your voice."

She laughed. "You must've had a bad day in court."

"Don't be a wise guy. So what's new?"

"Not much," she replied, then proceeded to recount a dozen events in her life, in such random order it was hard keeping up. That didn't matter; he enjoyed simply listening to her enthusiasm—how much she relished life. That's all he really wanted, for her to be happy.

" . . . and Shelly's opened up another office. That's his fifth or sixth, I think."

"You mean he has a chain of podiatrist offices?"

"Yeah, he's even got commercials on TV. They're kind of stupid, but funny too. One starts out with this baby counting its toes, and a voice says, 'If you can't count on your feet, what can you count on?' You know, he works on some of the Cubs' feet—Mark Grace, I think."

"I'm impressed."

"I asked Shelly to get you an autographed baseball. He's taking Mom and me out Saturday night to celebrate the grand opening. We're going to this neat restaurant with a huge salad bar. Wish you could come."

"Me too," he replied, without thinking.

"You mean you'd really come, even with Shelly there?"

He was surprised how easy the words came. "Sure, if that would please you. Unfortunately, I'm tied up with this murder case. When it's over, maybe we could arrange something."

"Daddy, I—" She stopped suddenly; someone behind her was chattering insistently.

"Who's that?" he asked.

"Mrs. Chang, my piano teacher. She wants me to get back to my lesson. 'You no break your concentration—very bad!' " She giggled.

"I didn't know you had a lesson. Go ahead, but do me a favor. Leave the phone off the hook for a few minutes. I don't get much of a chance to hear you play."

Lying back in bed, the receiver cradled to his ear, Rosen listened to his daughter playing Chopin and pictured her brow furrowed in concentration as her fingers danced across the keyboard. Again his mind wandered, and he heard Stevie's flute, the music's sweet sadness reflected in the boy's face.

Someone was knocking. Rosen hung up the receiver and returned the flute to his briefcase. Opening the door, he let Andi inside.

"Whew, it's cold!" she said, pushing back her hood and unzipping her jacket. Removing her gloves, she gripped her purse with both hands.

"Thanks for lending me your car. I've got to run an errand. I'll just get my coat and . . . "

"Wait a minute, Nate. Can I talk to you for a couple minutes?"

"Sure."

Andi sat on the end of the bed, her legs pressed tightly together. Still clutching her purse, she looked older and pale and made him feel sad. She started to speak, then looked down at her lap.

Rosen leaned back against the headboard and waited. He'd never known her to be at a loss for words. Maybe she was upset about Stevie's testimony against his grandfather, which seemed to guarantee a guilty verdict, but he sensed this was more personal.

"Nate, we didn't get much chance to talk after court adjourned today." She took a cigarette from her purse.

"If you're upset about the way Saul's case is going, I think it's too early to give up . . . "

"I'm not giving up on Saul." She lit the cigarette and inhaled deeply.

"What is it?"

She shrugged, but he waited, knowing she couldn't stand the silence.

"You . . . you know that the True Skys and I are pretty close. Didn't I tell you once that Grace is sort of an older sister to me?"

"Yes."

"I hate to . . . well, I feel like a traitor."

"Are you telling me you know something that will hurt Saul's case?"

"No." She shook her head violently. "God, no. It's just . . . I'm gonna have to leave town before the trial's over."

"Leave town?"

"Uh-huh. This weekend."

"Why?"

After stubbing out the cigarette in the empty metal trash basket, she withdrew a folded sheet of paper from her purse. "This was faxed to me this morning. It's a job offer, Nate. I'm finally gonna . . . I just can't believe it . . . I'm finally gonna leave this town."

She almost ran out of breath before finishing the sentence, and her knuckles were white clutching the paper.

"Really? What city?"

Her smile grew larger. "Chicago. Isn't it cool—that's where you're from. See, I talked to the editor last week, but there was nothing definite. That's why I didn't tell you Sunday. But then our story on Cantrell's mob connections, and my photos, were picked up by the wire services. I got a definite offer this morning."

"Which paper is it, the *Tribune* or *Sun Times?*"

"Uh, neither. It's a smaller paper, not quite the same circulation as the ones you mentioned."

"Which one?"

"You see, they liked my photographs and all, but they also wanted me because I'm a minority."

"You mean, being a woman?"

"Not exactly. Here."

She handed Rosen the letter, which he slowly unfolded. He read it twice.

"You're going to work for the *Polski Dziennik Glos?*"

"Yeah. It means *Polish Daily Voice.*"

"But the paper's printed in Polish."

"So?" She stuck out her jaw, as if daring him to take a swing. The color had returned to her cheeks.

"You don't know how to speak Polish."

"*Idz do diabla!*"

"Excuse me."

"It means 'go to hell.'" Andi took a small book from her purse. Thumbing through the pages, she added, "*Idz precz.* That means 'get lost.' The language ain't so tough. Besides, you don't have to speak Polish to take pictures. Did you know that there are almost as many Polish people in Chicago as there are in Warsaw? Why the hell is the mayor Irish?"

"So they took you because your name's Wojecki."

"No. They took me because my name's Wojecki and I'm a damn good photographer."

"Right. Sorry."

"Forget it." Kicking off her boots, she drew her long legs into a lotus position. "I'm just a little touchy. I feel bad about leaving Saul and Grace, and I'm a little scared about going to Chicago. I mean, I talked to Jack and he's all for me going—you know, he's selling the paper. And I've rented my house to this newlywed couple; I told you about that last Sunday. I'm just taking a few things with me—camera equipment, my portfolio, and some clothes. When I called the editor to accept the job, he told me I could move in with one of their reporters. She's looking for a roommate. He said she's got the best *kolackies* in the world. That's not what I think it is, is it?"

"It's a pastry. Looks like you've got everything covered. You're a lot more organized than you let on."

"I can take photography classes at the Art Institute. I hear there're lots of galleries downtown . . . the Loop. That's what they call downtown, right?"

He nodded.

"I really need to learn more about Chicago—and not just Polish. You do get in there now and then?"

"A couple times a year, to see my daughter."

"When you're in town, maybe you could . . . I don't mean that we have to . . . " Biting her lip, she looked down at the bed.

This time Rosen didn't wait for her to continue. "I know what you mean. I know what this is all about. Just like I know what Sunday night was all about."

Her cheeks reddened, but she didn't say anything. Didn't move.

"You want me to absolve you for leaving Grace and her family in their hour of need. Okay, I absolve you. Go to Chicago and be a success. It's just the way of the world. Besides, you got your story, your ticket out of here. That's what this was all about from the start, what we were all about."

He forced her chin up, so that she looked him in the eyes.

"Don't, Nate."

"That's why you called my boss, Nahagian, in the first place. To get Saul's case national publicity and your photos to the wire services. That's why you were so nice to me from the start. You couldn't wait to tell me how 'kinda cute' I was. Don't ever flatter a lawyer. He knows right away you're lying. You were using me to get a story."

"Don't."

"And that's what Sunday night was all about. You got your story and your ticket to Chicago. Our interlude on the living room floor . . . a little thank-you for my help."

She swallowed hard. "You make it sound so cold."

"Tell me, can you achieve orgasm with a man or just with your Hasselblad?"

Her eyes widened, as if she'd been slapped, and tears ran down her cheeks. But for the first time since he'd known her, Andi didn't say a thing.

He stared into her eyes, big and hurt like a child's—like Sarah's that first time he mentioned the divorce. Did his own eyes show the same look of pain when, as a boy, he was sent away by his father? No, damn it, he wasn't his father! Given the chance to forgive, when could Rosen not forgive? Besides, this wasn't doing either of them any good.

He gave her his handkerchief. "Look, Andi, I'm sorry. I've got no right to judge, to say such terrible things to you."

She shook her head. "You're right. Everything you said about me is—"

"No, let me finish. I knew what Sunday night was all about, but I let it happen anyway. Maybe it was a way for me to get back at my ex-wife, to justify in my own mind the Jewish divorce we never had. She made love to her new husband, so I made love to you. I'm not sure, except that it was wrong . . . I was wrong. You know, you remind me a little of Bess."

Hands shaking, she lit a cigarette. "Gee, thanks."

"Take it as a compliment. Both you and Bess are ambitious. When you want something, nobody stands in your way, especially me. You two should start a 'Skate Over Nate' club."

"You're just trying to cheer me up."

He looked at her hard, then suddenly began laughing.

"What's so funny?"

"You and me, and trying to change the way of the world. I was just being a little sensitive—that's an oxymoron for a lawyer. Go to Chicago, and knock 'em dead."

She dabbed her eyes dry. "You're not mad?"

"No, I'm not mad. In fact, next time I'm in town, we'll go to dinner, take a long walk along the lake, see the Cubs."

"You know, Nate, you really are a nice guy."

"Sure. Give me your car keys. I'll drop you home. Just promise me one thing," he said, opening the door.

"What's that?"

"You won't marry a podiatrist."

Chapter 18

It was nearly five o'clock. After dropping Andi at her house, Rosen drove back up to Main Street. He pulled into the corner gas station and hurried inside to ask directions.

"Good thing you're going up the hill now," the attendant said. A few snowflakes, shaped like tiny needles, struck the window behind him. "Big storm coming tonight—make it tough getting up there later." Shaking his head, he pointed to the thermometer just outside the door. "Eight below, not counting the wind. Folks used to say it couldn't snow when it got this cold. I think it's got something to do with all those trees they're cutting down in the Amazon."

Rosen's headlights bullied their way through the thickening snowfall as he drove on a road that corkscrewed up one of the hills behind town. There were no other cars out, just the noises of the old Mercury—the heater's wheezing and broken muffler's rumbling like a sick man gasping for air. What if the car broke down? Gripping the steering wheel, he stared through the windshield wipers. The way the road curved, and the sheet of snow on the pavement, would make it easy to slide onto the shoulder and off into the fields.

The homes grew larger as Rosen reached the hilltop. "Can't miss it," the attendant had said, and he was right. Alone at the end of a cul-de-sac, the house was a two-story brick with four colonnades and an attached garage. It was actually dug into the earth so that the second floor, rising above the hill, looked like its crest. The view from the back yard must have been magnificent.

There were no cars in the driveway, but they'd be kept in the garage on a day like this. Light from both floors glinted through the falling snow. Rosen had counted on someone being home for dinner. He parked along the curb a few feet from the driveway. Staring up at the great house topping the hill, he thought again of his old rabbi's warning against *bamot*—the unholy high places where Baal and other false gods were worshiped. He had already participated in the *inipi* ceremony on Saul True Sky's ridge, which somehow hadn't seemed a betrayal to his faith. But this house on the hill . . .

The snow swirled around his feet as Rosen skittered up the driveway to the front door. He rang the bell and rubbed his arms impatiently, until the door slowly swung open.

Judge Whistler wore a silver smoking jacket and held a drink in one hand. "Yes?" Rosen pushed back the hood of his parka. "What are you doing here?"

"I'd like to see you."

"You know it's improper for us to meet. I'm trying your client's case."

"I knew you'd say that. That's why I didn't call first."

"What's this all about?"

"I think you know. May I come in? It's really cold."

Rosen half-hoped he was wrong, and that the judge would send him away. Whistler hesitated, then nodded, letting him inside. They stood on a black slate floor in an ivory-colored hallway.

"Give me your parka," the judge said. He put it into a long closet filled with fur coats.

A large oil painting hung on the wall across from the closet. It was a portrait of some turn-of-the-century gentleman whom Whistler very much resembled, although the man in the painting was stouter and more self-assured.

"Your grandfather?" Rosen asked.

"Yes. He was a member of the state supreme court. I'm named for him."

"Quite a resemblance."

The judge stared wistfully at the painting. "No, not really."

Whistler led him through the foyer and up six steps to the second floor. The room ran the entire length of the house, the far wall made completely of glass. Outside, in the darkness, snowflakes scratched like small animals against the glass.

On their left stood a wet bar stocked with rows of liquor bottles. Past the bar stretched a long dining room table and twelve chairs; against the wall a cabinet and corner hutch were filled with fine china. All the furniture looked handcrafted from heavy, dark wood, as old and substantial as Judge Whistler's grandfather.

Across a polished wooden floor of tongue and groove, time leapt a hundred years. A contemporary couch and chairs of black leather, their edges mushrooming over the sides, were arranged around a glass-topped coffee table with granite base, all resting on a carpet of gray and white swirls. The couch faced a large fireplace, with built-in bookshelves along either side of the wall.

Directly above the mantelpiece hung an oil painting of the same dimensions as the one in the foyer. Pearl Whistler smiled down upon the room, her red hair lustrous as her lips, and the black evening dress showing the swell of her breasts. Even without the fireplace, her smile would have heated the room.

Whistler poured them both a drink. "My favorite sherry."

Rosen sat on the couch and took the glass from Whistler, who sat on the chair to his right. They sipped their drinks in silence, as old friends or strangers did. Since they'd first met at the preliminary hearing the previous summer, Rosen had liked Whistler for his dignity and common decency. But all along he'd been afraid it might come to this.

Nodding at Pearl's portrait, Rosen said, "She's a very beautiful woman."

The judge shook his head. "She's more than that. I like to think of her in an Aristotelian sense, as the ideal of beauty itself. You think I'm waxing romantic? That portrait was painted five years ago, when we were first married, and she hasn't aged a day—you've seen her. She doesn't drink or smoke, works out every day. Remember Oscar Wilde's story of Dorian Gray, about the portrait that aged while the man didn't?"

"As I recall, the portrait aged to show all the evil that the man had done."

"And what does that portrait up there tell you? Certainly not any evil on my wife's part?"

"Perhaps the evil men do because of her."

Whistler stared into his drink. "Are you married?"

"I'm divorced."

"Why did you and your wife . . . No, I'm sorry. That's not any of my business. Besides, we're not here about your wife."

"That's all right. I guess 'irreconcilable differences' is as good a term as any."

Leaning back in his chair, Whistler looked at Rosen. "Yes, it is—covers any number of sins of commission and omission. When I was an attorney, I refused to handle divorce cases. Didn't believe in divorce, not really because of religious reasons or even particularly moral ones. I suppose because marriage was a contract and, like any other legal document, you honored it. Later, I had to listen to my share of divorces in court. They sickened me—people airing their failures in public like so much dirty linen. I was the perfect man of virtue, like my grandfather. Another drink?"

Without waiting for Rosen to reply, Whistler took both glasses to the bar. "You know, my grandfather's portrait used to hang above the fireplace. Taking it down was one of my great acts of rebellion. I like to think of it as my guillotining King Louis or shooting the czar. Here." He handed Rosen the drink and returned to his chair. "Did you love your wife—I mean really love her, truly and passionately?"

"Yes . . . once."

"Then you were lucky. Even with the divorce, all the dirt and pain, you were lucky to have been in love. Most people never feel the heat of that kind of love. I didn't for the longest time, practically my entire life. I married a woman whose family knew my family—same club, same church, same handicap on the golf course. I accepted her, and why not? One was just as good as another, like rows of cereal boxes on the grocery shelf. We have two boys, grown-up now, of course. Do you understand what I'm saying?"

Rosen felt a queasiness in his stomach. "I understand."

"I read a poem once in school, by Wilfred Owen. It was about a soldier watching his friend die of poison gas. He says something like, 'In all my dreams, I see him guttering, choking, drowning.' Exactly the way I was with my first wife. For God's sake, we made love with the sheets tucked under the mattress." The air shuddered into his lungs. "I was guttering."

"And then you met Pearl."

He smiled. "Funny how paths cross and crisscross and sometimes you never know. Pearl actually baby-sat for us when she was a teenager; she's five years older than my eldest boy. Pretty thing. One night, I remember her coming over in her cheerleader's outfit—short skirt, tight sweater, and that beautiful red hair tied in a ponytail. I teased her about something or other, and she blushed. You know how something a woman does, the most casual of things, can stay with you the rest of your life?"

Rosen remembered the way Bess would play absently with a curl of her long black hair. Damn it! He clanked his drink upon the glass top of the coffee table.

Whistler didn't seem to notice. He was gazing at his wife's portrait. "Ten years went by, and I saw her at a party given by Belle and Albert Gates. I reminded her how she once baby-sat for us, and she blushed again. At that moment, I knew I had to have her."

"So you divorced your wife."

"Not just then. It was about a year. I started seeing Pearl. We'd have dinner, go for drives, even spent a weekend together in Denver. We never . . . I didn't commit adultery. I owed Eleanor that much. The boys were grown and had already moved away. Considering Eleanor had her own inheritance, my settlement was quite generous." He snickered. "I suppose it was conscience money on my part, but she took it quick enough. She's out East now, near the boys and their families. I don't see much of them." Again he looked at the portrait. "Not that I really mind. You know, I'm the only one in my family ever to have divorced, and probably the only one ever to marry for love. What do you think of that?"

The question could have been rhetorical, but from the way Whistler turned his head, Rosen knew the other man was waiting for an answer.

Rosen cleared his throat. "I think you want me to play judge."

Whistler began to reply but stopped suddenly, as he looked past Rosen to the stairs. Pearl stood just inside the room. She wore a tight black leotard and was dabbing her neck with a towel. Her hair, pulled back into a ponytail, sharpened her features, like a statue of the goddess Whistler imagined her to be.

"Finish your workout?" the judge asked. "Come in, my dear, we were just talking about you."

Had she been listening to their conversation? Pearl continued to pat her face, her gaze darting between the two men. Finally she dropped the towel onto the carpet, walked to the bar and poured a glass of Perrier. Joining the two men, she sat in a chair across from her husband, on the other side of Rosen. He smelled something in the air—her perfume, mixed with the sweat of her workout. That fragrance . . . familiar . . . of course. Of course.

Droplets of water beaded Pearl's upper lip—the Perrier, or was she nervous? "Mr. Rosen shouldn't be here. I mean, he's arguing a case before you. Isn't this some kind of legal impropriety?"

"Perhaps, but isn't it nice to have company to share this wonderful fireplace. We don't have too many mutual friends, Mr. Rosen. The age difference and such. Besides, dear, we're not discussing the case. We're talking about you. Mr. Rosen admires your portrait nearly as much as I."

"I still think it was wrong to let him come."

Rosen said, "You're very careful about appearances."

"Of course. Cal's a judge."

"No, I mean yours."

"I don't know what you're talking—"

"The judge and I were talking about love." The sickness Rosen had felt in his stomach returned. He wanted to get it over with, and sensed Whistler felt the same way. "Pearl, do you love your husband?"

She took a long drink of Perrier, her eyes peering over the glass. "Of course I do. Such a question."

"Have you been unfaithful to him?"

"How dare you. Cal, are you going to—"

"Suppose I were to tell you that—"

"You don't have any proof!"

Both her hands gripped the glass. She looked at her husband, but he was staring at her portrait.

Rosen said, "That's not the response of an innocent woman, is it?" Then he thought of a passage from the great sage Maimonides. "If people see a spice-peddler leave a woman, then they go inside and see her rising from the couch, tying her belt, and find moist saliva above the canopy, it is enough for a husband to dismiss her for harlotry."

"What the hell are you talking about?"

"Last summer, the day I arrived in Bear Coat, Andi took me to see Tin Town. We walked through the deserted houses, and in one of them I found a duffel bag. There was a bedroll inside, and a smell . . . a smell that's been bothering me all these months. Once or twice afterward I thought I smelled something like it—I even asked Jack Keeshin, thinking it was his cologne. But it wasn't. You'd passed by. It was your perfume mixed with something else. What I just smelled a minute ago—perfume mixed with the sweat of your workout. Only on the bedroll, it was the sweat of your lovemaking."

"I think you'd better leave."

"Bad enough that you committed adultery with Will True Sky. What was worse, you had your husband lie for him."

With great deliberation, Pearl put her glass upon the coffee table. "I said, you'd better leave. Cal, would you see Mr. Rosen out?"

Her husband's gaze remained fixed on her portrait.

From his shirt pocket, Rosen took the old iron nail Ike had given him and placed it on the table beside Pearl's glass. "It had to be Will. After Stevie Jenkins's testimony in court, I knew Saul was innocent, just as I knew Will was lying—that he killed Albert Gates."

"You're crazy. In court today, Stevie said that Gates named Saul as his killer."

"That's what the boy and, I suppose, most everyone else thinks, but it's not true. Gates was right-handed—I asked his wife—but he thrust his left hand at Stevie. You know what was in that hand—the rusted remains of a nail that once was like this one."

"So?"

"That's the evidence Will took from the police station, and why he knocked out Andi and stole her photos of the same object."

"Why would he do that? You're not making any sense."

"What would make Albert Gates angry enough to call the cops on Will?" Rosen asked. "Not arguing over $500 for a dead Indian's medicine bag. Besides, Gates had only given Will $50. According to his wife, the only thing that really angered Gates was being taken. That's what Gates discovered when he and Will returned that night to collect the *wotawe*."

Pearl was no longer protesting. She sat very quietly, like a defendant waiting to hear the judge pass sentence. Exactly the way her husband was sitting.

Rosen continued, "I examined the Indian remains a few days after the murder. Digging under the bones, I came up with what was left of an iron nail, exactly like what Gates held in his hand, what he must've found when he dug under the body. I also found the tip of one of his picks there. *Under* the body. You do understand."

She shook her head, more a shiver than a denial.

"The last Indians to roam the countryside died at Wounded Knee in 1890. The man who forged those iron nails didn't come to the ridge until 1910. How could those iron nails have gotten under the remains? It's a physical impossibility. But of course there was a way. Will put the skeleton there. The day of Belle's horse show, I went with Will and Stevie into the field. I tripped over some soft earth near a fence that Will was supposed to have fixed. That's where White Bear came from. Will saw the remains and the *wotawe* and figured that Gates would pay good money for it, but only, of course, if it wasn't on his own land. So Will dug up the bones, put them in his pickup, and reburied them on the ridge. I wonder how Gates felt when he brought up the nail from under the bones and realized that he'd been tricked."

Pearl stared at him. "How'd you know? How the hell'd you know?"

"People hear what they want to hear. People thought Gates said, 'Saul T . . . ,' then collapsed. But if you listen carefully to Stevie's testimony, Gates paused after he said the word. It was one word, one complete idea. 'Salty.' "

"Salty," she repeated with a laugh that caught in her throat.

"Just like Belle's grandfather Salty Gardner, who salted a stream with gold nuggets and sold it to Gates's grandfather. Belle told me how her husband never forgot that story. He said it was the last time anyone in his family was ever swindled. That's why he was so angry at Will. Wasn't he, Pearl?"

She picked up her drink, taking the time to think if it was worth lying. Then she shrugged. "He didn't mean to kill Gates. It's just that Albert got so crazy. He was threatening Will with prison—Will'd been in trouble with the law before. I guess you knew that. You seem to know everything."

"Not everything. Not how you got your husband to cover for him. Don't tell me you're in love with Will."

This time the laugh came hard and brittle. "In love with that breed?"

"You slept with him."

"We were using each other, that's all. He got to bed down the red-headed cheerleader of his high school dreams."

"And you?"

"We got . . . were going to get something much more important. That's right, *we,* Cal and me. After his divorce, between his ex-wife and their kids, Cal didn't get much more than this house."

"I'm sure he personally hunted down those minks hanging in your closet."

"Cal likes giving me presents, and I've got just as much right to live a decent life as anybody else. Certainly as much as Eleanor."

"It had something to do with bringing gambling into Tin Town, didn't it?"

She nodded. "Cal and I used all he had left buying up property here in town. It's almost worthless now, but wait till the poker chips start tumbling."

"Will promised to change his father's mind."

"Uh-huh. Even if he didn't, no way Saul's preventing us from getting Tin Town. I don't care what that fool O'Hara did at the condemnation hearing. His decision will be reversed. Nobody's going to let that old Indian stop progress. If something did happen to the old man, Will and Grace would own the land. Will promised me a share of the settlement, if I persuaded the town council to up its ante for the land."

"So you'd make money both ways."

Pearl smiled, crossing her legs and leaning back in the chair. "When Will called me the night he killed Gates, half out of his mind, I knew there'd be even more. All Cal had to do was give him an alibi. Nobody'd dare challenge Cal—even you didn't."

"No, I didn't." He looked at Whistler and shook his head. He didn't care about Pearl, but the judge . . . the judge was the law, and when he was corrupted, it cheapened what Rosen most believed in.

Pearl said, "You don't think . . . No, you don't understand about Cal. He'd never take part in a murder cover-up, even for me. After Will called, I told Cal about our affair. I made up some story about our having been together the whole evening and how I'd have to admit it to show that Will couldn't've killed Gates. Cal was real understanding—said he'd provide Will with an alibi. But he thought it was just our affair he was hiding."

As if waking from a deep sleep, Whistler looked from the portrait to his wife.

Rosen asked Pearl, "You'll testify that Will admitted murdering Gates?"

"I suppose so . . . I won't have to go to jail? I couldn't stand it."

Whistler said, "I couldn't stand it either."

Rosen shook his head in disgust. "I wouldn't worry, Pearl. I'm sure the district attorney will grant you immunity for helping him fry Will. I can just see you on the witness stand crying into your hankie and blushing—we men find that so endearing. Which lie are you going to use, that Will threatened you, or that you were blinded by your love for him?"

"Stop it," Whistler said.

"Then there'll be the story in *People* magazine and talk shows like 'Geraldo'—'older men who share their wives with murderers.' And the sleeze reporters hanging . . . "

"I said, stop it!" Whistler threw his glass into the fireplace. His jaw muscles tightened, then slowly relaxed. "We did that on our wedding night—threw our champagne glasses into the fire. Remember, Pearl?"

Her face was bone-white. "Yes, Cal, I remember."

He stood and walked past them to the end of the bookshelf. There was a small cabinet, waist-high, which the judge unlocked. He turned to face them with a pistol in his hand.

"I can't lose you. I've given up too much already."

"No, Cal! You're not going to . . . kill me?"

"Shut up," Rosen said. "Don't you understand?" To Whistler, "You haven't broken any law. That alibi for Will wasn't made under oath. Both you and Pearl are safe."

The judge shook his head. "Once this comes out, I'll have to step down from the bench. I haven't much money, and without my position, what do I have to offer a woman like her? How long before another Will True Sky, only this time she'll go with him." He looked up to her portrait. "Too bad such creatures are made of flesh and blood."

Whistler took a few steps back, then turned and walked to the end of the room. Opening the sliding glass door, he stepped into the darkness. The door remained ajar; snowflakes drifted into the room, glistening for an instant before melting on the wooden floor.

Rosen grabbed Pearl. He pulled her halfway across the room while she struggled against him.

"N . . . no, for God's sake, he's got a gun!"

When her nails raked his cheek, Rosen stopped and slapped her hard across the face.

Her eyes popped wide in surprise. "You can't . . . "

He shook her hard. "Don't you understand? Your husband's going to kill himself, because he doesn't think you'll stand by him. Never mind that he's right, you're going to convince him to put down the gun."

"But . . . "

"But nothing." Twisting her arm, he dragged her the rest of the way and pushed her through the doorway. She stumbled onto a wooden deck.

"Cal!"

Rosen blinked away snowflakes sharp as pinpricks in the frigid air. He watched Pearl struggle to her feet, then slip again, when suddenly a hand steadied her. Whistler stepped beside her. In his other hand the gun pointed, like an accusing finger, against his temple. Arms around his neck, she whispered frantically in his ear, while he watched her with the same gentle look he'd viewed her portrait with.

The gun moved slightly. Rosen was about to lunge for it, when Whistler slowly lowered the weapon.

Whistler kissed his wife on the forehead. "Go inside, you'll catch your death of cold. And you'd better change. We'll be expecting more company. Tom Cross Dog, I imagine."

Her lips moving, as if rehearsing what to tell the police, Pearl hurried inside.

Rosen took the gun from the judge. It felt warm in his hand, and he clutched it tightly, needing that warmth to stop him from trembling.

Whistler said, "I couldn't do it."

"I'm glad you changed your mind."

"I mean, not now, not in front of Pearl. Think what that might do to her."

Chapter 19

TUESDAY EVENING

Cross Dog's Blazer lumbered through the swirling snow on the road leading from Bear Coat. The town seemed deserted, except for the few cars huddling like puppies near the tired lights of a tavern. Occasionally the tires slid on a patch of ice, but the policeman didn't slow down. Rosen gripped the briefcase on his knees as if it were a second seat belt.

"Are you sure he's home?"

Cross Dog nodded. "I called the house from Judge Whistler's, and Will answered. I pretended to be calling for Grace." After a moment, he added, "She's out with that lady psychiatrist and . . . Keeshin. Just as well. I don't want her seeing any of this."

"It'll be rough on her, just the same. Her father's accused of murder, all along she half-suspects her son committed the crime, and now it turns out that her brother's guilty. Poor woman."

The policeman looked hard at the road. "Can't be helped. Besides, she got a shoulder to cry on now, don't she? One covered with a nice silk shirt."

Cross Dog wasn't the type to accept a kind word easily, but he needed one now.

Rosen said, "That was decent of you—leaving a patrolman at the Whistlers, instead of taking Pearl in."

"She ain't going anywhere in this weather. Tomorrow I'll take her over to the D.A. and let him decide what to do with her." He glanced at Rosen. "You really think the judge'd kill himself if he was left alone?"

"If you'd seen his face there in the darkness . . . Yes, I think he would have."

Cross Dog grimaced, then fell into his usual silence. Was he thinking about Judge Whistler's attachment to Pearl, or his own feelings toward

Grace? The great cold void that surrounded Whistler on his deck was the same that surrounded the policeman now, deepening both men's loneliness and leading to forbidden thoughts.

Within this same dark void, Rosen remembered his own loss the moment Bess told him she wanted a divorce. An unbearably hot August day, the sun so intense it might have been the light of God himself. He nodded at her words, grimacing in silence, as Cross Dog had just done, then walked to the window, rubbing his eyes against the radiant light. His anger had sustained him through the day. Only in the darkness of that night, sleeping alone in the third bedroom, did he feel the emptiness and the whispers that questioned his own existence.

Rosen stared into the black night. "Some say that evil is only the absence of God's light."

At first Cross Dog didn't reply. A minute later, he half-whispered, "I let her get away."

That was all, but it was enough. A simple confidence made the two men no longer strangers and, on this coldest of nights, sent a rush of warmth through Rosen's body.

It had stopped snowing by the time they left the last building on the edge of town. Another vehicle, four-wheel-drive like theirs, passed them on its way into Bear Coat, and once again they were alone. Their headlights revealed a smooth, white sheet, like a freshly made bed, with only a slight rumple from the other vehicle's tires. Clicking off the wipers, Cross Dog depressed the accelerator.

Rosen asked, "Aren't you going a little fast?"

"I want to get there before she does."

Rosen felt the land slowly rise long before he saw the ridge. A handful of stars shone dimly, reflecting off the snow into the gray sky. He looked for the moon, which hid behind a black cloud shaped like the head of an animal. He remembered the buffalo-skull altar at the *inipi* ceremony. No, the shape was more delicate.

"The cloud looks like a deer," Rosen said.

Cross Dog shook his head. "Elk."

"What Saul claims is his brother. You know, I have that courting flute here in my briefcase."

They drove up to Saul's house, where three vehicles were parked. Snow covered Will's service-station truck, Ike's van, and Grace's Toyota.

"Don't see Keeshin's car," Cross Dog said. "Good. Maybe we beat her here."

As the policeman checked the revolver on his hip, Rosen glanced at his watch—nearly eight. Pulling up the hoods of their parkas, both men stepped from the Blazer.

Rosen had never been so cold, and the clearing sky only further dropped the temperature. The snow crunched like glass under his boot heels. He burrowed his head deep inside the hood and rubbed his arms while Cross Dog knocked on the door. Each knock sounded like a gun-shot in the frozen air. When Stevie answered the door, they didn't wait to be invited inside.

Rosen stood very stiffly for a minute, slowly shedding the cold like the skin of a snake.

Cross Dog spoke quietly to the boy. "Where's your Uncle Will?"

"Upstairs in his room, taking a nap."

"A nap?"

"Uncle Will calls it his beauty sleep. He's got a date tonight with Wendy."

The entranceway led past a staircase to the kitchen. Stevie took their coats, then Rosen followed Cross Dog into a large, L-shaped room.

The room was paneled in dark, knotted wood, with white curtains brightening the windows. In the corner to Rosen's left stood an old sewing machine and, beside it, a handmade glass case filled with trophies, most topped with brass horses. Above the case, championship ribbons of green, red, and gold lined the wall. A large stone fireplace hissed and crackled with burning logs. Past the fireplace the room elbowed left to a handsome old dining table and chairs, not very different from Judge Whistler's.

Across from the fireplace Ike sat in a rocking chair, and Saul rested in the corner of a sofa, his feet on a low table that looked almost Japanese. They were watching a video, something starring a young Marlon Brando with a thick, black mustache.

"Is it almost ready?" Ike asked loudly.

Grace walked from the kitchen with a large bowl of popcorn. She stopped suddenly, almost spilling the bowl.

"Tom?"

The policeman looked as surprised as she. "Hello, Gracie. I thought you was out in Deadwood."

She stared at Rosen. "We got home about a half hour ago. Jack and Dr. Hartrey stayed for a little while. They just left. What're you both doing here? It's about Gates's murder, isn't it?"

Cross Dog nodded. He turned to her son. "Stevie . . ."

"No," she moaned, pulling the boy to her. "Mr. Rosen said Stevie had nothing to do with the killing. He promised . . . "

"You don't understand. Stevie, go tell your uncle I need to talk to him."

While Stevie climbed the stairs, Grace and the two men walked into the living room. She set the popcorn on the coffee table.

"Thanks," Ike said, taking a handful. "Sit down and join us. This is one of my favorites. Recognize it?"

"An old Brando movie," Rosen replied.

"*Viva Zapata,* about the Mexican revolutionary. You know, Zapata was an Indian. Maybe that's how Brando got into all that Indian-rights stuff in the sixties."

Cross Dog shook his head. "Another white man playing an Indian. They make us look good in the movies, then spit on us in the street."

"Maybe so. Personally, I like the Anthony Quinn part—Zapata's older brother. I could've played that part real well. See there how he's drunk and carrying on with that woman."

They watched the scene play out. Afterward, Ike blew his nose hard.

"That scene always gets to me—how Zapata lets his brother be gunned down for betraying the revolution. I guess that's what makes us men—doing what we have to do."

Ike was looking past them. Will ambled, barefoot, into the room, with Stevie trailing a few steps behind. He wore a red flannel shirt, torn jeans, and sneakers. He stretched broadly, stifling a yawn, then smiled.

"Whadda we got here, a party? Hi, Tom."

"I just come from talking to Judge Whistler and his wife. Pearl told us everything. I'm gonna have to take you in."

The smile stayed pasted on Will's face. "What the hell are you talking about?"

"About you murdering Albert Gates."

"C'mon, Tom. Stop kidding around."

"She told us everything. It's all down on paper, and tomorrow she tells it to the D.A."

Will shook his head. "That's crazy. Sure, I been sneakin' out with her.

Now maybe she gets mad 'cause I threw her over for Wendy. Just a jealous bitch. You know how that is." When the other man didn't reply, Will added, "It's her word against mine."

Cross Dog took a folded paper from his shirt pocket. "I had one of the boys get this search warrant from Judge O'Hara. Actually, there're two. The gas station's being searched right now. You and I are gonna have a look-see in your bedroom. We'll check the hamper in the basement as well."

"For what?"

"Evidence. Especially the uniforms you wear over at the gas station. I expect we'll find traces of Albert Gates's blood on one of them. He bled a helluva lot before he died."

Will ran a hand through his hair. "That was . . . hell, that was last summer. Them clothes been washed dozens of times."

Rosen said, "If a bloodstain's been in a fabric, a good lab can bring it out."

Cross Dog took Will's arm. "Let's take a look."

Will struggled in vain against the policeman's grip.

"Don't make me cuff you in front of your family."

Grace shook her head. "I don't understand. This don't make no sense at all. What Stevie said in court about Gates naming Father—what does Will have to do with all that?"

"Mr. Rosen will explain it all."

Taking a tattered card from his wallet, Cross Dog read Will his rights, then the two men walked upstairs.

Grace touched her forehead. "I need a drink of water."

Rosen wondered if he should follow her into the kitchen; perhaps she was going downstairs to hide Will's laundry. A moment later he heard her talking quietly on the phone. No need to ask whom she was calling.

Grace returned to sit on the sofa, her father moving beside her, while Rosen pulled up a rocking chair. Legs crossed, Stevie sat on the floor near Ike, who continued to watch the movie. Rosen closed his eyes for a moment, putting the events in their proper order, then began.

He told her what had really happened on the ridge the night of the murder. How Will had found the Indian remains on Gates's property, moved them to the ridge, and sold the *wotawe* to Gates. How he'd gone with Gates to the ridge at night to get the medicine bag, when Gates discovered the Indian remains had been brought there and "salted" to trick him, just as Belle's grandfather had tricked Cap Gates years before. How, in anger, Gates had threatened Will with jail and then been murdered by the young man. How Will had arranged for Pearl's husband to give him an alibi, in exchange for helping to bring gambling into Tin Town. And how, to be sure no one would make the connection between the rusted nail in Gates's hand and Will's reburying the remains, he'd first stolen the evidence from the police station, then burglarized Andi's house for the photos of the nail.

Through Rosen's account, Grace, Saul, and Stevie sat perfectly still, without expression, in a kind of solid silence, like those great stone gods of Easter Island. Only Grace's knuckles, white from clutching the sofa arm, betrayed any emotion.

The silence continued a few more minutes, until Cross Dog and Will returned. The policeman carried a brown grocery bag.

"Two sets of uniforms," he explained. "One clean, the other dirty. Could tell us something, though Will's already told me enough."

Will stared at the floor, his body trembling.

Blinking her eyes, Grace slowly looked up at her brother. "You mean, all that Mr. Rosen told us is true? You killed Albert Gates?"

Something sounding like a broken string of beads rolled from his mouth. He coughed hard, then tried again. "I . . . I didn't mean to kill him. It was an accident."

Rosen said, "You hit him on the back of the head with a large stone."

Will's foot began tapping uncontrollably. "He—he went all crazy when he found those nails under the bones. He knew I'd brung it there and figured out it was from his place . . . Hell, it was just like the other two he'd found years ago. Said I'd stolen his property and broken it all up moving it, that it mighta been his best specimen. Said I was gonna do time for this."

Wiping his eyes with his forearm, Will looked at his sister. "I was in jail once before. Gracie, you remember what I was like when I come out. I couldn't stand goin' back there. I tried talkin' to him, makin' him see how sorry I was, but he only got madder."

"Don't," she said, shaking her head.

"I don't even know how the stone got in my hand. I . . ."

"Don't."

" . . . just started hitting him."

"You bastard!"

She was on her feet, slapping him hard across the face.

"You were gonna let Father take the blame and make Stevie go half-crazy thinking his grandfather's a murderer!"

"I was scared, Gracie, scared to death!"

Her arms beat against his chest. "You bastard!"

"Gracie!"

Then Saul stood between them. He said only, "This is not done," then waited as Grace took a step back and dried her eyes.

She glared at her brother, but slowly her eyes softened. Her hand reached tentatively to touch his arm. "Oh, Will."

The air shuddered in his lungs as, once again, he looked down at the floor.

Rosen said, "You went up to the ridge with Gates after you closed the gas station, around ten."

Will nodded, still not looking up. "Went up in his Caddy. He said if we ran into my dad, I was to talk some sense into him."

"So you must've killed Gates between ten-fifteen and ten-thirty. What then?"

"I ran back to the gas station. I didn't know what to do. I needed somebody to figure things out for me, so I called Pearl. She came up with the idea of her husband giving me an alibi. I drove home a little after eleven, changed clothes, and called Gracie at the police station."

"You had no idea that Gates was still alive, or that Stevie came up the ridge later?"

"Christ no! I just got so scared. So damn scared."

Will sobbed, huddling in Gracie's arms like the little boy that he was.

Saul turned to Rosen. "I knew White Bear's spirit was restless. Now I understand why. I'm going with Will. I want you to come with us. He needs a good lawyer."

The doorbell rang, and Grace hurried to answer it.

"Will you come?" Saul asked.

Before Rosen could answer, Grace returned with Jack Keeshin. She held his hand tightly. Keeshin unzipped his coat to reveal a cream-colored fisherman's sweater.

"I understand Will's being arrested for the murder of Albert Gates."

Jaw clenched, Cross Dog nodded.

"It's unbelievable. Look, Grace asked me to come along when you book him."

"We won't be needing you."

Grace leaned against Keeshin. "Will can't go through this alone. I want Jack there. Will's got a right to a lawyer."

Her father said, "I'll be with my son. Mr. Rosen will come along."

Keeshin asked, "Is that right, Nate?"

Rosen glanced from Will to his father. "Sure."

"That's awfully good of you. You're certainly better at criminal law. And someone should stay with Grace."

Cross Dog pushed past them. "Let's get going."

"Tom, can I talk to you and Nate for a minute?" Keeshin nodded toward the door.

The three men walked into the hallway. The way Cross Dog slouched, looking away from Keeshin, reminded Rosen of a pitcher about to be yanked from the game.

Keeshin lowered his voice. "I must admit being less worried about Will than about the effect his arrest will have on the rest of the family, especially Grace. She's going to work in a few hours. I don't think she could stand having her brother in a jail cell a few feet away. Tom, I know the weather's bad and the highway's rough going, but would you consider taking Will into Deadwood? Won't he have to be brought there tomorrow anyway?"

The policeman finally made eye contact. "I'd already decided that. You're not the only one who . . . Forget it." He turned back to Will. "C'mon."

Saul, Will, Cross Dog, and Rosen bundled into their parkas and gloves. Grace and Keeshin stood together, arms intertwined.

Keeshin said, "I'm going to stay a few minutes, then go back home." To Grace, "I'll stop over later at the station."

The men barely heard his last few words, as Cross Dog had already opened the door and stepped outside.

Keeshin's vehicle, a Jeep Cherokee with BEAR COAT CHRONICLE lettered on both front doors, was parked beside the Blazer. Cross Dog handcuffed Will from behind, then put him into the back seat of the Blazer, tossing the bag of clothes into the cargo space. Saul sat beside his son. The policeman and Rosen closed their doors almost simultaneously, and the four-by-four moved slowly up the ridge.

Lifting his receiver, Cross Dog called in. "Wendy, I'm going into Deadwood. I'll call from there. Oh, Will has to cancel his date tonight. Something came up."

"Oh yeah?" Wendy said. "You tell him he's in big trouble."

Will looked out the window. "Christ, Tom, it's a helluva night for a ride up to Deadwood. Nobody'll be on the road. Ain't nothing out there for the next thirty miles."

"I been through worse. Your old man practically lives outdoors year-round. Just like our grandfathers. Ain't that right?"

Saul replied, "Our grandfathers also died in the snow. Remember what happened after Wounded Knee. That was a bad day for the Lakota."

"Seems like there's been a lot of them since then."

Will asked, "Tom, what's gonna happen to me?"

"I don't know. It sure ain't good—you killing Gates, not to mention messing with Judge Whistler's wife. All I can promise you is a fair trial. Maybe there'll be a change of venue, get you outta Bear Coat. Whaddya think, Mr. Rosen?"

"I think it's a good idea."

Will sniffled. "It was an accident, Tom. I swear it was."

"You better act real sincere at the trial and hope for an all-woman jury."

They topped the ridge, and, looking through the policeman's window, Rosen saw the murder scene—the snow-covered sweat lodge near a smaller mound containing the remains of White Bear. The cold and snow made the ridge seem clean, even antiseptic. Did any trace of Gates's blood remain, or had it seeped underground and been transformed into the earth itself, like the bloodstone that made the *chanunpa* and brought life to the Lakota?

The Blazer crunched down the ridge along a road Cross Dog must have sensed rather than seen. Snow swept across the headlights, but the sky continued to clear, and the broken houses of Tin Town shone pale in the moonlight, as if only tricks of the imagination.

Glancing at the two men behind him, Rosen suddenly realized that father and son hadn't spoken directly to one another since Will's arrest. At either end of the seat, they stared straight ahead; each might just as well have been alone. Like the great chasm between Rosen and his father. It could just as well have been the two of them sitting there. No—he shook his head—it wasn't the same, not at all. His father would never have come.

The Blazer jiggled over some rocks, then bounced onto the main high-way. Straightening the wheel, Cross Dog accelerated slightly to face another endless tract of snow. Although the engine throbbed as it picked up speed, the Blazer seemed only to move in place. The scenery remained the same, or rather, there was no scenery. Only the frozen air and a wind too solid to move against.

Watching the truck's long, black shadow sweep across the snow, Rosen remembered the Bergman movies he and Bess had seen in college. This could have been a scene from one of them—travelers riding in silence, each hiding his own secrets, long, black shadows gliding far ahead into a land as vacant as their hopes. Was this a dream? He rubbed his eyes.

Light glinted in the rearview mirror. Looking back, he saw a pair of headlights rapidly approaching. He was glad to have another car on the road, but it was moving too fast, as if chasing them. Cross Dog noticed it too, his head swiveling from the rearview to the sideview mirror. He edged the Blazer to the right.

The other car kept honking its horn, shattering the air like icicles. It was another four-by-four, and as it passed the Blazer, Rosen saw BEAR COAT CHRONICLE printed on its side.

"Keeshin's Cherokee!" Cross Dog said. "Maybe Grace is with him. If she gets hurt . . . !"

Its rear end wobbling, the Jeep slipped off the highway and pancaked a full circle, jerking to a stop. Cross Dog hit his brakes, letting the Blazer slide like a runner into home plate. Then he backed up until even with the other vehicle. Keeshin was already out of his truck, trudging toward the Blazer.

Cross Dog opened his door. "You son of a bitch!"

Keeshin said, "Easy, Tom," in a voice more chilling than the frigid air. "Keep coming, but very slowly. I'll take that." He glanced inside. "You too, Nate. Come around here."

"What's going on?"

"I want to show you."

As Rosen opened the door, his briefcase fell into the snow. He began to retrieve it, when Keeshin said, "Leave it. Hurry up."

Tightening his hood, Rosen walked around the truck. The other two men were standing apart—too far apart. He didn't understand why, until he saw the gun in Keeshin's hand. The butt end of another one, Cross Dog's, stuck out from the lawyer's pocket.

Keeshin shivered violently. "Over there by Tom. Saul, you and Will come out too. Hurry up, it's damn cold out here. For Chrissakes, I'm from southern California."

The other two men stepped from the car and stood beside Keeshin.

"Where's the key to the handcuffs?"

Cross Dog's jaw was set tight, but Will said, "In his right coat pocket."

"Get the key, Nate."

"What are you—"

"Just get the key, before my finger spasms on the trigger."

Reaching into Cross Dog's pocket, he saw the policeman frown and his eyes, two hot coals, stare into Keeshin.

"Good, now unlock Will's handcuffs."

Again Rosen did as instructed.

"Will, the key's in my Jeep, along with $150. That's all I had with me. Take off."

Will looked at his two free hands, then at Keeshin. "You mean I can go?"

"Yes." Keeshin gave a short hard laugh. "And hurry up, before we all become statues of the Snow Queen."

Rosen said, "He won't make it past Deadwood."

"Oh, yes he will. I'm babysitting you until he does."

"This isn't one of your games, Keeshin."

Cross Dog took a step forward. "Is she in the car?"

"Who? You mean Grace? Of course not. You think I'd involve her in something like this? I just couldn't let her brother be convicted of murder. I couldn't put her through another trial. You can understand that."

Rosen shook his head, and, despite the freezing cold, sweat slid down his back. There was something terribly wrong.

Will beamed. "Thanks, Jack. I'll never forget this."

He looked at his father and the smile faded. Turning away, he ran to the Cherokee, slowly pulled onto the road, then continued toward Deadwood.

After the Jeep was out of sight, Keeshin took a step back toward the Blazer. The other men began to follow, when he shook his head.

"Move back."

When they kept coming, Keeshin aimed his gun over their heads. The shot cracked like a whip. "Get back!"

The men did as they were told.

"I'm going now."

Rosen shook his head in disbelief. "You're leaving us out here to die."

"Probably. The odds of anybody coming out on this deserted road in the next hour or so—before you freeze to death—are negligible. But like any gambling, there always is that element of chance."

Cross Dog glared at the other man. "You'd better kill me now."

Keeshin slid into the car and started the engine. "No, I wouldn't want to do that." He began to pull away. "You see, Nate was wrong. It *is* a game."

Chapter 20

Gripping his briefcase while standing stiffly against the wind, Rosen looked up and down the empty road. Just as, when he was a law student in Chicago, he'd wait impatiently on the station platform for the "L." First he'd hear the distant rumbling, then its doors would slide open, and he'd huddle under the heat blowers all the way downtown.

But there was no train coming—no tracks, no buildings or great skyline in the distance. Only the dark sky that fitted over the white enameled plain as if both were parts of some great machine. Even the moon and stars seemed frozen in place. His boots felt tight in snow heavy as cement, and the bitter wind lacquered his face.

It would be all right; it had to be all right. Rosen remembered the stories his grandfather had told of the family walking through Poland after thieves had taken their horse and wagon. How cold it had been—the men had to chip the ice from their beards, while his grandmother wrapped open books around her legs to keep warm. Yet, God had kept them in his hand, until they reached their cousins' shtetl.

Having saved his family, God could save Rosen now. He could do anything—part the sea, send angels down ladders. Hadn't he even stopped the sun for Joshua? Rosen looked into the sky. If only it were the sun and not that moon, hard as a nickel-plated disk. If only it were the sun.

Standing a few feet away, Saul True Sky too was looking at the moon. His face was smooth and impassive as the moon's. Then the old Indian slowly turned and, boots crunching in the snow, moved closer. He said nothing, but there was a softness in his silence, the only softness Rosen could still feel.

"Here, over here."

Saul wasn't speaking, but the words were so clear, they could've been whispered in Rosen's ear. Looking around, he saw Cross Dog across the road, about fifty yards into the field.

Waving his arm, the policeman said again, "Over here."

So far away, yet so clear, like a whisper. As a little boy, Rosen had watched his brothers play telephone with a string stretched between two tin cans. He'd race from one end of the alley to the other and listen as Aaron and David sent messages. That was how Cross Dog sounded. In weather so bitterly cold, that's how everything sounded.

Taking his arm, True Sky led Rosen from the road. The field wasn't quite as smooth as it seemed. Cross Dog was on his knees, scratching with his hands like a dog against a snow-covered structure that appeared to be an igloo. At first Rosen thought it might have been a sweat lodge, but bits of brown and black, pushed from the hole Cross Dog was digging, revealed that it was an old haystack left over from harvest time. In a few minutes he had scraped away enough for the interior to resemble a small tent, piling loose hay on the bottom.

"All right, inside."

Rosen found it difficult to bend. Finally he fell forward and let the two men drag him between them. He set his briefcase in front of the entrance and, using both hands, crossed his legs.

It was better inside the haystack; no wind, and the two bodies pressing against him brought some life back into his arms. As the three men slowly exhaled, their breath sparkled like delicate crystal, only to shatter silently upon their laps.

True Sky cleared the brittle hay from a small piece of earth. "All this is *Inyan*—rock. Without this there is nothing. From Inyan came good but also evil. His youngest son Iya brings the cold down from the north. He's the one killing us." The Indian flattened one gloved hand upon the ground, as if feeling for a pulse. After a minute he added, "I'm old and ready to meet my grandfathers, but I'm sorry, lawyer, to bring you here. I'm sorry you're gonna die."

Cross Dog shook his head. "We're not gonna die. Not till I catch up to that son of a bitch. I'm not gonna let him get away with this. I'm not gonna let him get his hands on her."

"You would've made a great warrior if only, as a boy, you had cried for a dream. To talk with the Spirits, to have flown with them and seen our grandfathers. You need to have flown."

"The only thing I need to do is see Keeshin one more time."

214

The Indian began chanting something softly, while Rosen closed his eyes and saw himself standing before his father. He wanted to think of his mother and her warm, soft hands but couldn't, as if the cold had seeped into even his memory and had frozen his father's image in place.

That night so long ago, he'd been lost in the snowstorm and they'd all searched, no one daring to tell his father, who was at prayer. When the neighbor boy finally brought Rosen home, how his mother had hugged him, setting him beside her with hot tea and all the cookies he wanted. Neither of them remembered the lesson he was supposed to have done, until his father came home. How he'd looked at his son, his eyes arched in disappointment.

"Thank God the boy is safe," his mother had said, her warm hand caressing his face.

"Yes, but is that an excuse to forget his lesson?"

Eyes arched in disappointment, so cold. Colder than the storm outside. So damn cold. He shivered, snapping his eyes open, hoping the cold was just part of the nightmare. Instead, looking into the darkness, he realized the nightmare was part of the cold. He couldn't die like this, not so alone.

Fumbling with the zipper of his parka, he finally edged it halfway down, reached into his jacket, and found the fluorescent key chain, in the shape of a quarter note, that Sarah had given him last summer. It glowed like an amulet and, through the glove, he felt it warm as the touch of his mother's hand. Sarah.

He was losing the feeling in his legs and, while shifting his body, knocked over his briefcase. He decided to open it and prop it sideways, giving it twice the surface to block the wind. Clicking it open, he saw the courting flute.

Cross Dog handed the flute to True Sky. "Play something. The way sound carries in this cold, somebody might hear us. Hell, at least it's doing something."

True Sky held the flute in both his gloved hands, then flexed his fingers. He lifted the instrument to his lips.

"Don't get any saliva on it," the policeman said. "It'll stick to your skin like they been welded."

The old Indian blew gently into the flute. Through his heavy, aching eyes, Rosen saw the music thread its way into the sky like a thin blue vein. More notes led to more veins crisscrossing a horizon solid as marble.

He thought of his own veins in the arms and legs he could no longer feel. He was no longer cold, just tired, the sweet music making him want to fall asleep. Let it be Sarah at the piano playing Thelonius Monk, the way she did just for him. He wanted to fall asleep and dream of her playing something just for him. If it weren't for that damn light boring through the marble that encased him.

That and the rumbling wouldn't let him sleep. The light grew brighter each moment, then suddenly overwhelmed his eyes. He blinked hard, forcing his eyes to open, and saw an angel outlined in the glorious luminescence. It was unlike any angel the Torah had ever described—skinny and moving goat-footed toward him. Lifting Rosen into a warm, dark cloud.

He thought perhaps this was Heaven, but then why was he in such pain? His body ached; each movement forced tears down his leathery cheeks. The angel knelt over him, touching his body, and at each touch Rosen's toes, knees, the tips of his fingers burned. Were the angel's hands made of fire? Could this be Michael? The figure bent nearer, breaking into a smile and stroking his pointed chin. Blinking again, Rosen stared hard through the shadows and finally recognized the angel. It was Ike.

"You take it easy, lawyer," the old Indian said, clicking on a small overhead light. "Just rest up and get warm." After a moment he added, "Feel this?"

Rosen's toes tingled, as a dull throbbing snaked up his leg. "Oww."

"Feeling's coming back—that's good. Don't think there's any permanent damage. You were all bundled up real good. Saul, I'd have the doc check your nose and cheeks. You shoulda covered your face more like Mr. Lawyer here, but I guess you'll be all right. Just don't go rubbing anything. You gotta defrost real slowly, like a nice piece of prime rib."

Pushing up on his elbows, Rosen found himself facing backward, wedged between an old sink and the side door of Ike's van. The motor was running, and heat seeped over the front seat, collecting around the two men. He felt it tingle against his skin. Near the back of the van, beside a long toolbox, Saul sat cross-legged, the courting flute poised between his hands.

Adjusting his weight, Rosen scraped the knuckles of his right hand on the floor. His hand was clenched; slowly opening it, he saw Sarah's key chain. Its glow had faded under the overhead light but it still felt warm. He stared at the amulet a long time before returning it to his pocket.

He asked Ike, "How'd you find us?"

"I heard the music. It was from a courting flute. Can you believe I got to feeling horny just from hearing it?"

"You couldn't have heard it from the house."

"No. I was down the road about a half mile. I'd about decided to turn around, when I heard the music. Knew it was Saul."

"You were following us?"

"Keeshin really, which turned out to be the same thing. Saul and I didn't trust him with Gracie. In them old movies, he'd be the slick saloon owner with the black mustache."

"That's the reason you followed him?"

"He lied twice tonight. First, said he was gonna stay with Gracie, but he left just after you did. Told Gracie he was heading back into Bear Coat—his second lie. He started out that way, but when I left the house, I saw him cut his lights and loop back over the ridge, heading toward the highway that would take him north into Deadwood, same place you was going. Why head north on a night like this? I didn't have anything better to do, so I followed him. I would've been here a lot sooner if I hadn't run off the road twice. Second time I almost couldn't get back up. Had to jimmy some old planks of wood under the tires to get enough traction. From what Tom told me a few minutes ago, guess we was right not to trust Keeshin."

Rosen had forgotten about Cross Dog; now, turning his head, he saw the policeman in the driver's seat.

Cross Dog gripped the wheel. "I knew Keeshin was dirty. All along, I knew the son of a bitch was dirty. Just couldn't prove it. Last summer, when the town council started hassling Saul over his land, I kept following Keeshin. Every night on patrol I'd followed him but never could connect him to anything wrong. For awhile, I even thought he might've killed Gates."

Ike shook his head. "What he just did is bad enough—trying to save Will by killing three men. For Gracie, he told you? That's a strange kind of love."

"If it is love," Rosen said.

He felt the van moving forward.

Cross Dog said, "We've wasted enough time."

Stepping past Rosen, Ike climbed into the passenger seat. "Ain't you turning around? I think all three of you should get checked out at the medical center. I don't like the looks of Saul. His cheeks and—"

"We'll stop by the hospital after I catch up with Keeshin." More softly, "And I still need to bring in Will."

Craning his neck, Rosen saw snowflakes drift against the windshield. He couldn't help wondering what might happen if they were stranded again; Ike's van didn't seem any more reliable than Andi's old Mercury. It didn't matter, because nothing would change Cross Dog's mind, not even the fact that he was unarmed, while Keeshin carried at least two guns.

"Here." True Sky handed Rosen the courting flute.

"I never learned how to play."

"It takes time. You'll find your own tune."

Rosen dragged the briefcase onto his lap. The metal clasps were still almost too cold to touch, and he had to pry one of them from the lock. He lay the flute on the stacks of papers that no longer had any meaning. The case against Saul True Sky was over.

"Snow's getting thicker," Ike said. "You can barely make out Keeshin's tire tracks. Will's are already covered."

"Don't need no tire tracks," Cross Dog replied. "We know where they're goin'."

Rosen thought of Sarah playing Thelonius Monk for him back home, improvising on the great improviser, the notes toddling down the piano and across the room. He would see her again, after all. His fingers moved stiffly, itching to embrace her. He almost smiled but stopped, seeing True Sky sitting a few feet away. He remembered the first time he'd seen Stevie, the boy sitting still as a rock on the crest of the ridge.

"Last summer you told me about Stone Boy, but you never finished the story. What happened to him, after he saved his mother and uncles?"

The Indian shifted forward. "Stone Boy had everything, but still he wanted more. He became greedy, hunting only for the pleasure of killing, taking only the ears and claws—not even bothering with the meat. He bragged about what he'd done and wouldn't listen to his mother and uncles, who begged him to stop needlessly killing the animals held sacred by our people. Finally, the buffalo and other creatures could stand it no more. They revolted and attacked Stone Boy's lodge. Stone Boy and his uncles fought back bravely and killed animals by the thousands."

"Then he survived."

"In the end the Thunder Birds let loose the rain, which flooded his lodge and killed his mother and uncles. Still he fought until the animals defeated him. His magic was too strong for death, but they left him half-buried in the earth, where he still lies today."

Ike turned his head. "It's a good story, a real shoot 'em up. Made for the movies with somebody like Kirk Douglas, with his big dimple and smile, playing Stone Boy."

"It's a good story," True Sky agreed. "It teaches everything a man needs to know to be a man. Not only to be brave—that's easy, but to respect our grandfathers and the lives of all our brothers, like the buffalo. It tells what happens when one becomes greedy and forgets the right way. Even someone as mighty as Stone Boy could not escape."

It was different from any of the stories Rosen had heard as a boy, yet also talmudic in the making of its moral point. He thought at first of Noah, of the flood and the animals, but Noah was obedient, and this was about a man who fell from the righteous path. An Adam or Saul or Ahab . . . or Rosen himself. As far as his father was concerned, he might as well have been made of stone.

Closing his briefcase and putting it aside, Rosen stretched broadly. Despite his awkward position, the motor's hum and the heater's soft hissing made him drowsy. Shifting to one side, he was about to close his eyes when the van slowed.

"Something wrong?" he asked.

Ike said, "Take a look up ahead."

Kneeling, he looked over Ike's shoulder. Through snow fluttering like dander upon the windshield, he saw something dark and solid ahead, just off the road. As they drove closer, he recognized Cross Dog's Blazer, its front end smashed against an old fence post and the driver's door ajar.

"Keeshin," he half-whispered.

Cross Dog parked on the road a few yards from the collision. He kept the van running.

"You three can stay inside. If you do come out, keep away from the Blazer until I say it's okay. And don't touch anything."

Ike said, "Keeshin's got a couple guns."

"I'd like him to try it. You got a flashlight, Ike?"

"In the glove compartment. Here."

Cross Dog stepped from the van, crossed the headlights, and walked slowly in a wide arc toward the wreck. He swept the flashlight along the ground to his right.

219

Ike said, "I don't feel good about him going out there alone."

The last thing Rosen wanted to do was go back into the cold, but there was no choice. Putting his gloves over his tingling hands, he slid open the side door and stepped outside. Ike followed a half step behind, as Rosen blinked away a snowflake and followed the arc Cross Dog had made toward the Blazer. The truck had struck something much larger than a fence post—a thick wooden pole that once might've supported a gate.

Cross Dog leaned inside the vehicle.

Ike said, "Tom, you want us to—"

The policeman waved them back. After a minute, he stepped from the doorway and leaned heavily against the hood. When he finally looked up, it wasn't at them but the way they'd come, toward Bear Coat.

Ike asked, "He dead?"

For a long moment the policeman didn't answer. Finally his shoulders shrugged, and the word caught in his throat. "Ye . . . ah." Pushing past them, he added, "Don't touch anything," then lumbered along that same curving path back to the van.

With a shudder, Rosen stepped forward and opened the Blazer's door. A body slumped over the wheel, and it took a few seconds to realize that the dead man wasn't Jack Keeshin.

It was Will.

His forehead was covered with blood, which in the cold had thickened like taffy. Except for the blood, he might've been asleep, his face relaxed and arms resting casually on his lap. He wasn't wearing a seat belt, but the handle of Cross Dog's pistol stuck out from his coat pocket. Blood also smeared the windshield where his head had shivered the glass into a spider web.

Despite the cold, Rosen broke into a sweat, as his knees buckled and his hands clawed for the door frame. Over the years he'd seen many dead men. He'd heard policemen say they'd gotten used to it after awhile, but he never had. It didn't matter if men died old, like Albert Gates, or young, like Will. It didn't matter that Will had been a murderer, and that God's justice called for an eye for an eye. That's what Rosen's father would've said, and what Rosen had been fighting most of his life. God made man in his image, and life, any man's life, was holy. Would Grace and her father understand that or, like Job, bow their heads to the whirlwind?

"No," Rosen heard himself say aloud, even before realizing why. Keeshin had driven away in the Blazer; if he'd been accidentally killed, that would've been God's hand. But Will, who should've been inside a Jeep on his way to Deadwood, had died instead. God had nothing to do with that. Why was Will dead?

He turned to ask Ike, but found Saul staring at his son. The Indian's hand stretched to touch Will's shoulder, as if about to shake him gently awake. The snow stung Rosen's eyes; wiping them, he hurried away.

"Hey!" Cross Dog shouted, motioning with a flashlight for him to follow the same arcing path. Rosen did as instructed, joining the other two men just off the road, in a direct line with the Blazer and fence post.

The policeman squatted near the ground, looking at some footprints in the snow. Walking up to the road, he studied a set of tire tracks. He went back and forth several times between the two areas.

Rosen huddled with Ike near the van.

Ike said, "Between the snow and wind, in another half hour all these tracks'll be gone."

"What've you found?"

"Beats me. Don't believe all that stuff about us Indians being good trackers. Half the time I get lost on my way to the bathroom. 'Course, Tom here knows what he's doing. Did lots of hunting as a boy. Maybe that's why he's a cop."

They could have waited inside the heated van, but neither man suggested it. Perhaps they would have felt guilty leaving Cross Dog alone, or perhaps their suffering in the bitter cold let them, in some small way, share Saul's mourning for his dead son.

Finally Cross Dog clicked off the flashlight. "Can't see nothing more here. Might as well go inside."

"What about Saul?" Rosen asked.

"He'll come when he's ready."

They returned to the van. Rosen sat on an old water heater just behind the front seat.

"What did you find out?" When Cross Dog didn't reply, he added, "You know what happened to Will was no accident."

The policeman nodded. "I seen a lot of car accidents. If there'd been enough force to smash his head that hard into the windshield, the impact would've knocked him off his seat. He didn't have no seat belt on. Besides, what're the odds, with all this vacant field, of him hitting that old post? Somebody placed him there to look like an accident. The motor was still running when I got there, but the door was open. Guess whoever did it figured if the crack on the head didn't finish off Will, the cold would. Just as it woulda finished us off, if Ike hadn't come along."

"You said 'whoever did it.' Don't you mean Keeshin?"

Cross Dog frowned. "Yeah, I guess. Think of the way it'd look come tomorrow, if everything had gone like Keeshin planned. With all the snow and wind, there wouldn't be any tracks left. Tomorrow or the next day somebody'd come by and find the three of us froze to death along the side of the road. Then he'd find Will in my Blazer, my gun in his pocket."

"Sure," Rosen said, "and everybody in town would assume that Will had gotten your gun, stolen the Blazer, and left us to die while making his escape. Then he has his fatal accident. A terrible tragedy, and no witnesses."

"And for the rest of her life, Grace'd be left believing that her brother had murdered not only Albert Gates, but his own father. The son of a bitch."

Rosen knew the policeman wasn't referring to Will. Keeshin had to have done this. "But how did they change trucks? How did Keeshin catch up to Will?"

Ike said, "Maybe Will did have an accident, then Keeshin came along, finished the boy, switched trucks, and kept going?"

Cross Dog shook his head. "There'd be more of a mess in the snow. No, only one truck went off the road and into the post. Somehow, up here on the road, Will not only got himself killed but was taken from the Jeep and put into my Blazer."

How could Keeshin have done it? Rosen whispered, "Another one of his games."

"There's one more thing," the policeman said. "Just ahead on the road, there're two sets—"

He stopped suddenly, as the side door opened and Saul climbed inside. The old Indian sat in the same cross-legged position as before, but his shoulders hunched lower and his face, usually smooth and untroubled, was tight as a fist.

For a long time no one spoke. Cross Dog finally said, "I'm sorry we have to leave Will here, but the forensics team will have to come out and look everything over. I'll see they respect the body."

Saul barely nodded. "You know, it's not so much the death, but the way he died. My mother told me stories of her grandfather, Two Knives. He was a great warrior. He died in a raid against the Cheyenne. After he'd killed three of their braves, the others chased after him and shot him off his horse, breaking his arm in the fall. He took his knife and, pinning himself to the ground, sung his death chant, then took one more Cheyenne with him. That was the way to die. You faced your enemy and had time to sing your death chant. Not like this."

Cross Dog nodded. "It's not over. I'll face the enemy." He slowly turned the van around.

"We're going back to Bear Coat?" Rosen asked.

"Keeshin thinks we're all dead. He'll want to get back as quick as can be, to give himself an alibi. I could see his Jeep tracks going on toward Deadwood, but there's a turnoff not far ahead that circles back to town. With his four-wheel drive, he should be able to make it without much trouble. He's probably at the station right now, his arm around her."

"Another game," Rosen said.

The policeman shook his head. "That other thing I started to tell you. There were two sets of footprints up on the road near the tire tracks."

"Sure, Keeshin's and Will's."

"I guess, but one set looked awful big. Big and deep. Ike, you still carry that old hunting rifle?"

"Yeah, back there somewhere. I think under that old water heater."

"Dig it out, and see that it's loaded."

"That rifle only loads one bullet at a time."

Cross Dog accelerated the van. "One bullet is all I'll need."

Chapter 21

TUESDAY NIGHT

Grace had always wondered about her father's experiences within his vision pit. He had seen spirits, flown across the sky with his brothers the elk, and visited the lands of their grandfathers when the grass was tall and the buffalo wandered thick as the trees that covered the Black Hills. He had done all this while alone, within the dark bosom of the earth.

The vision pit was only for men, but there were times in the deep quiet of night, behind the plywood wall of the dispatch unit, when Grace saw things too. Now, her hand stroking Stevie's turtle doll, she saw her brother as a little boy running across the ridge, with the small bow and arrows their father had made for him. His hair was long, and he ran barefoot almost as quickly as the squirrels he was chasing. How proud their mother was of him, her little hunter. Never mind he was playing hooky from school or that, later on, he lost job after job for being late or leaving when he pleased. You couldn't chain a warrior to the white man's clock.

What would her mother have said now?

Closing her eyes, Grace saw her own son as a little boy, sitting at his grandfather's feet while listening to the old Lakota stories. How Stevie's eyes had widened, as he imagined the beautiful White Buffalo-Calf Maiden, sent by the buffalo people to give the Lakota the sacred pipe. Or Stone Boy magically bringing back to life his ten uncles.

Stevie would be all right. Thanks to Dr. Hartrey, he was getting better. He was getting better, and her father was innocent, and whatever the law was going to do to Will, she wouldn't go on worrying about him. God, she was tired of worrying.

The receiver crackled, and she logged a call from one of the squad cars about breaking up a barroom fight. 11:32. She thought of calling the sheriff's office in Deadwood—no. What could they tell her, other than that Will was in jail? Tom and her father were spending the night there; they'd tell her everything tomorrow. Maybe she should drive into Deadwood tomorrow morning. Maybe Jack would . . . She shook her head. Damn it, she wouldn't burden him with any more of this.

"Another quiet one." Skinny Al sat at Elroy's desk, slurping the last of his milk shake. He'd taken over Elroy Baker's job as assistant police chief. "You all right, Gracie?"

She nodded.

" 'Cause if you'd rather get away from here, I'll take over. You know how I hate filling out this paperwork."

The edges of her mouth tightened. "Thanks, Al. Maybe later."

"I heard Denny call in that fight. He should just toss 'em outside for ten minutes. If that don't cool 'em off, nothing will. Hell of a night. Sure glad I'm not on patrol."

Grace thought again of calling Deadwood, just to make sure Tom and the others had gotten there okay. Funny how she never worried about Tom. Like Stone Boy, he was tough enough to roll over whatever got in his way. Still . . .

"Hi there."

She looked up to see Jack smiling at her. She couldn't help but smile back.

"Buy a lady a cup of coffee?"

"I . . . uh . . . only came in a half hour ago. Don't think I should—"

"Nonsense. The last place you should be tonight is in a police station. Isn't that right, Al?"

Wiping his mouth with a napkin, the policeman nodded. "I just got through telling her that very thing. I can handle things here for awhile."

"Of course you can. Oh, by the way, the other day at the coffee shop you mentioned going to L.A. on vacation. That was the first week of February, right?"

"Yes, sir. Why?"

"I've got you a couple tickets for the Lakers game."

Al straightened in his chair. "Oh, that's great! My boy'd give his right arm to see the Lakers. How much do I owe you?"

"Forget it. I got the tickets through a friend who wasn't going to use them anyway. Just have a good time."

"I don't know how to thank you."

"Not at all. Friends do friends favors all the time."

Grinning like a crescent moon, Al scratched his head. "Well, I . . . Gracie, what're you sitting there for? Go out and have a cup of coffee with this gentleman. That's an order."

Again, she couldn't help but smile. "Yes, sir, Mr. Assistant Police Chief." To Jack, "I was thinking about calling the sheriff in Deadwood."

"Perhaps you should let it alone for tonight. I spoke to Nate Rosen before he and the others left your house. Nate may stay on to defend Will."

"That'd be wonderful."

"I'm sure he's taking care of everything. If you'd like, come along with me tomorrow morning when I drive Dr. Hartrey to the airport. Afterward, we'll go over to Deadwood together. All right?"

"Oh yes. I mean . . ." Glancing at Al, she lowered her voice. "It's not right getting you so involved with my family."

"Perhaps I have an ulterior motive."

"I don't understand."

"You will. Let's get your coat on."

Jack followed Grace to the closet. He zipped the coat up to her throat, snapped the collar in place, and tied the hood snug around her head. She remembered her mother doing the same thing before sending her off to school. Like she was somebody's little doll.

She felt her cheeks burning. "We're just going down the street to the coffee shop."

"Put your gloves on."

She giggled. "Now, Jack."

"Bye, Al."

"You two take your time."

Holding her tightly, Jack led her across the street, wind whistling through the tiny crevices between them. When Grace started to turn toward the coffee shop, Jack stopped her.

"How about my place? Not only is the coffee better, but so's the service." When she hesitated, he added, "Just coffee, and a little conversation."

"All right."

They hurried into the alley and up the outside stairway to his apartment on the second floor. She followed him through a narrow hallway into the living room.

Hanging up their coats, Jack said, "Make yourself comfortable while I put on the coffee. I just received a wonderful Kenyan blend. It'll just take a few minutes to grind the beans."

She loved his living room; there was nothing quite like it in Bear Coat. Everything was clean and new and somehow made Jack seem that much more important. Along the wall to her left were two glass cases, one filled with tennis trophies and the other with games of chance—cards and dice in leather cases. In the corner stood a small desk, on which lay a legal pad, a stack of letters, and a sterling-silver letter opener with the initials J.F.K. Straight ahead a large window overlooked Main Street; on either side of its curtains hung framed photographs of Jack with different tennis players, some of whom Grace had seen on television. There was one painting of a group of cigar-smoking dogs playing poker.

She sat in the white leather sectional, which faced walnut bookshelves holding a television and VCR surrounded by rows of law books. The matching leather chair stood a foot from her armrest. Chrome lamps, which seemed to grow from the floor on metal stems, illuminated the chair and sofa. A backgammon game lay open on the glass-topped table in front of her. Between the bookshelves and kitchenette stretched the darkened hallway leading to the bedrooms.

She heard the whir of the grinder and, a moment later, smelled the strong aroma of fresh coffee. She looked past the eat-in counter into the kitchenette and saw Jack take two mugs from the shelf. He had changed clothes from earlier in the evening and now wore a lime cardigan. The cardigan seemed a little old-fashioned, but Grace liked that too. It reminded her of all those men on TV she'd watched while growing up. Men in cardigans who read newspapers, smoked pipes, and always had time for their wives and children.

"Coffee'll be ready in another minute," he said. "Would you like anything else?"

"No, thanks. It smells real good."

He brought the steaming mugs on a silver tray, which he placed on the glass-topped table. He sat so close their sleeves touched. She inhaled his cologne and suddenly felt very warm.

"Two sugars, right?" he said, serving her. "Careful, it's very hot."

The coffee was strong but felt good going down. "Mmm."

It was nice, sitting quietly and sipping the coffee. Since the summer before, Grace had been to Jack's apartment many times. Sometimes in the evening, sometimes in the morning after work, but almost always they'd made love. He was gentle, so gentle that afterward she'd feel as if maybe it hadn't happened, maybe just a nice dream she'd woken from before it was quite over.

But this was nicer.

After a few minutes, he said, "A little while ago, I mentioned having an ulterior motive for being so interested in the welfare of your family. I hope what I'm about to say doesn't come as a total surprise."

Reaching into his shirt pocket, he took out an engagement ring. He rotated the band so that the diamonds sparkled under the light. She held her mug tightly in both hands, even after they began to burn.

He continued, "After all these months together, you must know how I feel about you. The picnics last summer, working out Stevie's problems together, the times alone up here when . . . " He hesitated, clearing his throat. "I've met lots of women—I've never made any secret of that—but nobody like you. What I'm trying to say is that I love you and want to marry you."

Grace stared at the ring until the diamonds blurred like headlights in the rain. Wiping her eyes, she didn't dare speak.

"What's the matter?" His hand touched her cheek. "Maybe I didn't do it right—haven't really had any practice at something like this. Should I get down on one knee? Like this?"

He was about to lower himself, when she caught his arm.

"No, don't do that." Her cheeks were burning. "I . . . I just don't know what to say."

"Surely you must've had some idea."

She shook her head.

"If I've embarrassed you, I'm truly—"

"No, it's not that. It's just . . . " She took a deep breath, then exhaled very slowly, her eyes still on the ring.

"Here." He put the ring in the palm of her hand.

She'd taken off her wedding band about a year after Steve died. Some folks thought that wasn't right; Edna, the day dispatcher, had worn hers for twenty years since her husband's death. But the Lakota part of Grace had told her a year was enough for the spirit to slip away. It didn't mean she'd forgotten him. God, no. Every day . . . alone in bed was worse. She watched Jack's ring sparkle in her hand.

She turned to him, but he was gone.

"Jack?"

He stood at the window, looking down into the street. Lifting his hand slowly, he waved at somebody outside.

"Jack, who's there?"

"I heard a car in the street." He was speaking quietly, as if to himself. "It's only an old drunk, that friend of your father's."

"Ike?"

He nodded. "What's he doing here? It's almost midnight."

"Bars close at midnight. Maybe he's on his way home and decided to stop by the police station to cheer me up or find out more about Will. I hope he hasn't got liquored up again. He's been sober for the last six months."

Again Jack nodded. He returned to the couch and kissed her. "I think I know why you're hesitating. Is it because of your late husband—a feeling of disloyalty?"

"No. I'll always have my love for Steve—"

"I understand."

"—but I know I got to get on with my life. It's not that."

"Then what?"

"You can't really want me, not after all those other women. I don't understand why you're even here in this little two-bit town."

He laughed. "How many times do I have to tell you? Those women are cheap and phony compared to you. I guess I'll just have to make your mind up for you. Justice of the peace next week?"

"But . . . "

He kissed her again, then held her hands tightly. "You've no idea how much I want to marry you."

He was about to slip the ring on her finger, when somebody knocked on the door.

His eyes narrowed. "Who in the world . . . ?"

"Probably Ike. Al must've told him I was with you. He probably just wants to know about Father and Will. Don't be too hard on him."

"No doubt he'll want to toast the happy couple, and with my best champagne. We may need a witness for the wedding, but surely not for the proposal." He stood, the ring in his hand. "Think about what I've been saying. I'll be right back."

As he stepped into the hallway, Grace looked at the table, where the two coffee mugs rested side by side. When they were first married and Steve's rig was on an overnight haul, she'd set both their cups on the kitchen table, ready for coffee the moment he stepped through the door. It'd be nice doing that again.

"Is that Ike?" she asked, glancing over her shoulder. "Jack?" When he didn't reply, she stood. "Jack?"

He backed into the room followed by Tom, who was holding an old rifle in one hand like a pistol. Seeing her, Tom stopped in his tracks.

"Gracie, what the hell are you doing here?"

She stared at the rifle pointed at Jack's chest. She couldn't understand. A hand was touching her arm.

Rosen stood beside her near the sofa. "You'd better sit down."

"What for? What's wrong? Jack?"

He had backed into the corner near the desk. "Grace, I . . . "

"Shut up," Tom said. "Don't even look at her."

Grace ran to Jack, who put one arm around her.

"I warned you." The edge in Tom's voice grew sharper, and his hand flexed the rifle butt.

Jack smiled. "You really should've called first. Grace and I would like to be alone." He opened his hand to show the ring. "You see, I've proposed marriage, and she was just about to accept. Weren't you, darling?"

For a moment Tom's jaw shut tightly and his face went smooth as a stone, like her father's did when talking to the white man. Then he said very quietly, "It's too bad Will won't be there for the wedding."

Grace shook her head hard. "For God's sake, Tom, what's this all about?"

Slowly his eyes softened, until he was finally the man she knew. "You tell her, Rosen."

The lawyer stared hard at Tom, then nodded. "I'm sorry, Grace. Will is dead."

"Dead?"

"He died on the highway—"

"No."

"Listen, Grace. Will was murdered. Keeshin murdered your brother."

She heard the words, but they didn't make any sense, like a drunkard's mumbling. None of this made any sense. The rifle . . . why was the rifle pointing at Jack? He was still smiling. This was just a joke. It had to be a joke, or he wouldn't be smiling.

Jack said, "Congratulations, Nate. Looks like you've won this set."

"Grace, he killed your brother and left us to die in the cold."

231

She shook her head.

"He's a crook. With your brother and father dead, he'd marry you and use your land to make a deal with the town. He'd cut himself into the gambling, as a front for the mob. In a few years, they'd be running all the action. Isn't that right, Keeshin?"

Grace felt her knees grow weak. She began to sink to the ground, but Jack still gripped her. Tom took a step toward them.

From behind Rosen, somebody shouted, "Hold it, Cross Dog!"

At that same instant, Jack grabbed the letter opener from the desk and held it to her throat.

Chick Cantrell stood just inside the bedroom hallway. He pointed a gun at Tom, who put his left hand under the rifle stock to balance it.

"Don't try it," Jack said. "You start shooting, and something might happen to Grace. You wouldn't want to take that chance. Now, very carefully, toss the rifle straight back, toward the door. That's right."

Cantrell stepped into the living room. He wore an old flannel shirt, jeans, and work boots. His hair and beard were matted, and even from the other end of the room Grace could smell him.

"What the hell are we gonna do now?"

As if he hadn't heard, Jack tossed the letter opener back onto the desk. Still holding Grace tightly, he unlocked the top drawer and took out a gun.

"There really isn't any choice. Get your things."

"For Chrissakes, we're right across the street from the police station. The whole stinking town must be crawling with cops."

"I don't think so. If Tom had stopped at the police station, he would've known Grace was here. Besides, he's the kind of man who wouldn't call any backup to bring me in. He'd want that John Wayne *mano-a-mano* finish." Pulling Grace back two steps, he glanced out the window. "I believe I'm right. It's awfully quiet out there. Get my overnight bag—top shelf of my bedroom closet. It's been packed for just such an emergency."

Cross Dog said to Cantrell, "That deep set of footprints in the snow—yours. I shoulda known. You were hiding in Keeshin's Jeep all along. When Will took the Jeep, you knocked him out, drove a few miles ahead and waited for Keeshin. After he drove the Blazer off the road into the post, you carried Will's body to the other car — that's why your bootprints were so deep. You finished him off, made it look like an accident, then you and Keeshin walked back up to the Jeep and drove away."

Cantrell stared at Jack. His mouth twitched. "You sure about them cops?"

"We'll find out soon enough. Now get your things, and be quick about it."

"You're sure you . . . ?"

"I'll be fine. I am the one holding the gun."

As the engineer hurried into the hallway, Jack wrapped his arm around Grace. She tried to twist away, but he was too strong.

Nuzzling her cheek, he said, "This would've made a nice wedding picture. You know, I was actually looking forward to getting married. It might've been fun."

"Till you got rid of her," Tom said.

Jack gave a short, hard laugh. "You make me into some kind of Bluebeard. I'm just a businessman, like thousands of others."

Rosen shook his head. "You murdered Will True Sky."

"Technically, no. You were right about Cantrell eliminating Will. But young True Sky was himself a murderer and had no qualms about letting his father take the blame. I think he would've let the old man fry, don't you?"

Grace felt her body shaking, and hot tears rolled down her cheeks. She was crying for her dead brother, and because Jack was right about Will, and because she'd been such a fool. Now, to have risked Tom's life as well.

Rosen said, "You were behind all of this, going back to last summer."

"Not Albert Gates's murder. That was all Will's doing."

"But you used even that to your advantage. You planned to make yourself a hero to Grace by helping her father with the condemnation hearing. When you won, you figured the town would be much more generous in making a deal, rather than risk an appeal. You had Cantrell hire Gil McCracken to kill Saul. When that failed, you took the next opportunity—Will's arrest. Had Saul died along with Will last night, all you would've needed to do was marry Grace and offer the land to the town for some gambling licenses."

"Very good, Nate. I really wish you played tennis."

"That's what you like—gentlemen's games like tennis and backgammon. Cantrell did all the dirty work. Hiring McCracken, gambling with Roy Huggins, courting the widowed mayor, even putting that poor idiot Elroy Baker on the take. He did the legwork, but everything was your idea. The spider patiently spinning its web."

"Why, Nate, you flatter me. Easy, darling." He pulled Grace back against him.

"You even used the F.B.I. investigation of Cantrell to your advantage. You ran your own exposé. The crusading editor—you might even have been elected mayor."

"I would have. But . . . " He shrugged.

Cantrell lumbered into the room, his gun tucked in his belt. He held a leather overnight bag in one hand, while the other dragged an over-stuffed green suitcase the size of a giant turtle.

Dropping the bags, Cantrell pulled out his gun. "You sure there ain't nobody outside?"

Keeshin said, "I told you—no."

"It's just that I don't like killing a cop. They look a lot harder for you."

"We have no choice. Besides, I've been more than generous."

"Bad enough taking care of Cross Dog and the lawyer. Doing a woman's about as bad as a cop."

Grace rubbed her eyes with her palms, the way her grandmother used to do. At least this time, she'd show her Lakota blood. Jack's breath was warm against her cheek. Staring into his eyes, she spit in his face.

Not breaking the stare, he wiped his face with his gun hand and said, "Chick, let's get on with it."

"All right, just let me see for myself if there're any cops outside."

As Cantrell passed Rosen, who stood beside the sofa, the lawyer suddenly tripped him. He fell hard against the coffee table, his head shattering the glass top.

"Hold it!" Jack shouted, when Rosen knelt on the floor. Cantrell's gun lay only a few feet away. Jack glanced from Rosen to Tom, then back to the lawyer.

Gently Rosen moved Cantrell's head; blood had filled the crevices of broken glass. "He's hurt pretty bad."

"Keep your hand away from the gun. Unfortunately, Chick will just have to stay behind with you two."

Jack's breathing had quickened. Grace saw his finger tighten on the trigger.

Rosen moved his hand an inch or two closer to the gun. "You needed Cantrell to kill us. You never do the dirty work yourself. So what now?"

Tom took a step closer.

Jack aimed at Tom. "It has to be done."

Clenching his fists, Tom shook his head slowly. "You shoulda killed me out on the road. Did you really think I'd let you hurt her?"

Rosen lunged for the gun on the floor. When Jack hesitated, Grace tore herself from his grip and Tom ran toward him. Jack's gun discharged and Tom jerked back, paused for an instant, then hurled himself forward. Arms flailing helplessly against the big man's iron grip, Jack stumbled backward. The gun fired once more into the ceiling, before both men crashed through the window, falling together into the cold black abyss.

"Tom!" Grace screamed. Staggering toward the window, she almost followed them into the darkness.

Rosen pulled her back. Huddling against the lawyer, she called Tom's name again, half blinded by her own tears. Through the jagged glass the wind's whispering sounded like the grandfathers of her people telling her something she couldn't understand. Not because she was a woman, but because she had turned her back on them long ago.

Chapter 22

THURSDAY MORNING

The furniture had been pushed back to the walls of Saul's living room. In the center of the room, Will's coffin, a simple wooden box, lay open on a long table. Rosen stood in line with Andi, behind five or six others waiting to pay their respects. He'd unzipped his coat but kept it on. He couldn't stay long.

The house was crowded with townspeople. In one corner a few Indian men, dressed in dark suits and white shirts, had congregated around Saul. Ike did most of the talking, while the others nodded solemnly. Rosen had already spoken to Saul, whose face remained smooth as a stone, revealing nothing—especially the pain. Because they'd probably never see each other again, Rosen had wanted him to smile, as friends do before saying goodbye. Of course, that couldn't happen, not with Will lying in his coffin a few feet away.

Wearing long print dresses, women kept going in and out of the kitchen, and soon Rosen smelled the rich aroma of turkey roasting in the oven. Belle Gates moved through the crowd, whispering condolences while shaking her head sadly. Wendy, the dispatcher, kept wiping her eyes, as did a number of other young women. Pearl Whistler was missing, but she and her husband had left town on an extended vacation. "Yeah," Andi had said earlier, "I bet she convinced him it was a second honeymoon."

Neither Grace nor Stevie was in the living room. She might be in the kitchen, and perhaps the boy was upstairs in his room, but Rosen had an idea where they both were, and the thought made him smile.

Ahead of him, an elderly Indian woman shuffled to the coffin. Her gray hair, thick as wire, was twisted into two long braids. From her purse she took a beautifully embroidered headband of red and green beads.

237

Looking into the casket, she said, "You were always good to us old ones. I remember how you brought my family groceries when John was home with a broken leg. And you'd take him to the doctor in your pickup and wait to bring him back. Here."

She placed the headband inside the casket and walked away.

Rosen approached the coffin with Andi. Will was dressed in an expensive blue suit and wore shiny black shoes that looked new. Despite his waxy pallor, he looked as handsome as he'd been in life. Only his forehead was marred, where the mortician had carefully stitched the wounds closed. Dozens of small gifts covered his body—beadwork like the headband, trinkets, even currency and coins.

From a manila envelope, Andi took an eight-by-ten photograph. It was a recent shot of Will, in a torn sweatshirt, sitting on the hood of his pickup. He had the cocky smile of a young Paul Newman.

She lay the photograph on Will's chest. "I had a good time whenever you took me out. We always had lots of fun, like the carnival up in Deadwood or the Corvette rallies out in Sturgis. Never really any hard feelings when we broke up, 'cause I knew you never meant any harm. You were just out for a good time. God bless you, Will."

Swallowing hard, she walked back to the hallway, where she'd left her camera bag.

It was Rosen's turn. Andi had told him that, at a Lakota wake, everyone was to give an offering and speak well of the dead. He placed a five-dollar bill beside the photograph and looked into the dead man's face.

What could be said about someone who'd allow his father to be wrongly accused of murder? Although estranged from his own father, Rosen could never have done that. Of all the commandments, the fifth was branded into his heart. "Honor thy father and thy mother." Yet, hadn't he dishonored his father? Before the Lord, wasn't he as guilty as Will? There was one difference between them, and because of that difference, Rosen knew what to say.

"You were a lucky man. You made mistakes, like we all do, but you were forgiven. You killed Belle Gates's husband, yet she's here. You let your father take the blame for you, yet he's here too. There couldn't be so many tears, so much forgiveness, without love."

Then he quietly recited the Kaddish, the Jewish prayer for the dead.

Rosen stepped aside and watched Wendy place a silver crucifix in the casket. She started to say something, then sobbed loudly. As she tried again, Rosen hurried away, hearing only the word "love." He walked over to Andi, who was adjusting her camera.

Checking the flash, she said, "Saul's letting me take pictures of the wake. They can't raise their dead up on scaffolds, like the old days, but they carry on their tradition the best they can."

"And you want to preserve it."

She nodded. "Besides, it's kind of a nice feeling with everybody together and the women cooking in the kitchen." She blinked hard. "God, that sounds terrible, Will's body lying there and me saying how nice things are."

"No, it's not terrible. It's a good home, filled with friendship and love. That's what you're supposed to feel."

"Guess you're right. Look, I'm going to take a few pictures, then we can go. Okay?"

"Sure."

Rosen heard a car coming up the road. Through the window, he saw Grace's Toyota pull up a few feet from the front-porch steps.

"I'll wait outside," he said, zipping up his coat.

Walking onto the porch, he blinked from the sunlight and inhaled the clean, cold air. The temperature, in the upper teens, seemed almost springlike compared to the blizzard a few days before.

As she stepped from the car, Grace nodded a greeting, then hurried around to the passenger side, her boots crunching in the snow. Stevie moved as quickly from the back seat. They both opened the door and helped Tom from the car.

The policeman struggled from his seat, then leaned against the car while retrieving his cane. His left arm, broken in the fall, rested snugly in a sling under his coat. Shaking off Grace and Stevie, who hovered on either side of him, he lumbered awkwardly like a trained bear up the porch steps.

"Hello, Tom," Rosen said. "I didn't expect you to be up and around so soon."

"It ain't so bad. Doctor said everything will heal up eventually. I sure look a lot better than Ike's van over there. If it was a horse, I'd have it shot."

Rosen glanced down the line of vehicles. Ike's van did indeed look like an old swayback, its roof caved in where Tom and Keeshin had crashed after falling from the second-story window.

"Now, Gracie," Tom groused, "gimme some room. I ain't a cripple."

She stayed beside him. "Why don't you tell Mr. Rosen what else the doctor said, that you should stay in bed a few more days."

"I said I'm all right."

"You promised to take it easy."

"You gonna chew my food for me too?"

"If I have to. Why you always have to be so stubborn, when all I'm trying to do is—"

"I ain't stubborn. It's just that I'm the police chief. What are folks gonna think?"

She looked at him and smiled softly. "They're gonna think how lucky they are. Ain't that right, Mr. Rosen?"

Before Rosen could answer, Tom cleared his throat and shifted against his cane. "I hear you're leaving today."

Rosen nodded. "As soon as Andi finishes taking some pictures inside. I'm driving with her as far as Chicago, then flying the rest of the way back to Washington."

Grace said, "She always wanted a job in some big city. We're all happy about it, but . . . the town won't be the same without her. It's nice you're keeping her company part of the way."

"After what happened to Tom and me Tuesday night, I was a bit apprehensive about that car of hers breaking down on the highway. But she showed me a written statement from her mechanic that the car's tuned up and in perfect condition."

"Hmm," Tom said, "hope it wasn't Oscar Two Hoops who worked on the car. He used to be Ike's drinking buddy. I remember once he poured four quarts of windshield wash where the oil shoulda gone. Drank the fifth quart himself."

The two men stared at each other, until the policeman broke out laughing.

Grace clicked her tongue. "Don't pay him no mind, Mr. Rosen. He's just teasing you. At least he's feeling better. Well, I better get inside. I just want to thank you again for everything you done. Clearing my father and all."

"I just wish I could've done more."

"What happened to Will was his fault. His and mine. If I hadn't been so blind . . . " Her eyes fixed on a point far in the distance, in the direction of town.

"Gracie," Tom said softly.

She roused herself. "I'd better get inside. Coming, Stevie?"

"In a couple minutes, Mom."

"You want to spend some time with the men." She smiled, tousling his hair. "All right, but come in before you get too cold."

She walked inside, closing the front door quickly, but not before Rosen again heard the quiet murmuring and smelled the roast turkey. He almost changed his mind about leaving.

"Too bad you're going," Tom said. "I'd kind of like you to see the town once it gets back to normal. Bear Coat's not a bad place to live. It was just all that crazy talk about the big money gambling would bring in. You know what talk like that can do to people."

"I know. That's why I wonder if it really is over. Has the town decided not to appeal Judge O'Hara's decision about Saul's land?"

"Roy Huggins wants to plow ahead, come hell or high water. But others, like Belle Gates, are sick over what happened. They'd rather take their chances with the way things are. 'Better the devil you know.' And we looked into the devil's own eyes, didn't we? I almost rode him straight down to hell."

"Stevie," Rosen asked, "would you please get my briefcase? It's in Andi's car, down there behind the green and white pickup. You may have to dig through a few boxes in the back seat."

Stevie ran toward the old Mercury.

"I shouldn't have mentioned Keeshin in front of the boy," Tom said. "They were pretty close for a while."

"He was an evil man."

"Maybe Stevie don't see it that way."

"If he doesn't now, he will once Keeshin's trial begins. I'm assuming Keeshin will live to stand trial with Chick Cantrell."

"Oh, he will, though I doubt he'll ever play tennis again—he may not even walk. From what the sheriff in Deadwood tells me, Keeshin and Cantrell are falling over each other trying to cut a deal, each begging to testify against the other and his mob connections. Whoever doesn't fry is gonna spend a long time in jail. I just wish that was enough to make up for all the bad they did here."

Rosen glanced back at the house. "Lawyers like me talk a lot about the efficacy of justice, but justice goes only so far. What really matters is the healing going on inside that house. Your people are from strong stock. They've been put through a lot of suffering, but they've endured."

"Sounds like you're speaking from experience."

"Sometimes I forget. I've had to bury my own dead on this trip."

"I don't understand. Somebody . . . ?"

"Not somebody. Something within me—the marriage my ex-wife and I once had. We've been divorced for years, but it's traveled along with me like a *wanagi,* the ghost that Saul's talked about. The one that should've been put to rest long ago. I've learned a lot about enduring from Saul's family and from you."

"Me?"

Rosen nodded. "You've finally forgiven Saul for what he did to your uncle years ago."

"For years Saul's been telling me that all I needed was to fly with the spirits. Well, Tuesday night I finally flew."

Stevie walked up the porch steps and handed the briefcase to Rosen, who opened it.

He took out the courting flute. "I understand it's an Indian custom not to keep a gift forever, but to pass it along to somebody who admires the object or has use of it. Is that right?"

Tom nodded. "But I think Stevie's a little young—"

"It's not for Stevie." He slipped the courting flute through Tom's coat and into the arm sling. "It seems that you'll be able to put this to good use."

Tom stared at him hard, then his eyes slowly softened and he smiled. "Guess maybe I could." Leaning the cane against his hip, he gripped Rosen's hand. "Thanks."

"You're welcome. In my profession, it always helps having a policeman as your friend."

Tom laughed. "Driving with Andi down the interstate, you're gonna need all the police friends you can muster. Well, I'd better get inside and pay my respects. Come on, Stevie."

Rosen laid a hand gently on the boy's shoulder. "How about walking me back to the car?"

Stevie shrugged. "Okay."

They walked past the line of cars, Rosen's hand still on the boy's shoulder, as it had been that day the previous summer when he'd sprained his ankle in Belle Gates's field.

"Before leaving, I wanted to apologize," Rosen said.

"What for?"

"Ever since I came to Bear Coat, I've been pretty rough on you. Believing in your grandfather's innocence, I was looking for the . . . guilty person."

"You mean murderer."

"That's right. For a while, I thought it might've been you."

Stevie nodded. "I know. Because I cut Mr. Gates the day of the murder—that's why his blood was on Grandfather's shirt. And because I cut you that night in the car on the way back from Deadwood, you thought I coulda killed somebody."

"And because everyone, including your mother and grandfather, wanted to protect you."

"I said, it's okay."

They had reached Andi's car. Taking his hand from Stevie's shoulder, Rosen crossed his arms and waited for the boy to look at him.

"It's not okay. I should never have suspected you."

"Why not?"

"Because of what your grandfather once told me, the story of Stone Boy." When Stevie's eyes narrowed, Rosen said, "You know the story."

"Yeah, but what's it got to do with anything?"

"As your grandfather once told me, the story teaches that man is capable of both the greatest good and the greatest evil. He said you'd learned that lesson well. When you stabbed Albert Gates—and me, for that matter—it was to protect your grandfather, just as Stone Boy set out on his adventures to protect his family. Murdering Gates behind his back—no true Lakota warrior would do that. Would your grandfather or Tom have done something like that?"

Stevie shook his head.

"Neither would you."

"But the way some say the story ends. Stone Boy destroys his family, because he hunts and kills the animals for no reason—just for the fun of it. Just because he thought he could get away with it, like . . . " He stopped suddenly and stared at the ground.

"That's right, like Jack Keeshin. Maybe you're a little mixed up, maybe the medication and Dr. Hartrey's counseling have helped you, but I think your grandfather had already set you on the right path. I think now your mother knows that too."

It was the first time that Rosen had seen Stevie smile, and in that smile, he saw the face of the boy's grandfather.

"Mom's gonna make a small tipi and watch over Uncle Will's soul, until it's ready to climb up to the Milky Way. That's the old way, you know, the way of our people."

"Yes," Rosen said, "so I've heard."

Just then, Andi walked up to the car and slung her camera into the back seat.

"Hope I'm not interrupting any important guy talk, but we'd better get going, if you want to arrive in Chicago by tomorrow afternoon."

Rosen shook the boy's hand. "Take care of your mom."

"I will."

Andi hugged Stevie tightly. "Don't take any crap from anybody. You're okay. You have your mom bring you to Chicago, and I'll show you the town. We'll see the Bulls, the Sox—"

"Cubs," Rosen blurted. "The Cubs."

Pulling out from the line of cars, Andi drove up Saul's ridge, the Mercury's muffler rumbling in the cold air.

"I thought you'd like to see the ridge one more time."

They climbed for a few minutes toward the clouds, then Andi stopped in front of the sweat lodge. She kept the motor running while Rosen got out.

He walked to the vision pit, which had filled with several inches of snow, and from there to the small pile, also frosted, where the remains of White Bear had been reburied. Standing beside the grave marker, he imagined the bones slowly decaying, returning to the earth from which they had been sustained in life. In the spring something new might grow, sustained by those very bones.

He felt a warm breeze bringing a faint scent of something green; no, that was only his imagination. It was much too early for spring. Yet, back at the house, he'd seen a new beginning for Tom, Grace, and Stevie.

"Life goes on," he whispered to himself, and remembered Sarah's invitation, when they'd talked on Tuesday.

"We're going to this neat restaurant . . . Wish you could come."

"We're" had included Bess and her new husband, Shelly.

As Rosen returned to the car, Andi shifted gears. "All set?"

He nodded, settling into the seat as the Mercury cruised down the dirt road that led to the highway. Looking back once at the ridge and the Black Hills looming in the distance, he asked, "Are you doing anything Saturday night? There's some people I'd like you to meet."